What Not

Also published by Handheld Press

HANDHELD CLASSICS

1 *What Might Have Been. The Story of a Social War*, by Ernest Bramah
2 *The Runagates Club*, by John Buchan
3 *Desire*, by Una L Silberrad
4 *Vocations*, by Gerald O'Donovan
5 *Kingdoms of Elfin*, by Sylvia Townsend Warner
6 *Save Me The Waltz*, by Zelda Fitzgerald
7 *What Not. A Prophetic Comedy*, by Rose Macaulay
8 *Blitz Writing. Night Shift & It Was Different At The Time*, by Inez Holden
9 *Adrift in the Middle Kingdom*, by J Slauerhoff, translated by David McKay
10 *The Caravaners*, by Elizabeth von Arnim
11 *The Exile Waiting*, by Vonda N McIntyre
12 *Women's Weird. Strange Stories by Women, 1890–1940*, edited by Melissa Edmundson
13 *Of Cats and Elfins. Short Tales and Fantasies*, by Sylvia Townsend Warner

HANDHELD MODERN

1 *After the Death of Ellen Keldberg*, by Eddie Thomas Petersen, translated by Toby Bainton
2 *So Lucky*, by Nicola Griffith

HANDHELD RESEARCH

1 *The Akeing Heart: Letters between Sylvia Townsend Warner, Valentine Ackland and Elizabeth Wade White*, by Peter Haring Judd
2 *The Conscientious Objector's Wife: Letters between Frank and Lucy Sunderland, 1916–1919*, edited by Kate Macdonald

What Not

A Prophetic Comedy

by Rose Macaulay

with an Introduction by Sarah Lonsdale

Handheld Classic 7

First published in the United Kingdom in 1918 by Constable.
This edition published in 2019 by Handheld Press Ltd.
72 Warminster Road, Bath BA2 6RU, United Kingdom.
www.handheldpress.co.uk

ISBN 978-1-912766-03-1

4 5 6 7 8 9 0

Series design by Nadja Guggi and typeset in Adobe Caslon Pro and Open Sans.

Printed and bound in Great Britain by TJ International, Padstow.

Contents

Sarah Lonsdale is a senior lecturer at City, University of London, and teaches journalism and English literature. Her research interests cover the links between journalism and literature, middlebrow fiction and the interwar women's movement. Her most recent book, *The Journalist in British Fiction and Film: Guarding the Guardians from 1900 to the Present* was published by Bloomsbury Academic in 2016. Her next book, *Rebel Women Between the Wars: Writers, Activists, Adventurers* will be published in 2020 by Manchester University Press.

Introduction

BY SARAH LONSDALE

Rose Macaulay wrote *What Not* in the final months of the First World War while men were still dying in huge numbers, and food rationing was beginning to bite on the Home Front. By 1918 many of the weary and grieving public were much lighter, some up to two stones lighter, than they had been at the outbreak of war, and, aware that they were in a fight for their lives, had submitted to a necessary wartime authoritarianism.[1] Enforced conscription had sent men up to the age of 40 to the Front; three five-penny meat coupons were the only official source of an adult's weekly meat ration; the press was severely restricted under the Defence of the Realm Acts (known as Dora); one leading newspaper, the *Globe*, had been closed down by the government for two weeks over an inaccurate story; hundreds of conscientious objectors to military service were in prison and Government edicts requisitioned anything from country houses to iron railings for the war effort. The optimism and confidence of Herbert Asquith's booming, Liberal Edwardian England had long since evaporated.

By the spring of 1918, however, victory over Germany was increasingly expected and writers and thinkers had begun debating what kind of Britain might emerge from the trauma of 'the war to end wars'. The central question of these debates was how to create a well-ordered society out of the social and economic chaos that dominated Europe, and of how to prevent another war. Contributions ranged from creating a state-controlled press and a 'Truthful Press Act', in response to the perceived lies published in the daily press during the conflict, to directing scientific research to ensure that populations were healthy in mind and body, and to eradicate the 'problem of feeblemindedness'.[2] Macaulay, who had been a published author since 1906, had satirised conditions in wartime Britain in her previous novel *Non-Combatants and Others* (1916), one of the first full-length pieces of fiction to scrutinise the effects of the war on the British Home Front. She then went on to do the same in *What Not: A Prophetic Comedy*, published at the end of March 1919 (see below for more discussion of the remarkable publication history of this novel). While the tone and style are recognisable, the setting is at once completely different and yet strangely familiar. This juxtaposition has the distorting effect of a mirage or hall of mirrors in the mind of the reader.

In this early passage, civil servants, having made their way to central London by underground train (and having been warned of the dangers of standing beneath a descending 'aero bus'), arrive at work:

> The Ministry of Brains, a vast organisation, had many sections. There was the Propaganda Section, which produced pamphlets and organised cinema shows ... there was the Men's Education Section, the Women's and the Children's; the section which dealt with brain-tests, examinations, certificates and tribunals, and the Section which was concerned with the direction of the intellects of the Great Unborn ... There were bonuses on the births of the babies of parents conforming to the regulations, and penal taxes on unregulated infants, taxes increasing in proportion to the flagrancy of the parents' disobedience so that the offspring of parents of very low mental calibre brought with them financial ruin. Everyone held a Ministry of Brains form, showing his or her mental category, officially ascertained and registered. (14)

At this point, the reader, having first brushed off the aero bus as a Macaulayesque flight of fancy, does a mental double-take. This is completely new territory. Her previous six novels, although all dealing with very different subjects, for example family inheritance

(*Abbots Verney*, 1906), delayed adolescent irresponsibility in Naples (*The Furnace*, 1907) and clashes between intellectualism, materialism and class (*The Lee Shore*, 1912), and set in different locations, from the sun-drenched Italian coast to the London suburbs, are, at least, all solidly embedded in Edwardian and Georgian contemporaneity. *What Not* is a bold departure, imagining a world where political, technological and workplace systems run on subtly distorted lines. Of the four pillars of the pre-War establishment, only the church, personified in the kindly, comforting and honest figure of Reverend Delmer, the vicar of Little Chantreys, remains unchanged (although bishops have had their palaces confiscated and taken over as housing for the poor). The further we get into the novel, the more distorted this hall of mirrors becomes: book bans, raids on poetry bookshops, heavy-handed censorship, state-controlled agriculture, a toppled prime minister replaced by a five-strong 'United Council', baby taxes leading to mass infanticide, the 'forcible repatriation' of Jews to Jerusalem. Despite the 'bright' tone, as described by the reviewer for the *Daily Mail*, *What Not* deals with some very serious, big and dark ideas prompted by the hypothesis that if a society will submit to conscription and rationing for the public good during wartime, it will submit to further authoritarian and anti-democratic policies if it is persuaded so to do, during the peace. Macaulay asks where, and what, the breaking point is of the 'strange, patient unaccountable dark horse', the people, when pushed to moral and ethical extremes. The novel thus explores the battle for the soul of Britain after a traumatic event that has left a national 'psychic wound' as Andrew Motion so eloquently described the aftermath of the Great War.[3]

Macaulay, who had lost her eldest brother Aulay to a violent death abroad at the hands of robbers in 1909, and whose younger brother Will was fighting with the King's Royal Rifles in France, certainly had an interest in continuing the debate she had begun in *Non-Combatants and Others* over how to prevent a future war. Born in 1881 into a middle-class family of intellectuals and clergymen, she read avidly from a young age and had begun publishing poetry in her early twenties. By the end of the War, by which time she had published nine books, she was beginning to make her way in literary London, and, thanks to her friend Naomi Royde-Smith, editor of the *Saturday Westminster*, was meeting 'people who seemed to me, an innocent from the Cam, to be more sparklingly alive than any in my home world'.[4] Endowed with, as Harold Nicolson described in a tribute after her death, a 'penetrating insight', she had a restless intellect and her novels are full of ideas and questions.[5] *What Not*, I would argue, contains more ideas and questions than any other of her novels. It is about the conflict between a new authoritarian and quasi-totalitarian political ideology and liberal, artistic Britain, about tradition versus modernity. It is about the social and personal sacrifices that must be made to create a better, if not perfect, society. It asks big questions about the role of the State in ordering and regulating people's lives, about the freedom of the press, and about the choices people make in love. It explores the social conditions that give rise to authoritarianism and in doing so presages the rise of fascism and Nazism in Italy and Germany. With equal prescience, it explores what happens when a charismatic, determined and slightly unhinged politician forces, through a mixture of persuasion and threat, a whole population to change its temperament and values. The novel resonates powerfully with the tumultuous politics experienced by modern Britain and the United States of America in 2016–19, and asks how much a society is prepared to submit to for the sake of an ideology.

Eugenics, *Brave New World* and utopias

From the mid-nineteenth century, steady progress in medicine, education, technology and transport had inspired in writers and philosophers optimistic dreams of a future utopian world where war was no longer necessary and a liberated, happy people engaged in craftwork and free love. William Morris' *News From Nowhere* (1890) and Edward Bellamy's *Looking Backward 2000–1887* (1888) are examples of these utopian fictions, based on a benevolent socialism. Both works, however, understand that in order to get from the 'present' of wage slavery, exploitation and constant threat of war, hard work and even revolution will be necessary. While Bellamy and Morris gloss over how utopia is achieved, *What Not* asks the tricky question: what do the idealists do when their visions of a perfect future come up against the hard rock of public dissent? What if people don't want a perfect society?

Macaulay must have had *News From Nowhere* partly in mind when she wrote the opening section of *What Not*, set in the London Underground in a crowded Bakerloo line carriage. Morris' *News From Nowhere* begins too in an underground carriage, 'that vapour bath of hurried and discontented humanity'. Whereas Morris' tube carriage is packed with argumentative socialists coming out of a meeting, Macaulay's carriage is packed with 'tired young men, lame young men, pale and scarred young men [who] bore a peculiar and unmistakeable impress stamped, faintly or deeply, on their faces, their eyes, their carriage, the set of their shoulders' (8). These are the victims of the failure of Victorian idealism and Edwardian liberalism to deliver peace across Europe. The novel is set 'After the Great War (but I do not say how long after)' (7). British society has peered into the abyss of total war and has withdrawn, terrified and has accepted rule by a five-man United Council. Macaulay is vague over whether there has been any form of democratic election to this council, although a semblance of democracy appears to be still in place. There is still a Parliament through which Bills and Acts have to pass. The Mental Progress Act demands that everyone must have their mental capacities tested and graded, from A to C3. Rules then state who may marry whom. Those in the lowest categories are not allowed to marry within their category, to prevent them from producing stupid children. If they ignore the regulations their babies are so heavily taxed that many are abandoned in ditches and at church doors across the country. Unregistered babies are collected by the Ministry of Brains and are dealt with 'in a secret room ... quite effectively' (117). A society thus regulated, so the idea goes, produces fewer stupid people and therefore reduces the chances of there being another war. The United Council, aware that during wartime people submitted to a whole raft of new and intrusive regulations, feels that the time is right to press home this extreme form of mass eugenics.

The ideas in the novel are both of, and well ahead of their time. The eugenics movement, which began in the United States in the late nineteenth century, was inspired by the studies of the British polymath Francis Galton, who concluded that the British upper classes' elevated position in society came from their genetic superiority. Eugenics debates had been widespread in British intellectual circles since the formation of the Eugenics Education Society in 1907, and in Europe the potential for misuse and the search for a 'Master Race', as pursued by Nazi Germany, was still a long way off. Rose Macaulay was certainly aware of eugenics arguments, counting Dean Inge, the prominent public intellectual and commentator, and supporter of eugenics, amongst her circle of friends in London. The ideas around eugenics originally came from more progressive ideas, that through selective breeding, the human race could direct its own evolution. In the United States and Britain, scientists of the Left, social reformers and feminists embraced eugenics as a way of preventing unwanted babies being born into disadvantaged households. By the late 1890s, however, some states in the USA had introduced the enforced sterilisation of certain groups of people and the prohibition from marrying of anyone who was 'imbecile, epileptic or feeble-minded'.[6] Although eugenics was never pursued in Britain to such extremes as in the United States, the 1913 Mental Deficiency Act created a criminal offence, punishable by two years in prison, of having 'carnal knowledge' of a woman deemed 'deficient'. While this was to protect 'deficient' women from sexual assault, rather than to prevent the creation of 'deficient' children, the Act provoked debate amongst British eugenicists over how to prevent 'deficients' from procreating. These ideas all fed into the most famous interwar novel to examine eugenics and reproductive science, Aldous Huxley's *Brave New World* (1932). Depicting a 'World State' at some unspecified future date (A F 632), social stability is made possible by mass-produced babies grown in artificial wombs, predestined to their future jobs by eugenic selection.

While there is no record of Huxley having read *What Not*, major themes of *Brave New World* bear uncanny resemblances to those in Macaulay's novel. Huxley was good friends with Naomi Royde-Smith at the same time that she and Macaulay were enjoying a close friendship. Royde-Smith and Huxley both worked for the literary pages of the *Westminster Gazette* and in early 1923 Huxley stayed at 44 Princes Gardens, Royde-Smith's spacious Knightsbridge apartment, for several months. This was also the time that Macaulay was a regular overnight guest and co-host with Royde-Smith of Thursday evening literary soirées.[7] So it is quite possible that Huxley either read *What Not*, or at least discussed its contents with Macaulay. Huxley's Alpha Double plus to Epsilon Minus caste system appears to have sprung straight from Macaulay's A to C3 grading system. Huxley's brainwashing techniques designed by *Brave New World's* 'Emotional Engineers' again appear to have been derived directly from the Mind Training programmes that all citizens in the Britain of *What Not* are forced to undergo. Finally, the small group of 'World Controllers' of A F 632 mimic the United Council of *What Not*: in both cases this elite and shadowy group has been accepted by the public after democracy has been deemed to have failed. Indeed it could be argued that the world of A F 632 is the world of *What Not* some few decades into the future.

The civil service and Orwell's *Nineteen Eighty-Four*

While themes from *What Not* can be found in *Brave New World* the offices of the Ministry of Brains, inhabited by slogan-producing, rubber-stamping, letter-writing civil servants, could also be those in Orwell's teeming Ministry of Truth in *Nineteen Eighty-Four* (1949):

> They worked underground, the registry people, like gnomes in a cave, opening letters and registering them and filing them and sending them upstairs, astonishingly often in the file which belonged to them ... a queer life, questing, burrowing, unsatisfied, underground. (66)

Macaulay had personal experience of this 'queer life' of a civil servant, having worked for the War Office since January 1917 and then for the Ministry of Information from early 1918. Indeed *What Not*, which is as much about working life as its wider themes, is dedicated to 'Civil Servants I Have Known'. Prior to joining the War Office, Macaulay's war work had also included a short period working on the land in rural Cambridgeshire, which she enjoyed, and as a VAD nursing auxiliary at a home for wounded soldiers near to where her family lived in Great Shelford, which made her miserable. By the time she joined the War Office, Macaulay and her recently widowed mother had moved to the semi-rural south Buckinghamshire village of Hedgerley. With its row of ancient cottages, scattered 'big houses' and Gothic Revival stone church, Hedgerley inspired the Little Chantreys of *What Not*, from where the novel's female protagonist Kitty Grammont, the efficient young civil servant at the Ministry of Brains, commutes into London. That tedious hour-and-a-half journey into Marylebone, and then down the Bakerloo line to Charing Cross, so minutely described in the opening pages of *What Not*, was endured and observed by Macaulay during her 13-hour working day: every bump, unaccountable delay, every dreary commuter with their newspaper.[8]

An expanding Whitehall and the absence of so many men, meant that women civil servants were much needed during the War. They were also much begrudged by men who clung jealously to their occupation of the higher administrative grades and it was generally expected that at the end of hostilities, women would return to the domestic sphere, or more menial occupations. Despite years of campaigning by the women's movement, at the outbreak of war women were still banned from taking the examinations that would permit them entry to more senior ranks. By the end of the First World War, some 170,000 women were employed across Whitehall, although most in positions far below their abilities. While most women worked as typists and stenographers, some were given more responsibility in drafting letters and making policy. The figure of 170,000 compares favourably with pre-war figures of 65,000, most of which number were telephonists with the Post Office. In *What Not* Rose Macaulay displays her under-acknowledged modernity in her depiction of the lives of middle-class working women. During one commuter conversation between Kitty Grammont and typist Ivy Delmer, the pair discuss their workloads, where to find cheap chocolate and how far you have to travel out of London before it is acceptable for a woman to be seen in breeches rather than a skirt. Very few novels of this time foreground professional women's lives in such detail. These aspects, at least, must have been refreshing for working women — teachers, nurses, administrators and factory inspectors — to read while swaying wearily in tube train carriages returning home in the evening to be asked by their mothers whether they had had a tiring day. Although little is known of Macaulay's work as a civil servant, her first biographer Constance Babington Smith quotes a contemporary of Macaulay's at the War Office who said she was 'rather hampered by her inability to keep an individual note out of her minutes'.[9] This disdain for civil service conventions is another point of similarity between Macaulay and Kitty Grammont, who had 'something of the elegant rake, something of the gamin, something of the adventuress, something of the scholar, with innocent amber-brown eyes gazing ingenuously from under long black lashes' (11).

Kitty's rebelliousness, against the bureaucracy, incompetence and policies of the Ministry she works for, also has echoes in *Nineteen Eighty-Four*. In Orwell's novel the protagonists Winston and Julia are employed within the Ministry of Truth which produces the *Times* for Party members as well as 'rubbishy newspapers which contained almost nothing except sport, crime and astrology' for the 'proles'.[10] Winston works in a parody of a newspaper newsroom where instead of producing original news copy, he and his colleagues either doctor *Times* archives to suit the Party's agenda or fabricate pieces of news to fill gaps left by the excision of articles whose existence would question Big Brother's authority. Likewise, Kitty, after working for the Propaganda Section, transfers to being a journalist for *Intelligence*, a Ministry of Brains official publication. Both Kitty and Winston ultimately rebel, although Kitty's rebellion comes from her innate self-confidence and brings her no jeopardy, whereas Winston's attempt to attack Big Brother ends in failure and torture.

The role of the press and journalism

Both Orwell and Macaulay, who were also prolific journalists, are concerned with the transmission of information from the loci of power — the Ministry of Information and the BBC — to the public, and in the role of newspapers and the media in controlling a population. The worlds of *What Not* and *1984* are highly mediated societies saturated with government messages, *Nineteen Eighty-Four* with its ubiquitous telescreens promoting 'Hate Week', and *What Not* with 'Safety-if-Possible' and Mind Training posters plastering city walls and village marketplaces. Both Kitty Grammont and Winston Smith fulfil roles that could be described as 'anti-journalists'; their functions are the antithesis to the idealised role of the journalist as fearless speaker of truth unto power.

While Orwell wrote *Nineteen Eighty-Four* having observed the rise of warmongering totalitarian states, Macaulay's speculation required greater imaginative leaps. Although she was writing *What Not* a year after the Russian revolutions of March and October 1917, no controlling political system had yet been established in Russia and the socialist soviets had yet to become the USSR. Her interest in both the censorship of some newspapers and in the populist irresponsibility of others and also of an overweening government propaganda machine — all explored in *What Not* — came from closer to home. The wartime elevation to the peerage and to government of Britain's two most powerful press barons, Lords Beaverbrook and Northcliffe, had caused concern amongst the London literary intelligentsia. As owners of, among other papers, the *Daily Mail, Times, Daily Express, Globe* and *Evening Standard*, they had access to millions of readers. Lloyd George's decision to bring them into the heart of government would have been something akin to Rupert Murdoch and the Barclay brothers being made cabinet ministers today. Macaulay was writing *What Not* at a time when the reputation of the British press was low. It was described by Norman Angell in his seminal post-war work *The Press and the Organisation of Society* (1922) as being a 'lynch press'.[11] In his soon-to-be-published novel *Kangaroo* (1923) D H Lawrence referred to the 'unspeakable baseness of the press and the public voice' in wartime London.[12] The failures of the British Press during the First World War led prominent press historian Phillip Knightley to claim: 'More deliberate lies were told than in any other period of history'.[13] Devastating post-war demolitions of false 'atrocity stories' published in newspapers — such as the claim that the Germans boiled down dead bodies to produce lubricating oil, a report initially published in the *Times* — appeared as early as the mid-1920s after several public and academic inquiries. Other stories, all later found to be mendacious propaganda, and satirised pointedly in Macaulay's previous novel *Non-Combatants and Others*, were printed as fact in the British press.[14]

Rose Macaulay had earned her living from 1911 by publishing poems and short pieces in newspapers, and had a particularly complex and often contradictory relationship with journalism. Eight of her novels have journalism either as a dominant or major theme and her next novel after *What Not*, *Potterism* (1920), concerns the rise of the popular press: it would be her first best-seller.[15] As a young girl she had wanted to be a foreign correspondent, as she confessed in a newspaper article in 1928, but she was, and always would be, she ruefully admitted, prevented from this because of her sex. In her novels where journalism is a setting, much of the discussion centres on the unfair stereotyping of women journalists and readers as being only interested in trivial or domestic topics. After the end of the First World War, concerned that her employment at the Ministry of Information would soon cease, Macaulay successfully applied for a 'behind-the-scenes' job on the liberal *Daily News*, although a nervous breakdown prevented her from taking up the position. Instead she wrote freelance articles for a wide range of newspapers and magazines, from *Time and Tide* and the *Spectator*, to *Good Housekeeping* and the *Daily Mail*. She was thus both an intellectual observer of, and an engaged contributor to, this powerful new phenomenon in society, the mass media.

What Not opens in a crowded Bakerloo Underground train where everyone is reading a newspaper: a 'fluffy typist' is reading a romantic short story in the *Daily Mirror*, a 'spruce young civil servant' the *Times*, 'an elderly gentleman' the *Morning Post* and 'a citizen with a law-abiding face' was reading the new Government daily, the *Hidden Hand*. It is almost a sociological study (the comments eerily foreshadow the Mass Observation newspaper surveys of the late 1930s) and one can imagine Macaulay, now in her mid-30s, making acute observations of her fellow travellers as she trundled towards work at Crewe House. This technique of defining people by the papers they read is seen in Macaulay's earlier novel, *The Making of a Bigot* (1914) where protagonist Eddy Oliver's father's home is defined by its reading matter. As well as the *Manchester Guardian* and the *Times*, laid out on the table by the window the family could read the *Spectator, Punch*, the *Morning Post*, the *Saturday Westminster*, the *Quarterly*, the *Church Quarterly*, the *Hibbert,* the *Cornhill*, the *Commonwealth*, the *Common Cause*, and *Country Life*, but did not take the *Church Times, Poetry and Drama*, the *Blue Review*, the *English Review*, the *Suffragette, Further* and any of the halfpenny dailies. 'All the same, it was a well-read home, and broad-minded too'.[16] The 'broad-minded' comment is somewhat ironic. The taking of the *Morning Post, Times* and *Manchester Guardian* in preference to the 'halfpenny dailies' indicates an erudite, upper middle class household, with the choice of *Spectator* and *Country Life* suggesting a Tory-leaning, traditionalist approach, underlined by the rejection of the *Suffragette*. Its preference for *Cornhill* over the *Blue Review* (a short-lived modernist literary magazine that lasted for only three issues in 1913) suggests the household's tastes in fiction were more Rudyard Kipling than D H Lawrence.

In *What Not*, newspapers have moved from being the independent cacophonic founts of information and opinion that they are in *The Making of a Bigot*, to instruments of government propaganda. Women's magazines support the government line, embedding targeted propaganda in apparently harmless texts, appealing to women's vanity and maternal instincts to encourage them to attend government Mind Training courses:

> The *Queen*, the *Gentlewoman*, the *Sketch* ... had articles on 'Why does a woman look old sooner than a man?', 'Take care of your mind and your complexion will take care of itself,' 'Raise yourself to category A, and you enlarge your matrimonial field,' 'How to train Baby's intellect,' and so forth. (59)

The *Times* and other newspapers support the government line and campaign for compulsory Mind Training, as the voluntary system employed thus far has not been having the desired effect, a reference to the Northcliffe Press's clamorous campaign for conscription during the War.

There is however, as in many of Macaulay's novels, a contradictory point of view in *What Not*. Rebellion against the Ministry of Brains' draconian edicts starts with the newspapers, led by the *Herald* (a left-wing popular paper) and the *Nation* (a radical liberal journal that had been banned from export overseas in April 1917 because it called for peace). To these two real-life papers Macaulay adds two fictitious ones: *Stop It*, the journal of the Stop It League, a campaigning group organised in opposition to the Ministry of Brains' news laws, and the *Patriot*, edited by Percy Jenkins, which reported 'not only the public misdemeanours of prominent persons, but with the scandals of their private lives' (160). In the original, 1918 version of *What Not*, Percy Jenkins tries to blackmail Nicholas Chester, the Minister of Brains, for £500 after discovering his hypocritical and scandalous secret marriage. The novel was withdrawn after Michael Sadleir, a director at *What Not*'s publisher Constable, recommended some excisions for fear of attracting a libel suit from a Fleet Street newspaper editor. Macaulay replaced the text with anodyne passages, and *What Not* was reissued in 1919.

In the novel these four newspapers are banned under the Defence of the Realm Act for being critical of government policy, and shortly afterwards a crowd, led by Percy Jenkins, marches on the Ministry. Newspapers are thus both mouthpieces for government propaganda and a bulwark against a government's anti-democratic tendencies; agents of a repressive regime yet also a rallying symbol of freedom of speech. Whether either of these contradictory arguments were held by Macaulay is hard to tell; she probably held both at different times. There is certainly more than a whiff of regret from Macaulay at the end of the novel that the Brains experiment didn't work and that Britain, condemned forever to be stupid, would stumble into another war.

Forbidden love in *What Not*

After a year at the War Office, Macaulay was transferred to Lord Beaverbrook's Ministry of Information. Under the Directorship of John Buchan, by then a well-known novelist and war historian, the Ministry of Information attracted many writers and intellectuals, including H G Wells and Wickham Steed. Macaulay worked for the Italian section of the Department for Propaganda in Enemy Countries under another press baron, Lord Northcliffe, as she was fluent in Italian. She and her family had lived on the Ligurian coast near Genoa from when she was six to thirteen, and she had a lasting love for southern Europe, setting many of her novels partially in and around the Mediterranean. *What Not* itself carries a lyrical section set on the Italian coast.

The chief of the Department's Italian section was the author and ex-priest Gerald O'Donovan who would become the love of Macaulay's life, her 'beloved companion', until his death in 1942. O'Donovan was a married man and for a long time Macaulay kept her relationship secret from members of her family, although the affair became common knowledge amongst Macaulay's literary circle fairly soon.[17] The deeply passionate feelings Macaulay felt for Gerald find expression in Kitty's secret and also illicit love for Nicholas Chester: 'It's queer, isn't it, how strong it is,' remarks the usually cool, detached and self-assured young woman, 'this odd, desperate wanting of one person out of all the world. It's an extraordinary, enormously strong thing.' Kitty's conflict between desire and reluctance to embark on a doomed affair (the pair can never marry. Nicholas Chester's own laws, under which he is uncertified for marriage, prevent it), written at the time when Macaulay was wrestling with her own feelings, must surely be autobiographical, as are her observations on the difficulty of an office-based love affair: 'When two people who love each other work in the same building ... they disturb each other, are conscious of each other's nearness ... There was no getting away ... no peace of mind' (126). There is something of the dark and charismatic Gerald in the 'beetle-browed' Chester, who through sheer willpower tries to force the British public to accept his draconian laws on marriage and procreation.

And herein lie some of the novel's problems. Although Chester is clearly a mesmerising, brilliant figure, there is no getting away from his vaunting hypocrisy. Although according to his own laws he is uncertified for marriage on account of his two siblings being classified as 'imbeciles' (136), his secret marriage to Kitty – under an assumed name – goes against everything he stands for. When he makes his decision, there is not a flicker of introspection, not a moment of questioning his own laws. His response to Kitty's doubts is simply: 'I don't care. What's the good of living if you can't have what you want?' (144). The affair is thus portrayed as utterly selfish, as well as reckless. Although it may have worked for Macaulay as a metaphor for her own feelings of guilt, it puts part of the novel's structure in jeopardy. Indeed, her publisher raised this criticism to which her biographer Constance Babington Smith says she replied, somewhat flippantly, 'People ought to take it not as a story but as a satire – the intelligent ones do, of course'.[18]

So, is Kitty Macaulay? They certainly share much in common: a University education (Macaulay studied at Oxford), the secret love affair, a job with the civil service, a commute into London from Buckinghamshire, a vivacious and witty personality, a beautiful complexion. But one wonders whether Macaulay would really have been quite as careless, thoughtless even, towards both her work and the love affair as Kitty is. After 1922 her guilt over her adulterous affair with O'Donovan led her to stop taking Holy Communion and going to confession, the Anglican church having been a central part of her life up until then. There is something of Macaulay in the other female protagonist of the novel, Ivy Delmer: the cautious, sensible and sensitive vicar's daughter who observes the glamorous Kitty with a mixture of envy and awe. She too falls for a man, but to marry him would be against the regulations.

Unlike Kitty, who marries anyway and carries on with her job of forcing others to submit to the laws she so thoughtlessly flouts, Ivy grows 'pale and depressed', and decides she must leave her job, now she no longer believes in what she is doing (157–59). Ivy is the guilty conscience. The Kitty-Ivy pairing is similar to other pairings in Macaulay's novels: the selfish, lazy and brilliant Jane Potter and the academic, loyal Katherine Varick in *Potterism* (1920); the shy, socially awkward tomboy Denham Dobie and the attractive, successful career woman Audrey Gresham in *Crewe Train* (1926). In *Keeping up Appearances* (1928) two women, upper-class socialite Daphne and lower middle-class journalist Daisy, occupy and torment the same person.

Truth and satire

It is these often irreconcilable inconsistencies that have led critics of Rose Macaulay's works, both contemporaneous and modern, to point out that it is hard to discern her true argument within her novels; that contradictions and satire combine to make it very difficult to find the meaning: to finish a novel and say, 'Yes, this is where she stands on this issue'. She was aware of this herself and indeed one of her early protagonists, Eddy Oliver, the journalist in *The Making of a Bigot*, is plagued by his inability to take a firm line on any argument. Did Macaulay really think that society should submit to laws on who should marry whom, for the sake of everlasting peace? It seems hard to accept, particularly as the unintended consequences of the Mental Progress Act are abandoned babies and state-sponsored infanticide. Yet these consequences are only because the people refuse to make the sacrifices required of them. If they would only submit to the new laws, their babies would not be taxed – indeed they might even receive a bonus – and their offspring would also be clever. While there does seem to be, at the end of the novel, a genuine regret that ideas like Mental Progress will never take root in Britain, the answer may in fact be found in the

Cheeper, Kitty's fatly chuckling, permanently charming and much-loved baby nephew. The Cheeper is illegitimate, the son of Kitty's brother Anthony and the bewitching Pansy Ponsonby, an actress who specialises in scantily-clad dancing. Had his parents paid any attention to social mores and regulations, the Cheeper would never have existed. Pansy's commentary on 'those silly laws' at the end of the novel may well also be Macaulay's (181). This view is reinforced if we read Macaulay's poem 'Sanity', written at about the same time as *What Not* and published in the collection *Three Days* (1919). The poem describes the chaos of war ('When the world's rims crumbled, and its walls fell down,/So raked were they, so beaten by hell's long guns') and the madness it unleashes in men.[19] In the poem the only refuge for 'poor reeling brains' is the countryside around Hedgerley, where she was then living, transposed as 'Little Chantreys' in *What Not*. This is where Pansy and the Cheeper live, as well as the down-to-earth Delmers, far from the long arm of the Ministry of Brains. Responding to the madness of war, Macaulay writes in 'Sanity', 'Let me hold in my mind/Things small, sweet and kind,/Apples, and the Chalfonts, and keep sane so.'

Another 'clue' to Macaulay's true views is the work done by Kitty at the Ministry of Brains, which mirrors Macaulay's work at the Ministry of Information. Macaulay's happy memories of Italy must have conflicted with her duties central to which were seeing Italy as an enemy country. This mirrors the conflicts Kitty Grammont felt in carrying out the policies she called 'these fantastic lunacies' at the Ministry of Brains. Ultimately, Kitty reconciles herself to these 'lunacies' in her clever, bored, offhand way, but one suspects that Macaulay had more serious misgivings. Here then, is her at times infuriating ambiguity; but her refusal to come down on one side or another also forces the reader to work hard at asking what their own viewpoint is.

What Not one hundred years on

How does *What Not* stand up today, one hundred years since its first publication? As a witty and affectionate account of a patient people putting up with wartime privations, the novel is a marvellous social document as well as an intriguing read. The cast of minor characters, particularly the occupants of End House, and the Delmers, are brilliantly sketched. As a rare literary depiction of the lives of professional women at an early stage in their engagement in public life, it is an important testimony. As war somewhere in the world is now part of everyday life, as various states in Europe and beyond now slip towards totalitarianism, and as advances in genetic science make the creation of 'perfect' babies a possibility, the themes of *What Not* are just as urgent and insoluble today.

With what stance should we respond to the ideas in the novel? As intellectuals interested in social progress, or as human beings, messy, loving, full of faults? Whatever the answer *What Not* is certainly an unfairly overlooked text, both in Rose Macaulay scholarship (it barely registers in academic studies of her work) and in the study of dystopian/utopian fiction. This latter oversight is particularly grave. Her ideas were spectacularly prescient and important, and, as we have seen, they laid the groundwork for the two twentieth-century novels about the future of the human race that are celebrated as the most visionary and thought-provoking ever written. To be sure, it is a difficult, and sometimes slippery book to grasp hold of, but it will certainly leave its mark long after you have turned the final page.

Endnotes

1 Several wartime diaries, both published and at the Imperial War Museum, refer to weight loss on the Home Front. Lillie Scales who kept a diary writes for example on May 12 1918: 'Most people are much thinner. I have lost two stone since the War began'; Lillie Scales, *A Home Front Diary 1914–1918* (Stroud: Amberley Publishing, 2014), 147.

2 Joanne Woiak, 'Designing a Brave New World: Eugenics, Politics and Fiction', *The Public Historian*, 29/3 (2007), 105–29, 109.

3 Andrew Motion, 'The Lost Generation', *The Guardian*, 5 July 2011.

4 Rose Macaulay, 'Coming to London' in *Coming to London* (ed.) John Lehmann (London: Phoenix House, 1957), 159.

5 Harold Nicolson, 'The Pleasures of Knowing Rose Macaulay' (1959), republished in Constance Babington Smith, *Rose Macaulay: A Biography* (London: Collins, 1972), 223.

6 Harry Laughlin, *Eugenical Sterilization in the United States* (Chicago: Psychopathic Laboratory of the Municipal Court of Chicago, 1922), 9 and *passim*.

7 Jill Benton, *Avenging Muse: Naomi Royde-Smith 1875 – 1964* (Bloomington: Xlibris, 2015), 85–86.

8 After January 1918 Rose's commute altered slightly, as she was based in Crewe House, Curzon Street.

9 Babington Smith 1972, 83.

10 George Orwell, *Nineteen Eighty-Four* (London: Penguin Modern Classics, 1949, 2004), 50.

11 Norman Angell, *The Press and the Organisation of Society* (Cambridge: Cambridge Minority Press, 1922, 1933), 28.

12 D H Lawrence, *Kangaroo* (Sydney: Collins, 1923, 1989), 250.

13 Phillip Knightley, *The First Casualty: The war correspondent as hero and myth maker from the Crimea to Iraq* (London: Andre Deutsch), 84.

14 Here is just a small selection: 'Baby Bayoneted ... an infant callously dragged from its sick mother and thrown from the window to bayonet point' (*Daily Express*, 10 October, 1914); 'German Atrocities ... One man whom I did not see told an official of the Catholic Society that he had seen with his own eyes German soldiery chop off the arms of a baby which clung to its mother's skirts' (*Times*, 28 August, 1914); 'Murdered priests – Germans' appalling record ... 27 priests in the Bishopric of Namur killed and 12 missing' (*Telegraph*, 16 December 1914); 'The Germans and their Dead ... There is a sickly smell in the air as if glue were being boiled. We are passing the great Corpse Utilisation Establishment' (*Times*, 19 April 1917).

15 These are, in chronological order, *The Making of a Bigot* (1914); *Non-Combatants and Others* (1916); *What Not* (1919); *Potterism* (1920); *Mystery at Geneva* (1922); *Crewe Train* (1926); *Keeping Up Appearances* (1928) and *Going Abroad* (1934)

16 Rose Macaulay, *The Making of a Bigot* (London: Hodder & Stoughton, 1914), 85–86.

17 Sarah LeFanu, *Rose Macaulay* (London: Virago, 2003), 152–3.

18 Babington Smith 1972, 91.

19 Rose Macaulay, 'Sanity', in *Three Days* (London: Constable, 1919), 24.

Further reading

Constance Babington Smith, *Rose Macaulay: A Biography* (London: Collins, 1972). The first of three Macaulay biographies, written by a cousin. Contains detailed family anecdotes as well as an appendix, 'The Pleasures of Knowing Rose Macaulay' containing fond reminiscences from prominent literary figures.

Rafaella Baccolini and Tom Moylan (eds), *Dark Horizons: Science Fiction and the Dystopian Imagination* (London: Routledge, 2003). Excellent collection of essays on dystopian fiction, despite omitting *What Not*.

Ethel Bilborough, *My War Diary 1914–1918* (London: Ebury Press with the Imperial War Museum, 2014). Fascinatingly detailed First World War diary, references many of the government regulations that people were subject to, particularly after 1917.

Helen Glew, *Gender, Rhetoric and Regulation: Women's Work in the Civil Service and London County Council* (Manchester: Manchester University Press, 2016). Scholarly yet fascinating and well written investigation into some of the earliest women civil servants.

Helen Jones, *Women in British Public Life, 1914–50* (London: Pearson Education, 2000). Very accessible overview of women civil servants, politicians, campaigners and educators during the interwar years as well as both World Wars.

Phillip Knightley, *The First Casualty: The war correspondent as hero and myth maker from the Crimea to Iraq* (London: Andre Deutsch, 1975; 2004). Now a classic account of the behaviour of the press during wartime.

Sarah LeFanu, *Rose Macaulay* (London: Virago, 2003). Critically acclaimed biography of Rose Macaulay.

Rose Macaulay (ed. Martin Ferguson Smith), *Dearest Jean: Rose Macaulay's Letters to a Cousin* (Manchester: Manchester University Press, 2011). Revealing and at times poignant letters, well annotated.

Kate Macdonald (ed), *Rose Macaulay, Gender and Modernity* (London: Routledge, 2018). First collection of scholarly essays on Rose Macaulay, focusing on her concerns over gender and genre, with the first full bibliography of Macaulay's work, and of critical work on her.

Note on the text

This text of *What Not* is based on the 1919 Constable & Company edition, dated 1918 but not published until 1919. This was the second edition, as its 'Note on the 1919 Edition' (see below) makes clear, published after what Rose Macaulay calls a 'slight alteration' in the text of the first edition, to avoid libel. The original passages have been reinstated here, by the kind permission of John Clute, the present owner of a first edition formerly owned by Michael Sadleir, a director of Constable, in which the pencilled excision marks are clear. The replacement passages have been retained in the Notes at the end of the volume, for comparison.

Other than this reinstatement, the text has only been altered to correct typographical errors in the original, and to modernise the spelling of a few words where it was felt that the older forms that Macaulay used might be distracting or intrusive.

To

Civil Servants

I have known

‘Wisdom is very unpleasant to the unlearned: he that is without understanding will not remain with her. She will lie upon him as a mighty stone of trial; and he will cast her from him ere it be long. For wisdom is according to her name, and she is not manifest unto many …

‘Desire not a multitude of unprofitable children …’

— Jesus, son of Sirach, c. 150 BC

‘It’s domestickness of spirit, selvishnesse, which is the great let to Armies, Religions, and Kingdomes good.’

— W Greenhill, 1643

‘It has come to a fine thing if people cannot live in their homes without being interfered with by the police … You are upsetting the country altogether with your Food Orders and What Not.’

— Defendant in a food-hoarding case, January 1918

Apology

One cannot write for evermore of life in war-time, even if, as at times seems possible, the war outlasts the youngest of us. Nor can one easily write of life as it was before this thing came upon us, for that is a queer, half-remembered thing, to make one cry. This is a tale of life after the war, in which alone there is hope. So it is, no doubt, inaccurate, too sanguine in part, too pessimistic in part, too foolish and too far removed from life as it will be lived even for a novel. It is a shot in the dark, a bow drawn at a venture. But it is the best one can do in the unfortunate circumstances, which make against all kinds of truth, even that inferior kind which is called accuracy. Truth, indeed, seems to be one of the things, along with lives, wealth, joy, leisure, liberty, and forest trees, which has to be sacrificed on the altar of this all-taking war, this bitter unsparing god, which may perhaps before the end strip us of everything we possess except the integrity of our so fortunately situated island, our indomitable persistence in the teeth of odds, and the unstemmed eloquence of our leaders, all of which we shall surely retain.

This book is, anyhow, so far as it is anything beyond an attempt to amuse the writer, rather of the nature of suggestion than of prophecy, and many will think it a poor suggestion at that. The suggestion is of a possible remedy for what appears to have always been the chief human ailment, and what will, probably, after these present troubles, be even more pronounced than before. For wars do not conduce to intelligence. They put a sudden end to many of the best intellects, the keenest, finest minds, which would have built up the shattered ruins of the world in due time. And many of the minds that are left are battered and stupefied; the avenues of thought are closed, and people are too tired, too old, or too dulled by violence, to build up anything at all. And besides these dulled and damaged minds, there are the great mass of the minds which neither catastrophe nor emotion nor violence nor age nor any other creature can blunt, because they have never been acute, have never had an edge, can cut no ice nor hew any new roads.

So, unless something drastic is done about it, it seems like a poor look-out.

This book contains the suggestion of a means of cure for this world-old ill, and is offered, free, to a probably inattentive and unresponsive Government, a close and interested study of whom has led the writer to believe that the erection of yet another Department might not be wholly uncongenial.

It will be observed that the general state of the world and of society in this so near and yet so unknown future has been but lightly touched upon. It is unexplored territory, too difficult for the present writer, and must be left to the forecastings of the better informed.

A word as to the title of this work, which may seem vague, or even foolish. Its source I have given. Food Orders we all know; What Not was not defined by the user of the phrase, except by the remark that it upset the country. The businesses described in this tale fulfil that definition; and, if they be not What Not, I do not know what is.

April 1918

Note to the 1919 reissue

As this book was written during the war, and intended prophetically, its delay until some months after the armistice calls for a word of explanation.

The book was ready for publication in November 1918, when it was discovered that a slight alteration in the text was essential, to safeguard it against one of the laws of the realm. As the edition was already bound, this alteration has naturally taken a considerable time.

However, as the date of the happenings described in *What Not* is unspecified, it may still be regarded as a prophecy, not yet disproved.

RM
March 1919

CHAPTER I

The Ministry

1

After the Great War (but I do not say how long after), when the tumult and the shouting had died, and those who were left of the captains and the kings had gone either home or to those obscure abodes selected for them by their more successful fellows (to allay anxiety, I hasten to mention that three one-time Emperors were among those thus relegated to distance and obscurity), and humanity, released from its long torment, peered nervously into a future darkly divined (nervously, and yet curiously, like a man long sick who has just begun to get about again and cannot yet make anything coherent of the strange, disquieting, terrifying, yet enchanting jumble which breaks upon his restored consciousness) — while these things happened, the trains still ran through the Bakerloo tube, carrying people to their day's work.

Compartments in tube trains are full of variety and life — more so than in trains above ground, being more congested, and having straps, also no class snobbery. Swaying on adjacent straps were a fluffy typist, reading 'The Love He Could Not Buy', in the *Daily Mirror*, a spruce young civil servant on his way to the Foreign Office, reading *The Times*, a clergyman reading the *Challenge*, who looked as if he was interested in the Life and Liberty movement, another clergyman reading the *Guardian*, who looked as if he wasn't, an elderly gentleman reading the *Morning Post*, who looked patriotic but soured, as if he had volunteered for National Service during the Great

War and had found it disappointing, a young man reading the *Post-War*, the alert new daily, and a citizen with a law-abiding face very properly perusing the *Hidden Hand*. The *Hidden Hand* was the Government daily paper. Such a paper had for long been needed; it is difficult to understand why it was not started long ago. All other papers are so unreliable, so tiresome; a government must have one paper on which it can depend for unfailing support. So here was the *Hidden Hand*, and its readers had no excuse for ignorance of what the government desired them to think about its own actions.

The carriage was full of men and women going to their places of business. There were tired young men, lame young men, pale and scarred young men, brown and fit young men, bored and *blasé* young men, jolly and amused young men, and nearly all, however brown or fit or pale or languid or jolly or bored, bore a peculiar and unmistakable impress stamped, faintly or deeply, on their faces, their eyes, their carriage, the set of their shoulders.

There were, among the business men and girls, women going shopping, impassive, without newspapers, gazing at the clothes of others, taking in their cost, their cut, their colour. This is an engrossing occupation. Those who practise it sit quite still, without a stir, a twinkle, a yawn, or a paper, and merely look, all over, up and down, from shoes to hat … They are a strange and wonderful race of beings, these gazing women; one cannot see into their minds, or beyond their roving eyes. They bear less than any other section of the community the stamp of public events. The representatives of the type in the Bakerloo this morning did not carry any apparent impress of the Great War. It would take something more than a great war, something more even than a food crisis, to leave its mark on these sphinx-like and immobile countenances. Kingdoms may rise and fall, nations may reel in the death-grapple, but they sit gazing still, and their minds, amid the rocking chaos, may be imagined to be framing some such thoughts as these: 'Those are nice shoes. I wonder if they're the ones Swan and Edgar have at 30s. She's trimmed her hat herself, and not well. That skirt is last year's shape. That's a smart coat. Dear me, what stockings; you'd think anyone would be ashamed.'

These women had not the air of reckless anticipation, of being alert for any happening, however queer, that, in differing degrees, marked the majority of people in these days. For that, in many, seemed the prevailing note; a series of events so surprising as to kill surprise, of disasters so appalling as to numb horror, had come and gone, leaving behind them this reckless touch, and with it a kind of greed, a determination to snatch whatever might be from life before it tumbled again into chaos. They had not been devoid of lessons in what moralists call Making the Best of It, those staggering years when everything had fallen and fallen, successively and simultaneously, civilisation, and governments, and hopes, and crowns, and nations, and soldiers, and rain, and tears, and bombs, and buildings, only not prices, or newspapers.

For, if everything had so fallen once, it might even now be riding for a fall again (in spite of the League of Nations and other devices for propping up the unsteady framework of a lasting peace). The thing was to get what one could first. The thing, in the opinion of one traveller in that train, was to wear cap and bells, to dance through life to a barrel organ, to defeat a foolish universe with its own weapons.

And always there was that sense in the background of a possible great disaster, of dancing on the world's thin crust that had broken once and let one through, and might break again. Its very thinness, its very fragility added a desperate gaiety to the dance.

2

Ivy Delmer (who was not the traveller alluded to above, and did not consciously think or feel any of these things) stood holding to a strap, with the novel which she was going to change in the lunch hour in one hand. Ivy Delmer, a shorthand typist at the Ministry of Brains, was young, ingenuous, soft-faced, naïve, and the daughter of a Buckinghamshire vicar. The two things she loved best in the world were marzipan and the drama. Her wide grey eyes travelled, with innocent interest, along the faces in the compartment; she was seeing if she liked them or not. Immaturely and unconsciously sexual, she looked with more hope of satisfaction at male faces than at female. Not but that she was susceptible to strong admirations for her own sex; she had a 'pash' for Miss Doris Keane and Miss Teddie Gerard, and, in private life, a great esteem for Miss Grammont, at the Ministry, whose letters she sometimes took down in shorthand. But everyone knows there is a greater number of interesting faces in trains belonging to another sex than to one's own, and it is no use pretending.

Having subjected the faces within her range to her half-unconscious judgment, and passed them with varying degrees of credit, Miss Delmer, for lack of anything better to do, read the advertisements and exhortations over the windows. With satisfaction she noted that she had seen all the advertised plays. She absorbed such temporal maxims and eternal truths as 'Let Mr Mustard mix your bath', 'God is not mocked', and the terrifying utterances of the Safety-if-Possible Council, 'Is it safe? That is the question. No. That is the answer'. 'If you hope to achieve safety in a street aero (1) Do not alight before the aero does. (2) Do not attempt to jump up into an aero in motion'. Then a picture: 'A will be killed because he is standing immediately beneath a descending aero bus. B will be killed because he and others like him have shaken the nerve of the aviator'. A series of warnings which left one certain that, wherever one might achieve safety, it would not be in, or anywhere at all near, a street aero. That, probably, is the object. In the old days it was the motor bus that was thus made a thing of terror by the princes of the nether world. Now, even as then, their efforts met with success, and the tubes were filled with a panic-stricken mob.

Ivy Delmer, taking an empty seat, saw Miss Grammont at the other side of the carriage. Miss Grammont had the *New Statesman* and the *Tatler* and was reading one of them. She was partial to both, which was characteristic of her attitude towards life. She was one of those who see no reason why an intelligent interest in the affairs of the world should be incompatible with a taste for Eve. She enjoyed both classical concerts and new revues. She might be called a learned worldling. Ivy Delmer was rather shy of her, because of her manner, which could be supercilious, because of her reputed cleverness, and because of her position at the Ministry, which was a long way above Ivy's. On the other hand, her clothes made one feel at home; they showed skill and interest; she had not that air of the dowd which some people who have been to college have, and which is so estranging to normal people.

Kitty Grammont, something of the elegant rake, something of the gamin, something of the adventuress, something of the scholar, with innocent amber-brown eyes gazing ingenuously from under long black lashes, a slightly cynical mouth, a small, smooth, rounded, child's face, a travelled manner, and an excellent brain, was adequately, as people go, equipped for the business of living. She had seen some life, in a past which, if chequered, had not lacked its gaiety, meant to see much more, in a future which she did not foresee clearly but which she intended should be worthy of her, and was seeing enough to go on with in a present which, though at moments it blackly bored her (she was very susceptible to boredom), was on the whole decidedly entertaining.

Ivy Delmer, looking at her across the compartment, with some surprise because she was so nearly punctual this morning, this not being one of her habits, admired her greatly, thinking how clever she was, how clearly, how unhesitatingly, how incisively her sentences came out when she was dictating, cutting their way, in that cool, light, dragging voice of hers, through her subject, however intricate, as a sharp blade cuts ice; quite different from some people's dictation, which trails to and fro, emending, cancelling, hesitating, indistinct, with no edge to it, so that one's shorthand has constantly to be altered, making a mess on the page, and bits of it read aloud to see how it goes now, which was a nuisance, because one can't rely always on being able to read off even one's own shorthand quite fluently straight away like that. Further — and this was nearer Ivy's heart — Miss Grammont wore, as a rule, charming shoes. She also smoked extraordinarily nice cigarettes, and often had delicious chocolates, and was generous with both.

All this made it a grief to Ivy Delmer that Miss Grammont's brother and his family, who lived in her father's parish, and with whom Miss Grammont often stayed, were not Approved Of. Into the reasons for this it will be more appropriate to enter later in this narrative.

3

Oxford Circus. The hub of the world, where seething mobs fought on the platform like wild beasts. Piccadilly Circus. Lucky people, thought Ivy Delmer, who got out there, all among gaiety and theatres. Trafalgar Square. There naval officers got out, to visit the Admiralty, or the Nelson Column.

Charing Cross. There people had got out during the Great War, to go and help the War Office or the Ministry of Munitions to run the business. So much help, so much energy, so many hotels … And now there were more than ever, because so much needed doing, and hotels are the means heaven has given us to do it with.

At Charing Cross Ivy Delmer and Kitty Grammont got out, for, without specifying the hotel where the Ministry of Brains carried on its labours, it may be mentioned without indiscretion that it was within a walk of Charing Cross.

Miss Grammont and Miss Delmer walked there, Miss Delmer well ahead and hurrying, because to her it seemed late, Miss Grammont behind and sauntering because to her it seemed superfluously early. The Ministry daily day began at 9.30, and it was only 9.40 now.

The summer morning was glittering on the river like laughter. A foolish thing it seemed, to be going into an hotel on a summer morning, to be sitting down at a government desk laden with government files, taking a government pen (which was never a relief, only a not-exactly) and writing pamphlets, or answers to letters which, if left long enough, would surely answer themselves, as is the way of letters, and all to improve the Brains of the Nation. Bother the Brains of the Nation, thought Miss Grammont, only she used a stronger word, as was the custom in what Mrs Delmer called her unfortunate family. Black doubt sometimes smote her as to not so much the efficacy of the work of her Department as its desirability if ever it should be perfectly accomplished. Did brains matter so greatly after all? Were the clever happier than the fools? Miss Grammont, whose university career had been a brilliant intellectual adventure, felt competent to speak for both these types of humanity. She knew herself to be happier when playing the fool than when exerting her highly efficient brain; the lunatic-asylum touch gave her more joy than the studious, and she wore learning like a cap and bells. But stupidity was, of course, a bore. It must, of course, be mitigated, if possible. And anyhow the object of the Ministry of Brains was not to make people happy (that could be left to the Directorate of Entertainments), nor to make them good (that was up to the Church, now, to the great benefit of both, divorced from the State), but to further social progress and avert another Great War.

Miss Grammont yawned, because the day was yet so young, and followed Miss Delmer up the steps of the hotel.

4

The Ministry of Brains, a vast organisation, had many sections. There was the Propaganda Section, which produced pamphlets and organised lectures and cinema shows (Miss Grammont had been lent temporarily to this section by her own branch); there was the Men's Education Section, the Women's, and the Children's; the Section which dealt with brain-tests, examinations, certificates, and tribunals, and the Section which was concerned with the direction of the intellects of the Great Unborn. Ivy Delmer was attached to this section, and Mr Delmer, when he heard about it, was not altogether sure it was quite nice for her.

'She surely shouldn't know they have any,' he had said to his wife, who was weeding, and replied absently, 'Any what, dear? Who?'

'Intellects,' the vicar said. 'The Unborn. Besides, they haven't.' He was frowning, and jerking out dandelions from the lawn with a spud.

'Oh, that's not it, dear', Mrs Delmer reassured him vaguely. 'Not the just unborn, you know. The — the ever so long unborn. All this arrangement of who ought to marry who. Quite silly, of course, but no harm for Ivy in that way. After all, there's no reason why she shouldn't know that children often inherit their brains from their parents.'

The vicar admitted that, even for their precious and very young Ivy, there was no great harm in this.

The Section in question was, as Mrs Delmer had stated, concerned with the encouragement and discouragement of alliances in proportion as they seemed favourable or otherwise to the propagation of intelligence in the next generation. There were numerous and complicated regulations on the subject, which could not, of course, be enforced; the Ministry's methods were those of stimulation, reward and punishment, rather than of coercion. There were bonuses on the births of the babies of parents conforming to the regulations, and penal taxes on unregulated infants, taxes increasing in proportion to the flagrancy of the parents' disobedience, so that the offspring of parents of very low mental calibre brought with them financial ruin. Everyone held a Ministry of Brains form, showing his or her mental category, officially ascertained and registered. If you were classified A, your brains were certified to be of the highest order, and you were recommended to take a B2 or B3 partner (these were the quite intelligent). To ally yourself with another A or a B1 was regarded as wasteful, there not being nearly enough of these to go round, and your babies would receive much smaller bonuses. If you were classed C1, C2, or C3, your babies would receive no encouragement, unless you had diluted their folly with an A partner; if you chose to unite with another C they were heavily fined, and if you were below C3 (ie uncertificated) they were fined still more heavily, by whomsoever diluted, and for the third and subsequent infants born under such conditions you would be imprisoned. (Only the Ministry had not been working long enough for anyone to have yet met with this fate. The children of unions perpetrated before the Mental Progress Act were at present exempt.) Families among the lower grades and among the uncertificated were thus drastically discouraged. You were uncertificated for matrimonial purposes not only if you were very stupid, but if, though yourself of brilliant mental powers, you had actual deficiency in your near family. If you were in this case, your form was marked 'A (Deficiency)'.

And so on: the details of the regulations, their intricacies and tangled knots, the endless and complicated special arrangements which were made with various groups and classes of persons, may be easily imagined, or (rather less easily, because the index is poor) found in the many volumes of the Ministry of Brains Instructions.

Anyhow, to room number 13, which was among the many rooms where this vast and intricate subject was dealt with, Ivy Delmer was summoned this Monday morning to take down a letter for Vernon Prideaux.

5

Vernon Prideaux was a fair, slim, neat, eye-glassed young man; his appearance and manners were approved by Ivy Delmer's standards and his capabilities by the heads of his department. His intellectual category was A; he had an impatient temper, a ready tongue, considerable power over papers (an important gift, not possessed by all civil servants), resource in emergency, competence in handling situations and persons, decided personal charm, was the son of one of our more notorious politicians, and had spent most of the war in having malaria on the Struma front, with one interesting break when he was recalled to England by his former department to assist in the drawing up of a new Bill, dealing with a topic on which he was an expert. He was, after all this, only thirty now, so had every reason for believing, as he did, that he would accomplish something in this world before he left it. He had been sucked into the activities of the new Ministry like so many other able young men and women, and was finding it both entertaining and not devoid of scope for his talents.

Ivy Delmer admired him a good deal. She sat at his side with her notebook and pencil, her soft, wide mouth a little parted, waiting for him to begin. He was turning over papers impatiently. He was in a rather bad temper, because of his new secretary, of whom he only demanded a little common sense and did not get it, and he would have to get rid of her, always a tiresome process. He couldn't trust her with anything, however simple; she always made a hash of it, and filled up the gaps, which were profound, in her recollection of his instructions with her own ideas, which were not. He had on Saturday given her some forms to fill up, stock forms which were always sent in reply to a particular kind of letter from the public. The form was supposed merely to say, 'In reply to your letter with reference to your position as regards the tax [or bonus] on your prospective [or potential, or existing] infant, I am to inform you that your case is one for the decision of the Local Tribunals set up under the Mental Progress Act, to whom your application should have been made'. Miss Pomfrey, who was young and full of zeal for the cause (she very reasonably wished that the Mental Progress Act had been in existence before her parents had married), had added on her own account to one such letter, 'It was the stupidity of people like you who caused the Great War', and put it this morning with the other forms on Prideaux's table for signing. Prideaux had enquired, fighting against what he knew to be a disproportionate anger with her, didn't she really know better by now than to think that letters like that would be sent? Miss Pomfrey had sighed. She did not know better than that by now. She knew hardly anything. She was not intelligent, even as B3s went. In fact, her category was probably a mistake. Her babies, if ever she had any, would be of a mental calibre that did not bear contemplation. They would probably cause another Great War.

So Prideaux, who had also other worries, was out of temper.

'Sorry, Miss Delmer … Ah, here we are.' He fidgeted about with a file, then began to dictate a letter, in his quick, light, staccato voice. Ivy, clenching the tip of her pink tongue between her teeth, raced after him.

> 'Sir,
>
> 'In reply to your letter of 26th May with reference to the taxation on babies born to your employees and their consequent demand for increased wages, I am instructed by the Minister of Brains to inform you that this point is receiving his careful attention, in connection with the general economic question involved by the terms of Ministry of Brains Instruction 743, paragraph 3 …'

Prideaux paused, and frowned nervously at his secretary, who was conducting a fruitless conversation over his telephone, an occupation at which she did not shine.

'Hullo … yes … I can't quite hear … who are you, please? … Oh … yes, he's here. … But rather busy, you know … Dictating. … Yes, *dictating*. … *Who* did you say wanted him, please? … Oh, I see … '

'What is it, Miss Pomfrey?' Prideaux broke in, making her start.

'It's the Minister's secretary,' she explained, without covering the receiver. 'He says will you go to the Minister. There's a deputation — of bishops, I think he said. About the new Instruction about Clergymen's Babies … But I said you were busy dictating …'

Prideaux had jumped to his feet, frowning, and was at the door.

'You'd better make a note that I'm never busy dictating or doing anything else when the Minister sends for me,' he shot at her as he left the room.

'And now he's cross,' Miss Pomfrey murmured sadly.

'I daresay he's only angry at being interrupted,' said Ivy Delmer, who had been at the same secretarial college as Miss Pomfrey and thought that her days in the Ministry of Brains were numbered.

'I do make him cross,' Miss Pomfrey observed, accepting the fact with resignation, as one of the sad, inevitable fatalities of life, and returned to her indexing. She had been set to make an index of those Ministry of Brains Instructions which had come out that month. She had only got to the 11th of the month. The draught fluttered the pages about. Ivy Delmer watched the Instructions waving to and fro in the breeze — number 801, Agriculturists, 798, Conscientious Obstructionists, 897, Residents in Ireland, 674, Parents of more than three children.

... How many there were, thought Ivy, as she watched. How clever the people who dealt with such things needed to be. She thought of her father's village, and the people in it, the agriculturists, the parents of more than three children, all the little human community of lives who were intimately affected by one or other of these instructions, and the fluttering pages emerged from the dry realm to which such as Ivy relegate printed matter and ideas, and took vivid human life. It mattered, all this complicated fabric of regulations and rules and agreements and arrangements; it touched the living universe that she knew — the courting boys and girls on stiles in Buckinghamshire lanes, Emmeline, the Vicarage housemaid, who had married Sid Dean last month, Mr and Mrs White at the farm, all the great stupid pathetic aggrieved public, neatly filed letters from whom covered every table in the Ministry, awaiting reply, their very handwriting and spelling calculated to touch any heart but a civil servant's …

Ivy found a moment in which to hope that everyone in the Ministry was being very careful and painstaking about this business, before she reverted to wondering whether or not she liked the colour which Miss Pomfrey had dyed her jersey.

Having decided that she didn't, and also that she had better go away and wait for Mr Prideaux to send for her again, she departed.

6

Vernon Prideaux, having given his assistance to the Minister in the matter of the third clause of the new Clergymen's Babies Instruction, left the Minister and the deputation together and returned to his room via the Propaganda Branch, which he visited in order to ask Miss Grammont to dine with him that evening. He and Kitty Grammont had known one another for some years. They had begun at Cambridge, where Prideaux had been two years the senior, and had kept up an intermittent friendship ever since, which had, since their association in the Ministry, grown into intimacy.

Prideaux found Kitty writing a pamphlet. She was rather good at this form of literature, having a concise and clear-cut style and an instinct for stopping on the right word. Some pamphleteers have not this art: they add a sentence or two more, and undo their effect. The pamphlet on which Miss Grammont was at this moment engaged was intended for the perusal of the working woman, and bore the conversational title, 'The Nation takes an interest in Your Affairs: will You not take an interest in the Affairs of the Nation?' Which, as Miss Grammont observed, took rather a long time to say, but may have been worth it.

'Dine with you? I'll be charmed. Where and when?'

'My rooms, eight o'clock. I've got my parents and the

Minister coming.'

'Oh, the Minister.'

'Do you mind?'

'No, I'm proud to meet him. I've never yet met him over food, so to speak, only officially. I admire our Chester more every day he lives, don't you? Nature made him and then broke the die.'

'Wonderful man,' Prideaux agreed. 'Extraordinary being … A happy touch with bishops, too. Picked that up in the home, no doubt; his father's one. Liking's another thing, of course … By the way, do you know what his category is? However, this is gossip. I must get back and discover what's the latest perpetration of my new secretary. See you tonight, then.'

He left the room. Kitty Grammont observed with satisfaction, for she was critical of such things, how well his clothes fitted him, wondered what he had nearly told her about the Minister's category, finished her pamphlet, and sent it out for typing. She had an idea that this pamphlet might not get passed by the censor, and wanted to find out. For the censor was cautious about pamphlets, wisely opining that you cannot be too careful. Pamphlets may, and usually do, deal with dangerous or indecent topics, such as the Future. If sufficiently dangerous and indecent, they become Leaflets, and are suppressed on sight. There were dangerous and explosive words, like Peace, War, and Freedom which the censor dealt with drastically. The danger of the word Peace dated, of course, from the days when Peace had not yet arrived and discussion of it was therefore improper, like the discussion of an unborn infant. By the time it did arrive, its relegation to the region of Things we do not Mention had become a habit, not lightly to be laid aside, so that a Ministry of Brains pamphlet entitled 'The Peace of Fools' had been strangled before birth, the censor being very naturally unable to believe that it did not refer in some mysterious way to the negotiations which had ended hostilities, whereas as a matter of fact it was all about the foolish content of stupid people who went on submitting to diseases which a little intelligent thought would have prevented. There had also perished, owing to the same caution on the censor's part, and, it must be presumed, to the same guilty conscience on the part of the Government, a booklet published by Messrs Mowbray in a purple paper cover with a gold cross on it, called 'The Peace which passeth understanding', not to mention a new edition of Burke's 'Regicide Peace', and one or two other works of which the censor, whose reading was obliged to be mainly twentieth century, mistook the date. And, if treatises concerning Peace were suspected from force of habit, works on War were discouraged also, on the sound British principle that the stress of a great Peace is not the time to talk of War; we must first deal with Peace, and then we may think about War; but One Thing At Once, and do not let us cry War, War, when there is no war. But there may be one day, argued the pamphleteers, and might it not be well to prepare our minds for it? To which the answer very properly was, No; Britons do not look ahead. They Come Through, instead. And anyhow it was treachery to those who were spending their energies on this righteous peace to discuss a premature war, which could neither be just nor lasting.

Another improper subject, naturally, was Liberty. That needs no explanation; it has always been improper in well-regulated countries, like Eugenics, or the Poor, and has received no encouragement from authority. Notwithstanding this, so many improper works upon it, in every conceivable form, have always been produced, that the censors had to engage a special clerk, who had just obtained a first class in English Literature at Oxford, and who therefore had books and pamphlets of all dates fresh in her memory, to check their researches and inform them when their energies were superfluous. Not that all the books of former centuries on this topic were to be encouraged, for, after all, one period is in some respects singularly like another, and the same reflections strangely germane to both. Naturally, therefore, when the literary clerk, seeing advertised a new and cheap edition of Robert Hall's 'Sentiments proper to the present crisis', and, remembering the trend of this work, sent for it (having sold her own copy at Blackwell's when she went down), and read such remarks as 'Freedom, driven from every spot on the continent, has sought an asylum in a country which she always chose for her favourite abode, but she is pursued even here and threatened with destruction … It is for you to decide whether this freedom shall yet survive, or be clothed with a funeral pall and be wrapped in eternal gloom' — very properly she reported the matter to headquarters, and the cheap edition was called in.

Equally naturally there perished (without the help of the literary clerk, who was not asked to judge of twentieth century literature) various collections of Free Verse, for which the Poetry Bookshop was successfully raided, a tract of the sort which is dropped about trains, published by the Evangelical Tract Society and called 'Throw off your Chains!', 'Citizens of a Free City', which was found at Mowbray's, and bore on its title page the statement 'Jerusalem … is free' (a manifest and seditious untruth, as we, of course, held Jerusalem, in trust for the Jews), and many others of like tendency, such as works on Free Food, Free Drink, Free Housing, Free Love, Free Thought, and Labour, in Chains. Even fiction was suspect. A novel entitled *The Dangers of Dora*, by the well-known author of *The Perils of Pauline* and *The Exploits of Elaine*, was suppressed, in spite of what should have been the reassuring fact that Dora, like Pauline and Elaine before her, triumphantly worsted all her foes in the end, and emerged smiling and safe on the last page. Publishers were known to demand the alteration of a title if the name Dora occurred in it, such wholesome respect did the Censor's methods inspire.

It will therefore be readily understood that even government departments had to go warily in this matter.

The Minister of Brains held pamphlet propaganda to be of the greatest importance. A week ago the workers in the propaganda section had been sent for and interviewed by the Minister in person. This personal contact had, for the time being, oddly weighted Miss Grammont's too irresponsible levity, kindled her rather cynical coolness, given her something almost like zeal. That was one thing about the Minister — he set other people on fire. Another was that his manners were bad but unexpected, and a third that he looked like a cross between M Kerensky, a member of the Geddes family, and Mr Nelson Keys.

Thus Miss Grammont, thoughtfully smoking a Cyprus cigarette, summed up the Minister of Brains.

CHAPTER 2

Little Chantreys

1

Ivy Delmer went home to Little Chantreys on the following Saturday afternoon, after a matinée and tea in town, in the same train, though not the same carriage as Kitty Grammont and Vernon Prideaux, who were presumably spending the week-end at the End House. Ivy travelled home every evening of the week. Miss Grammont had a flat in town, but spent the week-ends when she was not otherwise engaged, with her brother in Little Chantreys, which was embarrassing to Ivy.

As Ivy got out of the train she saw Miss Grammont's brother and the lady who could scarcely be called her sister-in-law, on the platform, accompanied by a queer-looking man of about forty, with ears rather like a faun's. Anyone, thought Ivy, could have guessed which house in Little Chantreys he was staying at. The week-end people who came to the End House differed widely one from another in body and soul; some looked clever, or handsome, others did not, some were over-dressed, some under, some, like Miss Grammont and her brothers, just right; there were musical people, sporting people, literary or artistic people, stagy people (these last were the friends of Miss Pansy Ponsonby, who was not Miss Grammont's sister-in-law), uncommon people, and common people; but they all, thought Ivy Delmer, had two looks in common — they looked as if they wouldn't get on very well with her father and mother, and they looked as if they didn't read the Bible.

This second look was differentiated according to the wearer of it. Some of them (like this man today) looked as if he didn't read it because it had become so inextricably bound up with vulgar superstition and an impossible religion that he despised it. Some, like Miss Grammont and her brother Anthony, looked as if they didn't read it because they already knew enough of it to be funny about it when they wanted to; others, like Miss Pansy Ponsonby, looked as if she had really once given it a try, but had found it dry and put off further perusal until such time as she lay dying and might want to do something about her future state. And Miss Grammont's brother Cyril looked as if it was a Protestant book, and rather vulgar. Some, again, looked innocent, as if they had never heard of it, others guilty, as if they never wanted to again.

Ivy Delmer walked home to the Vicarage, hoping rather that the End House wouldn't come to church tomorrow. It was taken, from time to time, with an unaccountable fit of doing this. It made Ivy uncomfortable. Whether or not it came to pray, she could not help having an uneasy suspicion that it stayed to mock.

2

'Hullo, old dear,' said Miss Pansy Ponsonby, in her rich and resonant drawl, as Kitty and her companion came out of the station. 'Here we all are again. And the Cheeper. He's a growin' boy, our Cheeper: he puts on weight. Takes after me: I put on weight when I forget my exercises and don't keep an eye on myself. Don't I, Tony? Mr Prideaux, isn't it? How do, Mr Prideaux? Vurry pleased you've come. You know Mr Amherst, don't you? You clever folks all know each other.' Miss Ponsonby, who was not an American, had once performed in the same company as Miss Lee White, and had caught an inflexion or two. She looked with the satisfaction of the hospitable hostess at the little group, and added, 'So here we all are. And vurry nice too.'

It was, indeed, not an unpleasing group. Dominating it was Miss Ponsonby herself, very tall, very beautiful, very supple (only a year ago she had been doing her celebrated eel-dance in Hullo, Peace!), with long and lovely violet eyes and the best kind of Icilma skin, adorned tastefully but quite unnecessarily, with pink paint, white powder, scarlet lip salve, and black lash-darkener. All this was from force of habit: Miss Ponsonby was quite adequately pink, white, scarlet and black in her own person. But, as Kitty observed, having been given by heaven such an absurd thing as a human face, what could one do but make it yet more absurd by these superimposed gaieties? You cannot take a face as a serious thing; it is one of nature's jests, and it is most suitably dealt with as the clown and the pierrot deal with theirs. This was Kitty's point of view; Pansy had none, only habits.

Pansy was guiding and controlling a motor-pram, in which lay the Cheeper, aged four months (he had no Christian name, having so far evaded both the registrar and the font, and presumably no surname, owing to the peculiar circumstances of his parents). The Cheeper's father, Anthony Grammont, was a fair, pale, good-looking, rather tired young man of seven and twenty, with a slightly plaintive voice; he looked as if he shared, only with more languor, Miss Ponsonby's placid and engaging enjoyment of the world; he had been in one of the hottest corners of France through the European War, and had emerged from it a bored and unambitious colonel, deaf of one ear, adorned with a Military Cross, and determined to repay himself for his expenditure of so much time, energy and health by enjoying the fifty or sixty years which, he piously hoped, remained to him, to the full. Which he was now doing. His professional life was passed on the Stock Exchange.

Mr Leslie Amherst, the man like a faun, who was staying with him, was an old friend of the Grammont family. He wrote, and was on the staff of a weekly journal. He was engaged just now on a series of articles on the Forces of Darkness in Darkest Europe. So far he had produced 1. The Legislature, 2. Capitalism, 3. Industrialism, 4. Nationalism, 5. Militarism, 6. The Press, and this week he was writing 7. Organised Religion. (It will no doubt shock some readers to learn that these forces had not all, in spite of the earnest hopes entertained for so long for their overthrowal, yet been overthrown; but truth compels me to state that they had not.) Though Amherst talked like a cynic, and had his affectations, he was an earnest thinker, and sometimes tired his host, who was not, and who had been left by his years of difficult continental sojourn with a supreme distaste for any further probing into the problems of Darkest Europe. Amherst had the advantage, in this matter, of having been a Conscientious Objector to Military Service, so the war had not tired him, and he retained for home use the freshness and vigour of attack which had, in the case of many of his fellow-countrymen, been all used up abroad.

The End House party was completed by Kitty Grammont, with her round, long-lashed eyes and her air of the ingenuous rake, and Vernon Prideaux, brisk and neat and clever. So there they all were; and very nice, too.

Kitty kissed her brother and Miss Ponsonby and dug the Cheeper in the ribs in the manner he preferred. She was very fond of them all, and found Miss Ponsonby immeasurably entertaining. Little had she thought, when of old she used joyfully to watch Miss Pansy Ponsonby twist and kick and curl herself about the stage and sing fascinating inanities in her lazy contralto, that they would ever be linked by no common bond. Of course she had known that her brother Anthony was showering flowers, chocolates, suppers, week-ends and air-trips at Miss Ponsonby's nimble feet (the toes of which could bend right back at the joints) but Anthony had been known to shower these things at the feet of others. Certainly Kitty had never expected that he would install this delightful and expensive being in a real house, have a real infant, and really settle down, albeit socially ostracised in Buckinghamshire because imperfectly married (that was the fault of Pansy's husband, Mr Jimmie Jenks, who, though he didn't want her himself, selfishly refused to sever the connection irrevocably).

'What's the afternoon news?' enquired Mr Amherst, as they walked up to the village.

'Haven't seen a paper for half an hour,' replied Prideaux, who kept his finger on the pulse of the nation and liked his news up to date. 'I've got two five o'clock ones with me, though. The Leeds strike is rather worse, the Sheffield one rather better. The aero bus men are coming out on Monday. Dangerous unrest among Sussex shepherds and Cotswold cowmen.' (Agricultural labour was now controlled by the State.) 'Lord Backwoods has been speaking to his constituents against the Bill for disfranchising Conscientious Obstructionists of the Mental Progress Acts. A thoroughly seditious speech, of course. Poor old chap, his eldest son has just got engaged to be married, so there'll be another family of Backwoods babies who ought never to exist. It will hit them heavily financially ... And the International Police have found another underground gun-factory near Munich, under a band-stand. And it's confirmed that old Tommy Jackson is to be Drink Controller.'

'Another good butler spoilt,' observed Anthony Grammont. 'He was a jolly good butler once. And he'll be a jolly bad Drink Controller.'

'Dear old Tommy,' murmured Miss Ponsonby absently, lifting the Cheeper out of his motor-pram with one strong white hand and balancing him on her ample shoulders. 'He was vurry kind to me in the dear old days, when I spent weekends at Surrey Towers. He used to give me tips on Correct Conduct. I didn't take them; Correct Conduct wasn't what the people there asked me for; but I was grateful to Tommy. '

'If,' said Anthony, 'there is any member of a government department, existing, fallen, or yet to come, who has not in the dear old days been vurry kind to you, my dear Pansy, I should be rather glad to know his name.'

'Why, certainly,' returned Pansy, with cheerful readiness. 'Nicky Chester, the Brains Minister who's making himself such an all-round eternal nuisance, doesn't even realise I exist, and if he did he'd think I oughtn't.'

'That's where you're wrong, Pansy,' Kitty said. 'He thinks everyone ought to exist who does anything as well as you do your things. You're Starred A, aren't you?'

'I've gone and lost the silly old bus ticket,' said Pansy indifferently, 'but that's what it said, I think.' Starred A meant (in the words of the official definition) first-class ability at a branch of work which would not appear to be a valuable contribution to the general efficiency of the State. The Cheeper, child of a starred A mother and a B3 father (Anthony's brains had been reduced by trench life; he had been quite intelligent at Oxford), was subject neither to bonus nor tax.

'Anyhow,' went on Pansy, grinning her wide, sweet, leisurely grin, 'I think I see Nicky Chester sendin' me round flowers or goodies after a show! He's seen me, you know: he was in a box the first night of Hullo, Peace! He laughed at the political hits, but my turns left him cold; I guess they weren't brainy enough.' She tossed the Cheeper in the air and caught him, strongly and easily. 'Make him supple young,' she observed, 'an' by the time he's six he'll be a star Child Gamboller, fit for revue. He takes after me. Already he can put both his big toes in his little mouth at once.'

'Very unusual, surely,' remarked Mr Amherst, looking at the Cheeper through his pince-nez as if he were an insect under a microscope. Mr Amherst was a fellow of an Oxford college, and had the academic touch, and was not yet entirely used to Pansy, a type outside his previous studies, and at no time would he be really used to anyone under eighteen years of age, let alone six months. Possibly this was what his reviewers meant when they said that he lacked the touch of common humanity.

His attention was diverted from the Cheeper by the parish church, which he inspected with the same curiosity and distaste.

'Organised Religion, I presume,' he commented. 'If you've no objection, Anthony, I will attend morning service there tomorrow. It may provide me with some valuable subject matter for my article.'

'We'll all go,' said Kitty. 'The End House shall set an example to the village. We'll take Cyril, too. He can get a dispensation. It's Brains Sunday, you know, and all patriotic clergymen will be preaching about it. Vernon and I are officially bound to be there.'

'I don't suppose it will be amusing,' said Anthony. ''But we'll go if you all want to.'

'Church,' said Pansy, meditatively regarding the Early Perpendicular tower. 'I went one Sunday morning.' She paused reminiscently, and added, without chagrin, 'The vicar turned me down.'

'He could hardly,' said Mr Amherst civilly, 'do otherwise. Your position is not one which is at present recognised by Organised Religion.'

'Oh, he recognised it all right,' Pansy explained. 'That was just the trouble; he didn't like it … He's not a bad old sort. He came to call afterwards, and told me all about it. He was quite upset. So was I, wasn't I, old thing?'

'Not in the least,' returned Anthony placidly.

'I'd only wanted to do the proper thing,' Pansy continued her unperturbed narrative, in her singularly beautiful voice. 'I was always brought up to go to church now and then. I was confirmed all right. I like to do the proper thing. It only seems fair to the Cheeper to bring him up in the way he should go. I wouldn't care for him to grow up an agnogger, like all you people. But Mr Delmer said my way of life was too ambiguous to square with comin' to church. Rather a sweet word, don't you think? Because it isn't ambiguous really, you know; not a bit, I'm afraid … So when the Cheeper turned up, it seemed to me he was a bit ambiguous, too, an' that's why I haven't had him made a little Christian yet. The vicar says he can square that up all right — he called on purpose to tell me — but somehow we've never had the time to fix it, have we, darlin'? Tottie O'Clare promised me she'd be godmother if ever I did have him done …'

'Pansy,' said Anthony, 'you're boring Amherst and Prideaux. They're not interested in babies, or baptisms, or Tottie O'Clare.'

Pansy smiled at them all out of her serene violet eyes. She looked like some stately, supple Aphrodite; she might, but for the delicate soupçon of powder and over-red lips, have sat for a madonna.

'Pansy,' said Kitty, 'it's the Sistine Madonna you're like; I've got it at last. You're the divine type. You might be from heaven. You're so restful. We all spin and buzz about, trying to get things done, and to be clever and fussy and efficient — and you just are. You happen, like spring, or music. You're not a bit like Chester, but you're ever so much more important. Isn't she, Vernon?'

'They're both,' said Prideaux tactfully, 'of enormous importance. And certainly, as you say, not in the least alike. Chester is neither like spring nor music, and certainly one wouldn't call him restful. And I should be a bit surprised to learn that heaven is where he either began or will end his career ... But, I ask you, look at that.'

They were passing the little Town Hall that stood in the village market place. Its face was plastered with an immense poster, which Prideaux and Kitty surveyed with proprietary pride, Amherst with cynical amusement, Anthony with bored resignation, and Pansy and the Cheeper with placid wonder at the world's folly.

'Ours is a wonderful government,' Kitty commented. 'And we are a wonderful ministry. Think of rural England all plastered with that ... I don't believe Chester laughs when he sees it, Vernon. I'm sure he looks at it proudly, like a solemn, earnest little boy.'

'And quite right too,' said Prideaux, screwing his glass into his eye the better to read. For this was a new Ministry of Brains poster; new this week. It read, in large type, 'Improve your Brains! Go in for the Government Course of Mind Training! It will benefit you, it will benefit your country, it will benefit posterity. Old Age must come. But it need not be a Doddering Old Age. Lay up Good Mental Capacities to meet it, and make it a Fruitful and Happy Time. See what the Mind Training Course has done for others, and let it Do the Same for You.'

Then, in smaller type, 'Here are a few reports from those who have benefited from it.'

> *From a famous financier.* Since I began the Course I have doubled my income and halved those of 750 others. I hope, by the time I have completed the Course, to have ruined twice this number.

From a Cabinet Minister. Owing to the Mind Training Course I have now remained in office for over six weeks. I hope to remain for at least three more.

From a newspaper proprietor. I have started eight new journals since I took the Course, overturned three governments, directed four international crises, and successfully represented Great Britain to the natives of the Pacific Islands.

From the editor of a notorious weekly paper. I took the Course because I seemed to be losing that unrivalled touch which has made my paper what, I may say, it is. Since taking it, more than my old force has returned, so that I have libelled nine prominent persons and successfully defended six libel actions in the courts. The M T Course teaches one to Live at one's Best.

From a Civil Servant. Every time a new government department is born I enter it, rendered competent by the Mind Training Course to fill its highest posts. When the Department falls I leave it, undamaged.

From a Publisher. My judgment has been so stimulated by the Course that since taking it I have published five novels so unpleasant that correspondence still rages about them in the columns of the *Spectator*, and which have consequently achieved ten editions. The Course teaches one why some succeed and others fail.

From a Journalist. I now only use the words decimated, literally, annihilated, and proletariat, according to the meanings ascribed to them in the dictionary, do not use 'pacifism' more than three times a day, nor 'very essential' or 'rather unique' at all.

From a famous Theologian. Before I undertook the Course I was a Bishop of a disestablished Church. Now my brain is clarified, my eyes are opened, and I am a leader of the Coming Faith. The Course teaches the Meaning of Life.

From a former Secretary of State. Since taking the Course I have recognised the importance of keeping myself informed as to public affairs, and now never refer in my public speeches to any speech by another statesman without having previously read a summary of it.

From a poet. I can now find rhymes to nearly all my lines, and have given up the old-fashioned habit of free rhythms to which I have been addicted since 1912. I can even find rhymes to indemnity, also a rhyme to War which is neither gore, claw, nor star.

From an inveterate writer of letters to newspapers. I no longer do this.

From a citizen. I was engaged to be married. Now I am not.

Then in large type again,

All this has happened to Others! Why should it not happen to You? Save yourself, save your country, save the world! How shall wisdom be found, and where is the place of understanding? So asked the Preacher of the ancient world, and got no answer, because then there was none. But the answer is now forthcoming. Wisdom is to be found in the Government Mind Training Course — the M T C, as it is affectionately called by thousands of men and women who are

> deriving benefits from it. Enter for it today. For further information apply Mind Training Section, Ministry of Brains, SW1.

Above the letterpress was a picture poster, representing two youths, and called 'Before and After'. 'Before' had the vacuity of the village idiot, 'After' the triumphant cunning of the maniac. The Mind Training Course had obviously completely overset a brain formerly harmless; if deficient.

'How long,' enquired Amherst, in his best Oxford manner, 'do you give yourselves? I address the enquiry, as a member of the public, to you, as servants of a government which can resort to such methods as that.'

'We have now remained in office for over six months,' said Kitty, 'and we hope to remain for at least three more … But it's for us to ask you, as a member of the public, how long you intend to give us? Personally I'm astonished every day that our hotel, and all the other hotels, aren't stormed and wrecked. I don't know why the Aero Bus Company, while it's on strike, doesn't sail over us and drop bombs. It shows we must be more popular than we deserve. It shows that people really *like* being coerced and improved. They know they need it. Look at the people going about this village; look at their faces, I ask you. They're like 'Before'. Look at the policeman at his door, half out of his clothes. He's god-like to look at; he's got a figure like the Discobolus, and the brain of a Dr Watson. He could never track a thief. He's looking at us; he thinks we're thieves, probably, just because we're ambiguous. That's the sort of mind he has. Look at the doctor, in his absurd little Ford. How much do you suppose he knows about curing people, or about the science of bodies? He patches them up with pills and drugs, and … But he didn't cut us, Tony. Why not?'

'He and the vicar don't,' explained Anthony. 'Professional attendance. There's the vicar, outside that cottage. See him put his hand up as we pass him.'

He returned the salute with some pride, and Pansy nodded agreeably. Amherst examined the vicar, who was small and sturdy and had a nice kind face.

Amherst shook his head when they had left him behind.

'Not nearly clever enough for the part,' he pronounced. 'To organise religion a man should have the talents of the devil, or at least of the intelligent civil servant. Prideaux would do it quite well; or Chester; only Chester might be too erratic for the popular taste. No wonder Christianity is the ineffective thing it is in this country, if it's left in the hands of officials like that. That man couldn't organise anything; I bet even his school treats go wrong—too few buns or something. That's the hope for the world, that inefficiency of most religious officials; that's why the public will succeed before long in throwing off the whole business, even before they succeed in downing Parliament and the British autocracy, who are a shade more acute. From my point of view your vicar's stupidity is all to the good. If he preaches tomorrow as the Brains Ministry want him to — and he looks loyal and patriotic enough to try — he'll be preaching against his own interests. But that's what all you Brains people are doing, of course. You don't seem to see that if you ever were to succeed in making the human race reasonably intelligent, your number would be up; you wouldn't be stood for a moment longer. You're sitting on a branch and trying to saw it off. Lucky for you your saws aren't sharper.'

'Chester would go on just the same if he did see,' Kitty said. 'He probably does. He's an idealist, but his eye for facts is very penetrating. And he'd think it worthwhile to perish in so good a cause.'

'The fact is,' added Prideaux, 'that he never would perish, even if the branch did fall; he'd climb on to another pretty quickly and rise as the People's Saviour. Our Nicky won't go under.'

3

They arrived at the End House, about which there is little to say except that it lay just beyond the straggling village, was roomy, comfortable, untidy, full of dogs all named after revue stars, and was an interesting mixture of the Grammont taste in art and decoration, which was the taste of clever people several of whom were artists, and of Pansy's taste, which is most shortly indicated by mentioning that if you saw the house before you saw Pansy you were surprised, and if you had seen Pansy first you were not. The drawing-room floor was littered with large and comfortable and brightly-hued cushions, obviously not mistakes but seats. This always a little flurried the vicar and his wife when they called; it was, as Mrs Delmer observed, so very Eastern, and suggested other habits belonging to the same dubious quarter of the globe, some of which there was only too good reason to believe had been adopted. The chimney-piece was worse, being adorned by photographs of Pansy's friends—her loving Tottie, hers everlastingly, Guy, warmly Phyllis and Harry, and so forth. (There was even hers Jimmie, which, if Mrs Delmer had known rather more of Pansy's domestic circumstances than she did, would have struck her as being in very doubtful taste.) Some of these ladies and gentlemen, fortunately, had elected to be taken head and shoulders only (and quite enough too, thought Mrs Delmer, wondering how far below the bottom of the photograph the ladies' clothes began) and some showed the whole figure. ('I should think they did!' said Mrs Delmer, on her first call, nervously retreating from the chimney-piece.

It may be mentioned that Mrs Delmer was not in the habit of witnessing revues, and was accustomed to an ampler mode of garment. These things are so much a question of habit.)

These photographs, and the excellent painting in the hall of Pansy herself in her eel dance, were among the minor reasons why Ivy Delmer was not allowed to enter the End House. There were three reasons why her parents did so; they might be stupid, but they were of an extraordinary goodness, and could not bear to leave sin alone, anyhow in their own parish, where it set such an unfortunate example, when they might, by sufficient battling, perhaps win it over to righteousness; also they had kind and soft hearts, and did not like the idea of Pansy alone all day with her infant son and the two most notoriously ill-behaved young servants in the village; and finally they were Christians, and believed that the teaching of their religion on the subject of sociability to sinners was plain. So, swallowing their embarrassed distaste, they visited the End House as one might visit a hospital, but kept their children from it, because it was a hospital whose patients might be infectious.

Into this house, standing hospitably open-doored in the May evening, its owner and his friends entered. It affected them in various ways. Anthony Grammont was proud of his house and garden, his Pansy and his Cheeper. He was young enough to be vain of being head of a household, even of an ambiguous household, and of course anyone would be proud of the dazzling and widely-known Pansy, whose name had always been one of the two in large type in advertisements of the shows in which she figured (she was as good as all that); and he was tired enough, mentally and physically, by his life of the last few years, its discomforts, its homelessness, its bondage, its painful unnaturalness, to sink with relief into Pansy's exotic cushions and all they stood for.

Kitty found the house and household inordinately cheering and entertaining; the mere sight of Pansy's drawing-room could rouse her from any depression.

Vernon Prideaux shuddered a little at the row of photographs — he detested photographs on chimney-pieces — and the Eve design on the chair covers; he was not so good at the comic-opera touch as Kitty was, and had a masculine sense of propriety and good taste, and had always preferred revue stars on the stage to off it. He had also, however, a wide tolerance for the tastes of others, and was glad that Tony Grammont had found domestic happiness.

Amherst's thoughts were brief and neat, and might be summed up thus: 'Forces of Darkness — number 8. The expensive, conscienceless, and unthinking female.'

Pansy went upstairs to put the Cheeper to bed, and Kitty went with her to see her nephew in his bath, putting both his big toes into his mouth at once.

The only other event of importance which happened before dinner was the arrival of Cyril Grammont, a brother of Anthony's, a Cambridge friend of Prideaux's, a Roman Catholic, a writer of epigrammatic essays and light verse, and a budding publisher. He and Pansy usually quarrelled. He had spent the war partly in Macedonia as a member of the Salonika Force, digging up fragments of sculpture from Amphipolis and the other ruined cities of those regions, tracking what he then held to be the pernicious influence of St Paul with the help of a pocket atlas of his journeys and the obviously evil habits and dispositions of the towns which had received his attentions, and partly in Palestine, where he had taken an extreme dislike to both Jews and Turks, had become convinced that they must be so wrong about everything that mattered that Christians must be right, and was forthwith converted from atheism to Christianity. He considered that war-time is no time for Christians, they have to do so much either explaining or protesting or both, so he had waited till the war was over, and had then proceeded to investigate the various forms into which Christianity had developed (they all seemed a little strange to him at first), in order to make his choice. An impartial friend with whom he discussed the subject told him that he would find Roman Catholicism best suited to his precise, clear-cut, and Latin type of mind, provided that he succeeded in avoiding all contact with the more luscious forms of Roman devotions, which, he was warned, would disgust him as much as patchouli, or Carlo Dolci. 'And anyhow,' added his friend, probably erroneously, 'it will outlast the other churches, for all its obscurantism, so if you want a going concern, join it.'

So Cyril enquired into Roman Catholicism, found that, in its best cathedral forms, it satisfied his artistic sense, and, in its sharply-cut dogma, his feeling for precise form (his taste in art was violently against the post-bellum school, which was a riot of lazy, sloppy, and unintellectual formlessness), and so, accepting as no stranger than most of the growths of a strangely sprouting world the wonderful tree which had grown from a seed so remarkably dissimilar, he took a firm seat upon its branches, heedless of the surprised disapproval of most of his friends, who did not hold that any organised religion could be called a going concern, except in the sense that it was going to pot.

So here was Cyril, at the End House for Sunday, neat, handsome, incisive, supercilious, very sure of himself, and not in the least like the End House, with its slatternly brilliance, its yapping dogs, its absurdities, its sprawling incoherence, its cushions, and its ambiguity.

In the evening Pansy danced her willow-tree dance for them. Her hair tumbled down, and she ceased to look like the Sistine Madonna and became more like a young Bacchanal. Some of her jokes were coarse (you have to be coarse sometimes in revue, and cannot leave the habit entirely behind you when you come off the boards) and Amherst, who was refined, was jarred. Then she quarrelled with Cyril, because he remarked, with his cheerful and businesslike air of finality, that of course if the Cheeper were not baptised he would go to hell. Upon her violent remonstrance he merely observed that he was sorry, but facts were facts, and he couldn't get them altered to please her. He talked like this partly to annoy Pansy, because it amused him to see her cross, and partly for the pleasure of unobtrusively watching Amherst's expression when the word hell was mentioned.

So, to unite the party, Kitty proposed that they should play the new card game, League of Nations, of which the point was to amass cards and go out while presenting an appearance of doing nothing at all.

Thus harmoniously and hilariously the night wore on, till at last the End House, like the other Little Chantreys houses, only much later, went to bed.

4

Little Chantreys slept under the May moon, round the market square with the Ministry of Brains poster in the middle.

The doctor slept with the sound sleep of those who do not know the width of the gulf between what they are and what they should be.

The sick, his patients, slept or woke, tossing uneasily, with windows closed to the soft night air. Every now and then they would rouse and take their medicine, with impatience, desperation, simple faith, or dull obedience, and look in vain for a bettering of their state. Those who considered themselves well, never having known what welfare really was, slept too, in stuffy, air-tight rooms, disturbed by the wailing of babies which they had not taught not to cry aloud, by the hopping of fleas which they had failed to catch or to subdue, by the dancing of mice which would never enter traps so obvious as those which they scornfully perceived in their paths, by the crowding of children about them, too close to be forgotten or ignored, by the dragging weight of incompetent, unfinished yesterday, and incompetent, unbegun tomorrow.

The vicarage slept. The vicar in his sleep had a puzzled frown, as if life was too much for him, as if he was struggling with forces above his comprehension and beyond his grasp, forces that should have revolutionised Little Chantreys, but, in his hands, wouldn't. The vicar's wife slept fitfully, waking to worry about the new cook, whose pastry was impossible. She wasn't clever enough to know that cooking shouldn't be done in this inefficient, wasteful way in the home, but co-operatively, in a village kitchen, and pastry should be turned out by a pastry machine. Mrs Delmer had heard of this idea, but didn't like it, because it was new. She wasn't strong, and would die one day, worn out with domestic worries which could have been so easily obviated ...

The young Delmers slept. They always did. They mostly ought not to have been born at all; they were, except Ivy, who was moderately intelligent, below standard. They slept the sleep of the unthinking.

The vicarage girl slept. She would sleep for some time, because her alarum clock was smothered by a cushion; which would seem to indicate more brains on her part than were to be found in the other inmates of the vicarage.

So Little Chantreys slept, and the world slept, governments and governed, forces of darkness and forces of light, industry and idleness, the sad and the gay; pathetic, untutored children of the moment looking neither behind nor ahead.

The morning light, opening dimly, like a faintly tinted

flower, illumined the large red type of the poster in the Little Chantreys market place. 'IMPROVE YOUR BRAINS!' So Brains Sunday dawned upon a world which did indeed seem to need it.

CHAPTER 3

Brains Sunday

1

Ivy Delmer had been right in her premonition. The End House was in church, at matins (the form of Sunday midday worship still used in Little Chantreys, which was old-fashioned). Ivy looked at them as they sat in a row near the front. Mr Anthony Grammont and Miss Ponsonby sat next each other and conversed together in whispers. Miss Ponsonby was attired in pink gingham, and not much of it (it was not the fashion to have extensive clothes, or of rich materials, lest people should point at you as a profiteer who had made money out of the war; even if you had done this you hid it as far as was convenient, and what you did not hide you said was interest on war loans). Miss Ponsonby, with her serene smile, looked patient, resigned, and very sweet and good. Next to her was Miss Grammont, who looked demure in a dress of motley, and, beyond her again, Mr Prideaux, who looked restless and impatient, either as if he were thinking out some departmental tangle, or as if he thought it had been a silly idea to come to church, or both. At the end of the row were Mr Amherst, who was studying the church, the congregation and the service through his glasses, collecting copy for his essay, and Mr Cyril Grammont, who looked like a Roman Catholic attending a Protestant church by special dispensation. (This look cannot be defined, but is known if seen.)

Ivy looked from the End House to her father, surpliced at the lectern, reading the Proper Lesson appointed for

Brains Sunday, Proverbs 8 and 9. 'Shall not wisdom cry, and understanding put forth her word? She standeth in the top of high places, by the way, in the places of the paths. She crieth at the gates, at the entry of the city, at the coming in at the doors … O ye simple, understand wisdom, and, ye fools, be of an understanding heart … Wisdom hath builded her house, she hath hewn out her even pillars' (that was the Ministry hotel, thought Ivy) … 'She hath sent forth her maidens, she crieth upon the highest place of the city' (on the walls of the Little Chantreys town hall). 'Whoso is simple, let him turn in hither … Forsake the foolish and live, and go in the way of understanding … Give instruction to a wise man and he will get wiser; teach a just man and he will increase in learning … The fear of the Lord is the beginning of wisdom, and the knowledge of the holy is understanding …' Which set Ivy Delmer wondering a little, for she believed her parents to be holy, or anyhow very, very good, and yet … But perhaps they had, after all, the beginning of wisdom, only not its middle, nor its end, if wisdom has any end. She looked from her father, carefully closing the big Bible and remarking that here ended the first lesson, to her mother, carefully closing her little Bible (for she was of those who follow lessons in books); her mother, who was so wonderfully good and kind and selfless, and to whom old age must come, and who ought to be preparing for it by going in for the Government Mind Training Course, but who said she hadn't time, she was so busy in the house and garden and parish. And half the things she did or supervised in the house and garden ought, said the Ministry of Brains, to be done by machinery, or co-operation, or something. They would have been done better so, and would have left the Delmers and their parishioners more time. More time for what, was the further question? 'Save time now spent on the mere business of living, and spend it on better things,' said the Ministry pamphlets. Reading, Ivy supposed; thinking, talking, getting *au fait* with the affairs of the world. And here was Mrs Delmer teaching each new girl to make pastry (no new girl at the vicarage ever seemed to have acquired the pastry art to Mrs Delmer's satisfaction in her pre-vicarage career) — pastry, which should have been turned out by the yard in a pastry machine; and spudding up weeds one by one, which should have been electrocuted, like superfluous hairs, or flung up like dynamite, like fish in a river ... But when Mrs Delmer heard of such new and intelligent labour-saving devices, she was as reluctant to adopt them as any of the poor dear stupid women in the cottages. It was a pity, because the Church should lead the way; and really now that it had been set free of the State it quite often did.

Ivy looked with puzzled, thoughtful eyes, which this morning, unusually, were observing people rather than their clothes, at the rest of the congregation, her own brothers and sisters first. The young Delmers were several in number; there was Betty, who had just left school, and showed no signs of 'doing' anything, except her hair, the flowers, and occasionally the lamps. For the rest, she played tennis for prizes and hockey for Bucks, went out to tea, and when in doubt dyed her clothes or washed the dogs. There was Charlie, at Cambridge. Charlie was of those for whom the Great War had been allowed to take the place of the Little Go, which was fortunate in his case, as he had managed to get through the one but would probably in no circumstances have got through the other. And there was Reggie, who had got through neither, but had been killed at Cambrai in November 1917. There also some little ones, Jane and John, aged twelve and eleven, who, though separated by the length of a seat, still continued to hold communication by Morse, and Jelly, who was named for a once famous admiral and whose age cannot be specified. Jelly was small and stout, sat between his mother and Ivy and stared at his father in the choir-stalls, and from time to time lifted up his voice and laughed, as if he were at a Punch and Judy show.

On the whole an agreeable family, and well-intentioned (though Ivy and Betty quarrelled continuously and stole each other's things), but certainly to be numbered among the simple, who were urged to get understanding. Would they ever get it? That was the question, for them and for the whole congregation here present, from the smallest, grubbiest school-child furtively sucking bulls'-eyes and wiping its sticky hands upon its teacher's skirt, to the vicar in the pulpit, giving out his text.

'The fool hath said in his heart, there is no God'; that was the text. Ivy saw a little smile across the clever and conceited face of Mr Amherst as it was given out. He settled himself down to listen, expectant of entertainment. He believed that he was in luck. For Mr Amherst, who did not say in his heart that there was no God, because even in his heart he scorned the affirmation of the obvious, was of those who are sure that all members of the Christian Church are fools (unlike Mr Arnold Bennett, who tries and fails, he did not even try to think of them as intellectual equals), so he avoided, where he could, the study of clever Christians, and welcomed the evidences of weakness of intellect that crossed his path. He believed that this was going to be a foolish sermon, which, besides amusing them all, would help him in his article on Organised Religion.

Ivy could not help watching the End House people. Somehow she knew how the sermon was affecting them. She didn't think it funny, but she suspected that they would. Her father wasn't as clever as they were; that was why he failed to say anything that could impress them except as either dull or comic. Brains again. How much they mattered. Clergymen ought to have brains; it seemed very important. They ought to know how to appeal to rich and poor, high and low, wise and simple. This extraordinary thing called religion — (Ivy quite newly and unusually saw it as extraordinary, seeing it for a moment with the eyes of the End House, to all of whom, except Miss Ponsonby and, presumably, Cyril Grammont, it was like fairy lore, like Greek mythology, mediæval archaic nonsense) — this extraordinary lore and the more extraordinary force behind it, was in the hands, mainly (like everything else), of incompetents, clerical and lay, who did not understand it themselves and could not help others to do so. They muddled about with it, as Miss Pomfrey muddled about with office papers … It would not be surprising if the force suddenly demolished them all, like lightning …

But such speculations were foreign to Ivy, and she forgot them in examining the hat of Mrs Peterson, the grocer's wife, which was so noticeable in its excessive simplicity — its decoration consisted wholly of home-grown vegetables — as to convince beholders that Mr Peterson had not, as some falsely said, made a fortune during the war by cornering margarine.

2

Mr Delmer was talking about the worst form of unwisdom — Atheism; a terrible subject to him, and one he approached with diffidence but resolution, in the face of the unusual pew-full just below him.

'It is an extraordinary thing,' he was saying, 'that there are those who actually deny the existence of God. We have, surely, only to think of the immeasurable spaces of the universe — the distance He has set between one thing and another …

It is reported of the Emperor Napoleon that, looking up at the stars one night, he remarked …' Ivy, who had heard this remark of the Emperor Napoleon's before, let her attention wander again to the hats of Mrs Peterson and others. When she listened once more, the vicar had left Napoleon, though he was still dealing with the heavenly bodies.

'If an express train, performing sixty miles an hour, were to start off from this planet — were such a thing possible to imagine, which of course it is not — towards the moon, and continue its journey without stops until it arrived, it would reach its destination, according to the calculations of scientists, in exactly 1 year, 8 months, 26 days.' (Ivy, who had left school lately enough to remember the distance set by the creator between the earth and the moon, began to work this out in her head; she did not think that her father had got it quite right.)

'And, in the face of this, there are those who say that God does not exist. A further thought, yet more wonderful. If the same train, travelling at the same rapid rate, were to leave this earth again, this time for the sun, the time it would take over this journey would be — I ask you, if you can, to imagine it, my friends — no less than 175 years, I week, and 6 days.' (Ivy gave it up; it was too difficult without pencil and paper.) … 'Is it possible that, knowing this, there are still those who doubt God? Yet once more. Imagine, if you can, this train again starting forth, this time bound for the planet Jupiter. Scientists tell us, and we must believe it,' (All right, thought Ivy, with relief, if he'd got it out of a book), 'that such a journey would take, if performed when Jupiter was at its furthest, 1097 years, 9 months, 2 weeks, 5 days, 10 hours, and a fraction. Can it really be that, confronted with the dizzy thought of these well-nigh incredibly lengthy journeys from one heavenly body to another, there are yet men and women who attribute the universe to the blind workings of what they are pleased to call the Forces of Nature? I ask you to consider earnestly, could any force but God have conceived and executed such great distances? And Jupiter, my friends, is comparatively near at hand. Take instead one of those little (but only apparently little) nameless stars twinkling in the firmament. Imagine our train starting off into space once more …'

Ivy failed to imagine this; her attention was occupied with the End House seat. The train's last journey had been too much for the tottering self-control of the Grammont family and Vernon Prideaux (nothing ever broke down Mr Amherst's self-control, and Pansy's thoughts were elsewhere). Prideaux's head rested on his hand, as if he were lost in thought; Kitty and Anthony were shaking, unobtrusively but unmistakably; and Cyril's fine, supercilious chin, set firmly, was quivering. Cyril had, from childhood, had more self-control than the other two, and he was further sustained by his conviction that it would be unthinkably bad form for a Catholic to attend a Protestant service and laugh at it in public.

They oughtn't, thought Ivy, rather indignantly, to laugh at her father's sermon when he wasn't meaning to be funny. If he saw he would be hurt. One shouldn't laugh in church, anyhow; even Jane and John knew that. These people were no better than Jelly.

'This Sunday,' continued the Vicar, his last star journey safely accomplished, 'is the day that has been set aside by our country for prayer and sermons with regard to the proposed increase in the national brain-power. This is, indeed, a sore need: but let us start on the firm foundation of religion. What is wisdom apart from that? Nothing but vanity and emptiness. What is the clever godless man but a fool from the point of view of eternity? What is the godly fool but a heavenly success?' ('He's talking sedition,' whispered Kitty to Prideaux. 'He'd better have stuck to the trains.')

But, of course, the vicar continued, if one can combine virtue and intelligence, so much the better. There was, eg Darwin. Also General Gordon, St Paul, and Lord Roberts, who had said with his last breath, in June 1915, 'We've got the men, we've got the money, we've got the munitions; what we now want is a nation on its knees.' (Ivy saw Prideaux sit up very straight, as if he would have liked to inform Mr Delmer that this libel on a dying soldier had long since been challenged and withdrawn.) One can, said the vicar, find many more such examples of this happy combination of virtue and intelligence. There was Queen Victoria, Florence Nightingale, and Lord Rhondda (who in the dark days of famine had led the way in self-denial). Not, unfortunately, the Emperor Napoleon, Friedrich Nietzsche, or the Kaiser Wilhelm II. The good are not always the clever, nor are the clever always the good. Some are neither, like the late Crown Prince of Germany (who was now sharing a small island in the Pacific with the Kaiser Wilhelm and MM Lenin and Trotzky, late of Petrograd, and neither stupid nor exactly, let us hope, bad, but singularly unfortunate and misguided, like so many Russians, whom it is not for us to judge).

But we should try to be both intelligent and good. We should take every step in our power to improve our minds. (Prideaux began to look more satisfied; this was what sermons today ought to be about.) It is our duty to our country to be intelligent citizens, if we can, said the vicar. Reason is what God has differentiated us from the lower animals by. They have instinct, we reason. Truly a noble heritage. We are rather clever already; we have discovered fire, electricity, coal, and invented printing, steam engines, and flying. No reason why we should not improve our minds further still, and invent (under God) more things yet. Only one thing we must affirm; the State should be very careful how it interferes with the domestic lives of its citizens. The State was going rather far in that direction; it savoured unpleasantly of Socialism, a tyranny to which English men did not take kindly. An Englishman's home had always been his castle (even castles, thought some aggrieved members of the congregation, were subject to unpleasant supervision by the police during food scarcity). No race was before us in its respect for law, but also no race was more determined that their personal and domestic relations should not be tampered with. When the State endeavoured to set up a Directorate of Matrimony, and penalised those who did not conform to its regulations, the State was, said the vicar, going too far, even for a State. The old school of *laissez-faire,* long since discredited as an economic theory, survived as regards the private lives of citizens. It is not the State which has ordained marriage, it is God, and God did not say 'Only marry the clever; have no children but clever ones.' He said, speaking through the inspired mouth of the writer of the book of Genesis, 'Be fruitful and multiply and replenish the earth.' ('And, through the inspired mouth of Solomon, "Desire not a multitude of unprofitable children",' murmured Anthony Grammont, who knew his Bible in patches, but was apt to get the authorship wrong.)

The vicar said he was now going to say a bold thing; if it brought him within reach of the law he could not help it. He considered that we ought all, in this matter, to be what are called Conscientious Obstructionists; we ought to protest against this interference, and refuse to pay the taxes levied upon those less intelligent infants sent to us by heaven. He did not say this without much thought and prayer, and it was, of course, a matter for everyone's own conscience, but he felt constrained to bear his witness on this question.

This came to Ivy as a shock. She had not known that her father was going to bear his witness this morning. She watched Prideaux's face with some anxiety. She admired and feared Prideaux, and thought how angry he must be. Not Miss Grammont; Miss Grammont didn't take these things quite seriously enough to be angry. Ivy sometimes suspected that the whole work of the Ministry of Brains, and, indeed, of every other Ministry, was a joke to her.

It was a relief to lvy when her father finished his sermon on a more loyal note, by an urgent exhortation to everyone to go in for the Mind Training Course. We must not be backward, he said, in obeying our country in this righteous cause. He, for his part, intended to go in for it, with his household (Mrs Delmer looked resigned but a little worried, as if she was mentally fitting in the Mind Training Course with all the other things she had to do, and finding it a close fit) and he hoped everyone in the congregation would do the same. Ivy saw Prideaux's profile become more approving. Perhaps her father had retrieved his reputation for patriotism after all. Anyhow at this point the And Now brought them all to their feet, they sang a hymn (the official hymn composed and issued by the Brains Ministry), had a collection (for the education of imbeciles), a prayer for the enlightenment of dark minds (which perhaps meant the same), and trooped out of church.

3

'He ought, of course,' said Prideaux at lunch, 'to be reported and prosecuted for propaganda contrary to the national interest. But we won't report him; he redeemed himself by his patriotic finish.'

'He is redeemed for evermore by his express train,' said Kitty.

'A most instructive morning,' said Amherst.

'Protestants are wonderful people,' said Cyril.

'I always said that man was a regular pet lamb,' said Pansy. 'And hadn't he pluck! Fancy givin' it us about that silly old baby tax with you two representatives of the government sitting under him an' freezin' him. I guess I'll have the Cheeper christened first opportunity, just to please him, what, old dear?'

Anthony, thus addressed, said, 'As soon and as often as you like, darling. Don't mind me. Only I suppose you realise that it will mean thinking of a name for him — Sidney, or Bert, or Lloyd George or something.'

'Montmorency,' said Pansy promptly. 'Monty for short, of course. That'll sound awfully well in revue.'

It should be noted as one up for Mr Delmer that his sermon, whether or not it brought many of his parishioners to the Government Mind Training Course, had anyhow (unless Pansy forgot again) brought one infant soul into the Christian Church.

4

Mrs Delmer said to Ivy, 'I suppose we shall all have to go in for it, dear, as father's told everyone we're going to. But I don't quite know how I'm going to get the time, especially with this new boy so untrustworthy about changing the hens' water when he feeds them and crushing up the bones for them. Perhaps he'll be better when he's taken the course himself. But I half suspect it's not so much stupidity as naughtiness … Well, well, if father wants us to we must.'

Jane said, kicking stones along the road as she walked, 'Shall I be top of my form when I've taken the Course, mother? Shall I, mother? Will John? John was lower than me last week. *Shall* we, mother?'

Mrs Delmer very sensibly observed that, if all the other children in the parish took the course too, as they ought, their relative capacities would remain unchanged. 'But if both you and John took a little more pains over your homework, Jane,' she took the opportunity to add, whereupon Jane very naturally changed the subject.

Betty's contribution was '*Brains!* What a silly fuss about them. Who wants brains?'

Which was, indeed, a very pertinent question, and one which Nicholas Chester sometimes sadly asked himself.

Who, alas, did?

CHAPTER 4

Our Week

1

Brains Week ('Our Week', as it was called by the ladies who sold flags for it) having opened thus auspiciously, flourished along its gallant way like a travelling fair urging people to come and buy, like a tank coaxing people to come in and purchase war bonds, like the War Office before the Military Service Acts, like the Ministry of Food before compulsory rationing. It was, in fact, the last great appeal for voluntary recruits for the higher intelligence; if it failed then compulsion would have to be resorted to. Many people thought that compulsion should in any case be resorted to; what was the good of a government if not to compel? If the Great War hadn't taught it that, it hadn't taught it much. This was the view put forward in many prominent journals; others, who would rather see England free than England clever, advocated with urgency the voluntary scheme, hoping, if it might be, to see England both.

It was a week of strenuous and gallant effort on the part of the Government and its assistants. Every Cinema showed dramas representing the contrasted fates of the Intelligent and the Stupid. Kiosks of Propaganda and Information were set up in every prominent shop. Trafalgar Square was brilliant with posters, a very flower-garden. The Ministry of Brains' artists had given of their best. Pictorial propaganda bloomed on every city wall, 'Before and After', 'The Rich Man and the Poor Man' (the Rich Man, in a faultless fur coat, observing to the Poor Man in patched reach-me-downs, 'Yes,

I was always below you at school, wasn't I? But since then I've taken the Mind Training Course, and now money rolls in. Sorry you're down on your luck, old man, but why don't you do as I've done?') and a special poster for underground railways, portraying victims of the perils of the streets — 'A will be safe because he has taken the Mind Training Course and is consequently facing the traffic. B will not, because he has refused to improve his mind and has therefore alighted from a motor bus in the wrong direction and with his back to oncoming traffic; he will also be crushed by a street aero, having by his foolish behaviour excited the aviator. B will therefore perish miserably, AND DESERVES TO.'

There were also pictures of human love, that most moving of subjects for art. 'Yes, dear, I love you. But we are both C2' (they looked it). 'We cannot marry; we must part for ever. You must marry Miss Bryte-Braynes, who has too few teeth and squints, and I must accept Mr Brilliantine, who puts too much oil on his hair. For beauty is only skin-deep, but wisdom endures for ever. We must THINK OF POSTERITY.'

Nor was Commerce backward in the cause. Every daily paper contained advertisements from our more prominent emporiums, such as 'Get tickets for the M T Course at Selfswank's. Every taker of a ticket will receive a coupon for our great £1000 lottery. The drawing will be performed in a fortnight from today, by the late Prime Minister's wife.' (To reassure the anxious it should be said that the late Prime Minister was not deceased but abolished; the country was governed by a United Council, five minds with but a single thought — if that.) 'By taking our tickets you benefit yourself, benefit posterity, benefit your country, and stand a good chance of winning A CASH PRIZE.'

And every patriotic advertiser of clothes, furs, jewellery, groceries, or other commodities, tacked on to his advertisement, 'Take a ticket this week for the M T Course'. And every patriotic letterwriter bought a Brains Stamp, and stamped his envelopes with the legend 'Improve your Brains now'.

Railway bookstalls were spread with literature on the subject. The *Queen*, the *Gentlewoman*, the *Sketch*, and other such periodicals suited, one imagines, to the simpler type of female mind, had articles on 'Why does a woman look old sooner than a man?' (the answer to this was that, though men are usually stupid, women are often stupider still, and have taken even less pains to improve their minds), 'Take care of your mind and your complexion will take care of itself', 'Raise yourself to category A, and you enlarge your matrimonial field', 'How to train Baby's intellect', and so forth. Side by side with these journals was the current number of the *Cambridge Magazine*, bearing on its cover the legend 'A Short Way with Fools; Pogrom of the Old Men. Everyone over forty to be shot', 'We have always said,' the article under these headlines very truly began, 'and we do not hesitate to say it again, that the only way to secure an intelligent government or citizenship in any nation is to dispose, firmly but not kindly, of the old and the middle-aged, and to let the young have their day. There will then be no more such hideous blunders as those with which the diplomacy of our doddering elders has wrecked the world again and again during the past centuries.'

The *Evening News* had cartoons every day of the Combing Out of the Stupid, whom it was pleased to call Algies and Dollies. The *New Witness* on the other hand, striking a different note, said that it was the fine old Christian Gentile quality of stupidity which had made Old England what it was; the natives of Merrie England had always resented excessive acuteness, as exhibited in the Hebrew race at their expense. The *Herald* however, rejoiced in large type in the

Open Door to Labour; the *Church Times* reported Brains Sunday sermons by many divines (in most of them sounded the protest raised by the vicar of Little Chantreys against interference with domestic rights, the Church was obviously going to be troublesome in this matter) and the other journals, from the *Hidden Hand* down to *Home Chat* supported the cause in their varying degrees and characteristic voices.

Among them lay the Ministry of Brains pamphlets, 'Brains. How to get and keep them', 'The cultivation of the Mind', etc. In rows among the books and papers hung the Great Thoughts from Great Minds series — portraits of eminent persons with their most famous remarks on this subject inscribed beneath them. 'It is the duty of every man, woman, and child in this country so to order their lives in this peace crisis as to make the least possible demand upon the intelligence of others. It is necessary, therefore, to have some of your own.' (An eminent minister.) 'I never had any assistance beyond my wits. Through them I am what I am. What that is, it is for others rather than for myself to judge.' (A great journalist.) 'It was lack of brains (I will not say whose, but it occurred before the first Coalition Government, mind you) which plunged Europe into the Great War. Brains — again, mark you, I do not say whose — must make and keep the Great Peace.' (One of our former Prime Ministers.) 'I have always wished I had some.' (A Royal Personage.) 'I must by all means have a Brains Ministry started in Liberia.' (The Liberian Ambassador.) Then, after remarks by Shakespeare, Emerson, Carlyle, Mr R J Campbell, Henry James, President Wilson, Marcus Aurelius, Solomon, Ecclesiasticus ('What is heavier than lead, and what is the name thereof but a fool?') and Miss Ella Wheeler Wilcox, the portrait gallery concluded with Mr Nicholas Chester, the Minister of Brains, looking like an embittered humorist, and remarking, 'It's a damned silly world.'

2

'Amen to that,' Miss Kitty Grammont remarked, stopping for a moment after buying *Truth* at the bookstall and gazing solemnly into the Minister's disillusioned eyes. 'And it would be a damned dull one if it wasn't.' She sauntered out of Charing Cross tube station and boarded an Embankment tram. This was the Monday morning after Brains Week had run its course.

The fact had to be faced by the Ministry: Brains Week had proved disappointing. The public were not playing up as they should.

'We have said all along,' said *The Times* (anticipating the *Hidden Hand*, which had not yet made up its mind), 'that the Government should take a strong line in this matter. They must not trust to voluntary effort; we say, and we believe that, as always, we voice the soundest opinion in the country, that it is up to the Government to take the measures which it has decided, upon mature consideration, to be for the country's good. Though we have given every possible support to the great voluntary effort recently made, truth compels us to state that the results are proving disappointing. Compulsion must follow, and the sooner the Government make up their minds to accept this fact the better advised it will be. Surely if there is one thing above all others which the Great War (so prolific in lessons) has taught us, it is that compulsion is not tyranny, nor law oppression. Let the Government, too long vacillating, act, and act quickly, and they will find a responsive and grateful nation ready to obey.'

Thus *The Times*, and thus, in a less dignified choice of language, many lesser organs. To which the *Herald* darkly rejoined, 'If the Government tries this on, let it look to itself.'

'It'll have to come,' said Vernon Prideaux to Kitty Grammont at lunch. They were lunching at one of those underground resorts about which, as Kitty said, you never know, some being highly respectable, while others are not. Kitty, with her long-lashed, mossy eyes and demure expression, looked and felt at home among divans for two, screens, powdered waitresses, and rose-shaded lights; she had taken Prideaux there for fun, because among such environments he looked a stranger and pilgrim, angular, fastidious, whose home was above. Kitty liked to study her friends in different lights, even rose-shaded ones, and especially one who, besides being a friend, was her departmental superior, and a coming, even come, young man of exceptional brilliance, who might one day be ruling the country.

'If it does,' said Kitty, 'we shall have to go, that's all. No more compulsion is going to be stood at present. Nothing short of another war, with a military dictatorship and martial law, will save us.'

'We stood compulsory education when there was no war,' Prideaux pointed out. 'We've stood vaccination, taxation, every conceivable form of interference with what we are pleased to call our liberty. This is no worse; it's the logical outcome of State government of the individual. Little by little, precept upon precept, line upon line, these things grow, till we're a serf state without realising it … After all, why not? What most people mean by freedom would be a loathsome condition; freedom to behave like animals or lunatics, to annoy each other and damage the State. What's the sense of it? Human beings aren't up to it, that's the fact.'

'I quite agree with you,' said Kitty. 'Only the weak point is that hardly any human beings are up to making good laws for the rest, either. We shall slip up badly over this Mind Training Act, if we ever get it through; it will be as full of snags as the Mental Progress Act. We shall have to take on a whole extra Branch to deal with the exemptions alone.

Chester's clever, but he's not clever enough to make a good Act. No one is … By the way, Vernon, you nearly told me something the other day about Chester's category. You might quite tell me now, as we're in the Raid Shelter and not in the Office."

'Did I? It was only that I heard he was uncertificated for marriage. He's got a brother and a twin sister half-witted. I suppose he collared all the brains that were going in his family.'

'He would, of course, if he could. He's selfish.'

'Selfish,' Prideaux was doubtful. 'If you can call such a visionary and idealist selfish.'

'Visionaries and idealists are always selfish. Look at Napoleon, and Wilhelm II, as Mr Delmer would say. Visions and ideals are the most selfish things there are. People go about wrapped in them, and keep themselves so warm that they forget that other people need ordinary clothes … So the Minister is uncertificated … Well, I'm going up to Regent Street to buy a birthday present for Pansy and cigarettes for myself.'

'I must get back,' said Prideaux. 'I've a Leeds Manufacturers' deputation coming to see me at 2.30 about their men's wages. Leeds workmen, apparently, don't let the Mental Progress Act weigh on them at all; they go calmly ahead with their uncertificated marriages, and then strike for higher wages in view of the taxable family they intend to produce. These fellows coming today have got wind of the new agreement with the cutlers and want one like it. I've got to keep them at arm's length.'

He emerged above ground, breathed more freely, and walked briskly back to the Ministry. Kitty went to Regent Street, and did not get back to the office until 3.15.

3

Kitty had lately been returned from the Propaganda Branch to her own, the Exemption Branch. Being late, she slipped into her place unostentatiously. Her in-tray contained a mass of files, as yet undealt with. She began to look through these, with a view to relegating the less attractive to the bottom of the tray, where they could wait until she had nothing better to do than to attend to them. Today there were a great many letters from the public beginning 'Dear Sir, Mr Wilkinson said in parliament on Tuesday that families should not be reduced to destitution through the baby-taxes …' That was so like Mr Wilkinson (parliamentary secretary to the Brains Ministry). Whenever he thoughtlessly dropped these *obiter dicta*, so sweeping, so far removed from truth, which was almost whenever he spoke, there was trouble. The guileless public hung on his words, waiting to pick them up and send them in letters to the Ministry. These letters went to the bottom of the tray. They usually only needed a stock reply, telling the applicants to attend their local tribunal. After several of these in succession, Kitty opened a file which had been minuted down from another branch, MB4. Attached to it were two sheets of minutes which had passed between various individuals regarding the case in question; the last minute was addressed to MB3, and said 'Passed to you for information and necessary action.' It was a melancholy tale from an aggrieved citizen concerning his infant, who was liable to a heavy tax, and who had been drowned by his aunt while being washed, before he was two hours old, and the authorities still demanded the payment of the tax. Kitty, who found the helplessness of MB4 annoying, wrote a curt minute, 'Neither information nor action seems to us necessary,' then had to erase it because it looked rude, and wrote instead, more mildly, 'Seen, thank you. This man appears to be covered by MBI.187, in which case his taxation is surely quite in order and no action is possible. We see no reason why we should deal with the case rather than you.'

It is difficult always to be quite polite in minutes, cheap satire costing so little and relieving the feelings, but it can and should be done; nothing so shows true breeding in a Civil Servant.

Kitty next replied to a letter from the Admiralty, about sailors' babies (the family arrangements of sailors are, of course, complicated, owing to their having a wife in every port). The Admiralty said that My Lords Commissioners had read the Minister of Brains' (ie Kitty's) last letter to them on this subject with much surprise. The Admiralty's faculty of surprise was infinitely fresh; it seemed new, like mercy, each returning day. The Minister of Brains evoked it almost every time he, through the pens of his clerks, wrote to them. My Lords viewed with grave apprehension the line taken by the Minister on this important subject, and They trusted it would be reconsidered. (My Lords always wrote of themselves with a capital They, as if they were deities.) Kitty drafted a reply to this letter and put it aside to consult Prideaux about. She carried on a chronic quarrel with My Lords, doubtless to the satisfaction of both sides.

Soothed and stimulated by this encounter, she was the better prepared in temper when she opened a file in which voluminous correspondence concerning two men named Stephen Williams had been jacketed together by a guileless registry, to whom such details as that one Stephen Williams appeared to be a dentist's assistant and the other a young man in the diplomatic service were as contemptible obstacles, to be taken in an easy stride. The correspondence in this file was sufficiently at cross purposes to be more amusing than most correspondence. When she had perused it, Kitty, sad that she must tear asunder this happily linked pair, sent it down to the registry with a regretful note that 'These two cases, having no connection, should be registered separately,' and fell to speculating, as she often did, on the registry, which, amid the trials that beset them and the sorrows they endured, and the manifold confusions and temptations of their dim life, were so strangely often right. They worked underground, the registry people, like gnomes in a cave, opening letters and registering them and filing them and sending them upstairs, astonishingly often in the file which belonged to them. But, mainly, looking for papers and not finding them, and writing 'No trace', 'Cannot be traced', on slips, as if the papers were wild animals which had got loose and had to be hunted down. A queer life, questing, burrowing, unsatisfied, underground … No wonder they made some mistakes.

Kitty opened one now — a bitter complaint, which should have gone to MB5, from one who considered himself placed in a wrong category. 'When I tell you, sir,' it ran, 'that at the Leamington High School I carried off two prizes (geography and recitation) and was twice fourth in my form, and after leaving have given great satisfaction (I am told) as a solicitor's clerk, so that there has been some talk of raising my salary, you will perhaps be surprised to hear that the Local Intelligence Board placed me in class C1. I applied to the County Board, and (owing, as I have reason to know, to local feeling and jealousy) I was placed by them in C2. Sir, I ask you for a special examination by the Central Intelligence Board. I should be well up in Class B. There are some walking about in this town who are classed B1 and 2, who are the occasion of much local feeling, as it surprises all who know them that they should be classed so high. To my knowledge some of these persons cannot do a sum right in their heads, and it is thought very strange that they should have so imposed on the Intelligence Officers, though the reasons for this are not really far to seek, and should be enquired into ...'

A gay and engaging young man with a wooden leg (he had lost his own in 1914, and had during the rest of the war worked at the War Office, and carried the happy QMG touch) wandered in from MB5 while Kitty was reading this, and she handed it over to him. He glanced at it.

'We shall perhaps be surprised, shall we ... How likely ... The public overestimate our faculty for surprise. They have yet to learn that the only thing which would surprise the Ministry of Brains would be finding someone correctly classified ... I shall tell him I'm A2 myself, though I never got a prize in my life for geography or recitation, and I can't do sums in my head for nuts. I ought to be somewhere about B3; I surprise all who know me ... What I came in to say was, do any of you in here want a sure tip for the Oaks? Because I've got one. Silly Blighter; yes, you thought he was an absolute outsider, didn't you, so did everyone else; but he's not. You take the tip, it's a straight one, first hand. No, don't mention it, I always like to do MB3 a good turn, though I wouldn't do it for everyone ... Well, I'm off, I'm beastly busy ... Heard the latest Chester, by the way? Someone tried the Wheeldon stunt on him — sent him a poisoned thorn by special messenger in a packet "To be opened by the Minister Himself". Jervis Browne opened it, of course, and nearly pricked himself. When he took it to Chester, Chester did the Sherlock Holmes touch, and said he knew the thorn, it came off a shrub in Central Africa or Kew Gardens or somewhere. I think he knew the poison, too; he wanted Jervis-Browne to suck it, to make sure, but J-B wasn't having any, and Chester didn't like to risk himself, naturally. His little PS would have done it like a shot, but they thought it would be hard luck on the poor child's people. And while they were discussin' it, Chester ran the thing into his own finger by mistake. While J-B was waitin' to see him swell up and turn black, and feelin' bad lest he should be told to suck it (he knows Chester doesn't really value him at his true worth, you see), Chester whipped out his penknife and gouged a great slice out of his finger as you'd cut cheese, all round the prick. He turned as white as chalk, J-B says, but never screamed, except to let out one curse. And when he'd done it, and had the shorthand typist in from J-B's room to tie it up, he began to giggle — you know that sad, cynical giggle of his that disconcerts solemn people so much — and said he'd have the beastly weapon cleaned and take it home and frame it in glass, with the other mementoes of a people's hate … I say, I do waste your time in here, don't I? And my own; that's to say the government's. I'm off.'

'Gay child,' Kitty murmured to her neighbour as he went. 'He blooms in an office like an orchid in a dust-bin. And very nice too. I remember being nearly as bright at his age; though, for my sins, I was never in QMG. A wonderful Branch that is.'

Thereupon she threw away her cigarette, wrote five letters with extraordinary despatch and un-departmental conciseness of style, and went to have tea in the canteen.

4

The Minister was having tea too, looking even paler than usual, with his left hand in a sling. Kitty put up her eye-glasses and looked at him with increased interest. As ministers go, he was certainly of an interesting appearance; she had always thought that. She rather liked the paradoxical combination of shrewdness and idealism, sullenness and humour, in his white, black-browed, clever face. He looked patient, but patient perforce, as if he rode natural impatience on a curb. He looked as if he might know a desperate earnestness, but preferred to keep it at arm's length with a joke; his earnestness would be too grim and violent to be an easy and natural companion to him. He looked as if he might get very badly hurt, but would cut out the hurt and throw it away with the cold promptness of the surgeon. He was not yet forty, but looked more, perhaps because he enjoyed bad health. At this moment he was eating a rock bun and talking to Vernon Prideaux. One difference between them was that Prideaux looked an intelligent success, like a civil servant, or a rising barrister or MP, and Chester looked a brilliant failure, and more like a Sinn Feiner or a Bolshevist. Only not really like either of these, because he didn't look as if he would muff things. He might go under, but his revolutions wouldn't. Kitty, who too greatly despised people who muffed things, recognised the distinction. She had a friend whose revolutions, which were many, always did go under …

There was a queer, violent strength about the Minister.

But when he smiled it was as if someone had flashed a torch on lowering cliffs, and lit them into extraordinary and elf-like beauty. Kitty knew already that he could be witty; she suddenly perceived now that he could be sweet — a bad word, but there seemed no other.

He ate another rock bun, and another. But they were small. His eyes fell on Kitty, eating a jam sandwich. But his thoughts were elsewhere.

'Yes, it was me that had to tie it up for him,' Ivy Delmer was saying to another typist. 'Luckily I've done First Aid. But I felt like fainting … The *blood* … I don't *like* him, you know; his manners are so funny and his dictating is so difficult; but I must say I did admire his pluck … He never thanked me or anything — he wouldn't, of course. Not that I minded a scrap about that …'

5

When Kitty got home to her flat that evening, she found the Boomerang on the floor. (It was on the floor owing to the lack of a letter-box.) The Boomerang was a letter from herself, addressed to Neil Desmond, Esq, and she wrote it and despatched it every few months or so, whenever, in fact, she had, at the moment, nothing better to do. On such days as Bank Holidays, when she spent them at the office but official work did not press, Kitty tidied the drawers of her table and wrote to break off her engagement. The drawers got tidied all right, but it is doubtful whether the engagement could ever be considered to have got broken off, owing to the letter breaking it being a boomerang. It was a boomerang because Neil Desmond, Esq. was a person of no fixed address. He wrote long and thrilling letters to Kitty (which, if her correspondence had been raided by the police, would probably have subjected her to arrest — he had himself for long been liable to almost every species of arrest, so could hardly be further incriminated), but when she wrote to the address he gave he was no longer ever there, and so her letters returned to her like homing pigeons. So the position was that Neil was engaged to Kitty, and Kitty had so far failed to disengage herself from Neil. Neil was that friend who has been already referred to as one whose revolutions always went under. Kitty had met him first in Greece, in April 1914. She had since decided that he was probably at his best in Greece. In July he had been arming to fight Carson's rebels when the outbreak of the European War disappointed him. The parts played by him in the European War were many and various, and, from the British point of view, mostly regrettable. He followed Sir Roger Casement through many adventures, and only just escaped sharing in the last of all. He partook in the Sinn Fein rising of Easter 1916 (muffed, as usual, Kitty had commented), and had then disappeared, and had mysteriously emerged again in Petrograd a year later, to help with the Russian revolution. Wherever, in fact, a revolution was, Neil Desmond was sure to be. He had had, as may be imagined, a busy and satisfactory summer and autumn there, and had many interesting, if impermanent, friends, such as Kerensky, Protopopoff (whom, however, he did not greatly care for), Kaledin, Lenin, Trotzky, Mr Arthur Ransome, and General Korniloff. (It might be thought that the politics of this last-named would not have been regarded by Neil with a favourable eye, but he was, anyhow, making a revolution which did not come off.) In January, 1918, Neil had got tired of Russia (this is liable to occur) and gone off to America, where he had for some time been doing something or other, no doubt discreditable, with an Irish-American league. Then a revolution which seemed to require his assistance broke out in Equador, which kept him occupied for some weeks. After that he had gone to Greece, where Kitty vaguely believed him still to be (unless he was visiting, with seditious intent, the island in the Pacific where the world's great Have-Beens were harmoniously segregated).

'The only thing for it,' Kitty observed to the cousin with whom she lived, a willowy and lovely young lily of the field, who had had a job once but had lost it owing to peace, and was now having a long rest, 'The only thing for it is to put it in the agony column of the — no, not *The Times*, of course he wouldn't read it, but the *Irish-American Banner* or something. "KG to ND. All over. Regret."'

'You'll have to marry him, darling. God means you to,' sang her cousin, hooking herself into a flame-coloured and silver evening dress.

'It certainly looks as if he did,' Kitty admitted, and began to take her own clothes off, for she was going to see Pansy in a new revue. (Anthony would have been the last man to wish to tie Pansy down to home avocations when duty called; he was much too proud of her special talents to wish her to hide them in a napkin.)

The revue was a good one, Pansy was her best self, lazy, sweet, facetious, and extraordinarily supple, the other performers also performed suitably, each in his manner, and Kitty afterwards had supper with a party of them. These were the occasions when office work, seen from this gayer corner of life, seemed incredibly dusty, tedious and sad …

CHAPTER 5

The Explanation Campaign

1

It will be generally admitted that Acts are not good at explaining themselves, and call for words to explain them; many words, so many that it is at times wondered whether the Acts are worth it. It occurred about this time to the Ministry of Brains that more words were called for to explain both the Mental Progress Act recently passed and the Mind Training Act which was still a Bill. For neither of these Acts seemed to have yet explained itself, or been explained, to the public, in such a manner as to give general satisfaction. And yet explanations had to be given with care. Acts, like lawyers' deeds, do not care to be understood through and through. The kind of explaining they really need, as Kitty Grammont observed, is the kind called explaining away. For this task she considered herself peculiarly fitted by training, owing to having had in her own private career several acts which had demanded it. It was perhaps for this reason that she was among those chosen by the authorities for the Explanation Campaign. The Explanation Campaign was to be fought in the rural villages of England, by bands of speakers chosen for their gift of the ready word, and it would be a tough fight. The things to be explained were the two Acts above mentioned.

'And none of mine,' Kitty remarked to Prideaux, 'ever needed so much explanation as these will … Let me see, no one ever even tried to explain any of the Military Service Acts, did they? At least only in the press. The perpetrators never dared to face the public man to man, on village greens.'

'It ought to have been done more,' Prideaux said. 'The Review of Exceptions, for instance. If questions and complaints could have been got out of the public in the open, and answered on village greens, as you say, instead of by official letters which only made things worse, a lot of trouble might have been avoided. Chester is great on these heart-to-heart talks … By the way, he's going to interview all the Explanation people individually before they start, to make sure they're going about it in the right spirit.'

'That's so like Chester; he'll go to any trouble,' Kitty said. 'I'm getting to think he's a really great man.'

2

Chester really did interview them all. To Kitty, whom already he knew personally, he talked freely.

'You must let the people in,' he said, walking about the room, his hands in his pockets. 'Don't keep them at official arm's length. Let them feel *part* of it all … Make them catch fire with the idea of it … It's sheer stark truth — intelligence *is* the thing that counts — if only everyone would see it. Make them see stupidity for the limp, hopeless, helpless, animal thing it is — an idiot drivelling on a green'–Kitty could have fancied that he shuddered a little — 'make them hate it — want the other thing; want it so much that they'll even sacrifice a little of their personal comfort and desires to get it for themselves and their children. They must want it more than money, more than comfort, more than love, more than freedom … You'll have to get hold of different people in different ways, of course; some have imaginations and some haven't; those who haven't must be appealed to through their common sense, if any, or, failing any, their feeling for their children, or, even, at the lowest, their fear of consequences … Tell some of them there'll be another war if they're so stupid;

tell others they'll never get on in the world; anything you think will touch the spot. But first, always, try to collar their imaginations … You've done some public speaking, haven't you?'

Kitty owned it, and he nodded.

'That's all right, then; you'll know how to keep your finger on the audience's pulse … You'll make them laugh, too …'

Kitty was uncertain, as she left the presence, whether this last was an instruction or a prophecy.

3

The other members of Kitty's party (the Campaign was to be conducted in parties of two or three people each) did not belong to the Ministry; they were hired for it for this purpose. They were a lady doctor, prominent on public platforms and decorated for signal services to her country during the Great War, and a freelance clergyman known for his pulpit eloquence and the caustic wit with which he lashed the social system. He had resigned his incumbency long ago in order to devote himself the more freely to propaganda work for the causes he had at heart, wrote for a labour paper, and went round the country speaking. The Minister of Brains (who had been at Cambridge with him, and read his articles in the labour paper, in which he frequently stated that muddle-headedness was the curse of the world) had, with his usual eye for men, secured him to assist in setting forth the merits of the Brains Acts.

They began in Buckinghamshire, which was one of the counties assigned to them. At Gerrards Cross and Beaconsfield it was chilly, and they held their meetings respectively in the National School and in the bright green Parish Hall which is the one blot on a most picturesque city. But at Little Chantreys it was fine, and they met at six o'clock in the broad open space outside the church. They had a good audience. The meeting had been well advertised, and it seemed that the village was as anxious to hear the Brains Acts explained as the Ministry was to explain them. Or possibly the village, for its own part, had something it wished to explain. Anyhow they came, rich and poor, high and low, men, women, children, and infants in arms (these had, for the most part, every appearance of deserving heavy taxation; however, the physiognomy of infants is sometimes misleading). Anthony Grammont and Pansy were there, with the Cheeper, now proud in his baptismal name of Montmorency. The vicar and his wife were there too, though Mr Delmer did not approve much of the Reverend Stephen Dixon, rightly thinking him a disturbing priest. It was all very well to advocate Life and Liberty in moderation (though Mr Delmer did not himself belong to the society for promoting these things in the Church), but the vicar did not believe that any church could stand, without bursting, the amount of new wine which Stephen Dixon wished to pour into it. 'He is very much in earnest,' was all the approval that he could, in his charity, give to this priest. So he waited a little uneasily for Dixon's remarks on the Brains Acts, feeling that it might become his ungracious duty to take public exception to some of them.

The scene had its picturesqueness in the evening sunshine — the open space in which the narrow village streets met, backed by the little grey church, and with a patch of green where women and children sat; and in front of these people standing, leisurely, placid, gossiping, the women innocently curious to hear what the speakers from London had to say about this foolish business there was such an upset about just now; some of the men more aggressive, determined to stand no nonsense, with a we'll-know-the-reason-why expression on their faces. This expression was peculiarly marked on the countenance of the local squire, Captain Ambrose. He did not like all this interfering, socialist what-not, which was both upsetting the domestic arrangements of his tenants and trying to put into their heads more learning than was suitable for them to have. For his part he thought every man had a right to be a fool if he chose, yes, and to marry another fool, and to bring up a family of fools too. Damn it all, fools or not, hadn't they shed their blood for their country, and where would the country have been without them, though now the country talked so glibly of not allowing them to reproduce themselves until they were more intelligent. Captain Ambrose, a fragile-looking man, burnt by Syrian suns and crippled by British machine-guns at instruction classes (a regrettable mistake which of course would not have occurred had the operator been more intelligent), stood in the forefront of the audience with intention to heckle. Near him stood the Delmers and Miss Ponsonby and Anthony Grammont. Pansy was talking, in her friendly, cheerful way, to Mrs Delmer about the Cheeper's food arrangements, which were unusual in one so young.

In the middle of the square were Dr Cross, graceful, capable-looking and grey-haired; Stephen Dixon, lean and peculiar (so the village thought); Kitty Grammont, pale after the day's heat, and playing with her dangling pince-nez; a tub; and two perambulators, each containing an infant; Mrs Rose's and Mrs Dean's, as the village knew. The lady doctor had been round in the afternoon looking at all the babies and asking questions, and had finally picked these two and asked if they might be lent for the meeting. But what use was going to be made of the poor mites, no one knew.

Dr Cross was on the tub. She was talking about the already existing Act, the Mental Progress Act of last year.

'Take some talking about, too, to make us swallow it whole,' muttered Captain Ambrose.

Dr Cross was a gracious and eloquent speaker; the village rather liked her. She talked of babies, as one who knew; no doubt she did know, having, as she mentioned, had two herself. She grew pathetic in pleading for the rights of the children to their chance in life. Some of the mothers wiped their eyes and hugged their infants closer to them; they should have it, then, so they should. How, said the doctor, were children to win any of life's prizes without brains? (Jane Delmer looked self-conscious; she had won a prize for drawing this term; she wondered if the speaker had heard this.) Even health — how could health be won and kept without intelligent following of the laws nature has laid down for us ('I never did none o' that, and look at me, seventy-five next month and still fit and able,' old William Weston was heard to remark), and how was that to be done without intelligence? Several parents looked dubious; they were not sure that they wanted any of that in their households; it somehow had a vague sound of draughts … After sketching in outline the probable careers of the intelligent and the unintelligent infant, between which so wide a gulf was fixed, the doctor discoursed on heredity, that force so inadequately reckoned with, which moulds the generations. Appealing to Biblical lore, she enquired if figs were likely to produce thorns, or thistles grapes. This started William Weston, who had been a gardener, on strange accidents he had met with in the vegetable world; Dr Cross, a gardener too, listened with interest, but observed that these were freaks and must not, of course, be taken as the normal; then, to close that subject, she stepped down from the tub, took the infants Rose and Dean out of their perambulators, and held them up, one on each arm, to the public gaze. Here, you have, she said, a certificated child, whose parents received a bonus for it, and an uncertificated child, whose parents were taxed. Observe the difference in the two — look at the bright, noticing air of the infant Rose ('Of course; she's a-jogglin' of it up and down on her arm,' said a small girl who knew the infant Rose). Observe its fine, intelligent little head (Mrs Rose preened, gratified). A child who is going to make a good thing of its life. Now compare it with the lethargy of the other baby, who lies sucking an india-rubber sucker (a foolish and unclean habit in itself) and taking no notice of the world about it.

'Why, the poor mite,' this infant's parent exclaimed, pushing her way to the front, 'she's been ailing the last two days; it's her pore little tummy, that's all. And, if you please, ma'am, I'll take her home now. Holdin' her up to scorn before the village that way — an' you call yourself a mother!'

'Indeed, I meant nothing against the poor child,' Dr Cross explained, realising that she had, indeed, been singularly tactless. 'She is merely a type, to illustrate my meaning … And, of course, it's more than possible that if you give her a thoroughly good mental training she may become as intelligent as anyone, in spite of having been so heavily handicapped by her parents' unregulated marriage. That's where the Government Mind Training Course will come in. She'll be developed beyond all belief …'

'She won't,' said the outraged parent, arranging her infant in her perambulator, 'be developed or anythin' else. She's comin' home to bed. And I'd like to know what you mean, ma'am, by unregulated marriage. Our marriage was all right; it was 'ighly approved, and we got money by this baby. It's my opinion you've mixed the two children up, and are taking mine for Mrs Rose's there, that got taxed, pore mite, owing to Mr and Mrs Rose both being in C class.'

'That's right,' someone else cried. 'It's the other one that was taxed and ought to be stupid; you've got 'em mixed, ma'am. Better luck next time.'

Dr Cross collapsed in some confusion, amid good-humoured laughter, and the infant Rose was also hastily restored to its flattered mother, who, being only C3, did not quite grasp what had occurred except that her baby had been held up for admiration and Mrs Dean's for obloquy, which was quite right and proper.

'One of nature's accidents,' apologised Dr Cross. 'They will happen sometimes, of course. So will stupid mistakes ... Better luck next time, as you say.' She murmured to Stephen Dixon, 'Change the subject at once,' so he got upon the tub and began to talk about Democracy, how it should control the state, but couldn't, of course, until it was better educated. 'But all these marriage laws,' said a painter who was walking out with the vicarage housemaid and foresaw financial ruin if they got married,' they won't help, as I can see, to give *us* control of the state.'

Dixon told him he must look to the future, to his children, in fact. The painter threw a forward glance at his children, not yet born; it left him cold. Anyhow, if he married Nellie they'd probably die young, from starvation.

But, in the main, Dixon's discourse on democracy was popular. Dixon was a popular speaker with working-men; he had the right touch. But squires did not like him. Captain Ambrose disliked him very much. It was just democracy, and all this socialism, that was spoiling the country.

Mr Delmer ventured to say that he thought the private and domestic lives of the public ought not to be tampered with.

'Why not?' enquired Stephen Dixon, and Mr Delmer had not, at the moment, an answer ready. 'When everything else is being tampered with,' added Dixon. 'And surely the more we tamper (if you put it like that) in the interests of progress, the further removed we are from savages.'

Mr Delmer looked puzzled for a moment, then committed himself, without sufficient preliminary thought, to a doubtful statement, 'Human love ought to be free,' which raised a cheer.

'Free love,' Dixon returned promptly, 'has never, surely, been advocated by the best thinkers of Church or State,' and while Mr Delmer blushed, partly at his own carelessness, partly at the delicacy of the subject, and partly because Pansy Ponsonby was standing at his elbow, Dixon added, 'Love, like anything else, wants regulating, organising, turning to the best uses. Otherwise, we become, surely, no better than the other animals …'

'Isn't he just terribly fierce,' observed Pansy in her smiling contralto, to the world at large.

Mr Delmer said uncomfortably, 'You mistake me, sir. I was not advocating lawless love. I am merely maintaining that love — if we must use the word — should not be shackled by laws relating to things which are of less importance than itself, such as the cultivation of the intelligence.'

'*Is* it of less importance?' Dixon challenged him.

'The greatest of these three,' began the vicar, inaptly, because he was flustered.

'Quite so,' said Dixon; 'but St Paul, I think, doesn't include intelligence in his three. St Paul, I believe, was able enough himself to know how much ability matters in the progress of religion. And, if we are to quote St Paul, he, of course, was no advocate of matrimony, but I think, when carried out at all, he would have approved of its being carried out on the best possible principles, not from mere casual impulse and desire … Freedom,' continued Dixon, with the dreamy and kindled eye which always denoted with him that he was on a pet topic, 'what is freedom? I beg — I do beg,' he added hastily, 'that no one will tell me it is mastery of ourselves. I have heard that before. It is no such thing. Mastery of ourselves is a fine thing; freedom is, or would be if anyone ever had such a thing, an absurdity, a monstrosity. It would mean that there would be nothing, either external or internal, to prevent us doing precisely what we like. No laws of nature, of morality, of the State, of the Church, of Society … '

Dr Cross caught Kitty's eye behind him.

'He's off,' she murmured. 'We must stop him.'

Kitty coughed twice, with meaning. It was a signal agreed upon between the three when the others thought that the speaker was on the wrong tack. Dixon recalled himself from Freedom with a jerk, and began to talk about the coming Mind Training Act. He discoursed upon its general advantages to the citizen, and concluded by saying that Miss Grammont, a member of the Ministry of Brains, would now explain to them the Act in detail, and answer any questions they might wish to put. This Miss Grammont proceeded to do. And this was the critical moment of the meeting, for the audience, who desired no Act at all, had to be persuaded that the Act would be a good Act. Kitty outlined it, thinking how much weaker both Acts and words sound on village greens than in offices, which is certainly a most noteworthy fact, and one to be remembered by all politicians and makers of laws. Perhaps it is the unappreciative and unstimulating atmosphere of stolid distaste which is so often, unfortunately, to be met with in villages … Villages are so stupid; they will not take the larger view, nor see why things annoying to them personally are necessary for the public welfare. Kitty wished she were instead addressing a northern manufacturing town, which would have been much fiercer but which would have understood more about it.

She dealt with emphasis on the brighter sides of the Act, ie the clauses dealing with the pecuniary compensation people would receive for the loss of time and money which might be involved in undergoing the Training Course, and those relating to exemptions. When she got to the Tribunals, a murmur of disapproval sounded.

'They tribunals — we're sick to death of them,' someone said. 'Look at the people there are walking about the countryside exempted from the Marriage Acts, when better men and women has to obey them. The tribunals were bad enough during the war, everyone knows, but nothing to what they are now. We don't want any more of those.'

This was an awkward subject, as Captain Ambrose was a reluctant chairman of the Local Mental Progress Tribunal. He fidgeted and prodded the ground with his stick, while Kitty said, 'I quite agree with you. We don't. But if there are to be exemptions from the Act, local tribunals are necessary. You can't have individual cases decided by the central authorities who know nothing of the circumstances. Tribunals must be appointed who can be relied on to grant exemptions fairly, on the grounds specified in the Act.'

She proceeded to enumerate these grounds. One of them was such poverty of mental calibre that the possessor was judged quite incapable of benefiting by the course. A look of hope dawned on several faces; this might, it was felt, be a way out. The applicant, Kitty explained, would be granted exemption if suffering from imbecility, extreme feeble-mindedness, any form of genuine mania, acute, intermittent, chronic, delusional, depressive, obsessional, lethargic ...

Dixon coughed twice, thinking the subject depressing and too technical for the audience, and Kitty proceeded to outline the various forms of exemption which might be held, a more cheerful topic. She concluded, remembering the Minister's instructions, by drawing an inspiring picture of the changed aspect life would bear after the mind had been thus improved; how it would become a series of open doors, of chances taken, instead of a dull closed house. Everything would be so amusing, so possible, such fun. And they would get on; they would grow rich; there would be perpetual peace and progress instead of another great war, which was, alas, all too possible if the world remained as stupid as it had been up to the present …

Here Kitty's eye lighted unintentionally on her brother Anthony's face, with the twist of a cynical grin on it, and she collapsed from the heights of eloquence. It never did for the Grammonts to encounter each other's eyes when they were being exalted; the memories and experiences shared by brothers and sisters rose cynically, like rude gamins, to mock and bring them down.

Kitty said, 'If anyone would like to ask any questions …' and got off the tub.

Someone enquired, after the moment of blankness which usually follows this invitation, what they would be taught, exactly.

Kitty said there would be many different courses, adapted to differing requirements. But, in the main, everyone would be taught to use to the best advantage such intelligence as they might have, in that state of life to which it might please God to call them.

'And how,' pursued the enquirer, a solid young blacksmith, 'will the teachers know what that may be?'

Kitty explained that they wouldn't, exactly, of course, but the minds which took the course would be so sharpened and improved as to tackle any work better than before. But there would also be forms to be filled in, stating approximately what was each individual's line in life.

After another pause a harassed-looking woman at the back said plaintively, 'I'm sure it's all very nice, miss, but it does seem as if such things might be left to the men. They've more time, as it were. You see, miss, when you've done out the house and got the children's meals and put them to bed and cleaned up and all, not to mention washing-day, and ironing — well, you've not much time left to improve the mind, have you?'

It was Dr Cross who pointed out that, the mind once improved, these household duties would take, at most, half the time they now did. 'I know that, ma'am,' the tired lady returned. 'I've known girls who set out to improve their minds, readin' and that, and their house duties didn't take them any time at all, and nice it was for their families. What I say is, mind improvement should be left to the men, who've time for such things; women are mostly too busy, and if they aren't they should be.'

Several men said 'Hear, hear' to this. Rural England, as Dr Cross sometimes remarked, was still regrettably eastern, or German, in its feminist views, even now that, since the war, so many more thousands of women were perforce independent wage-earners, and even now that they had the same political rights as men. Stephen flung forth a few explosive views on invidious sex distinctions, another pet topic of his, and remarked that, in the Christian religion, at least, there was neither male nor female. A shade of scepticism on the faces of several women might be taken to hint at a doubt whether the Christian religion, in this or in most other respects, was life as it was lived, and at a certainty that it was time for them to go home and get the supper. They began to drift away, with their children round them, gossiping to each other of more interesting things than Mind Training. For, after all, if it was to be it was, and where was the use of talking?

4

It was getting dusk. The male part of the audience also fell away, to talk in the roads while supper was preparing. Only the vicar was left, and Captain Ambrose, and Anthony Grammont, and Pansy, who came up to talk to Kitty.

'My dear,' said Pansy, 'I feel absolutely flattened out by your preacher, with his talk of "the other animals", and organised love. Now Mr Delmer was sweet to me — he said it ought to be free, an' I know he doesn't really think so, but only said it for my sake and Tony's. But your man's terrifyin'. I'm almost frightened to have him sleep at the End House tonight; I'm afraid he'll set fire to the sheets, he's so hot. Won't you introduce me?'

But Dixon was at this moment engaged in talking to the vicar, who, not to be daunted and brow-beaten by the notorious Stephen Dixon, was manfully expounding his position to him and Dr Cross, while Captain Ambrose backed him up.

'They may be all night, I should judge from the look of them,' said Kitty, who by now knew her clergyman and her doctor well. 'Let's leave them at it and come home; Tony can bring them along when they're ready.'

The End House had offered its hospitality to all the three Explainers, and they were spending the night there instead of, as usual, at the village inn. Kitty and Pansy were overtaken before they reached it by Anthony and Dr Cross and Dixon.

Pansy said, with her sweet, ingratiating smile, 'I was sayin' to Kitty, Mr Dixon, that you made me feel quite bad with your talk about free love.'

'I'm sorry,' said Dixon, 'but it was the vicar who talked of that, not I. I talked of organised love. I never talk of free love: I don't like it.'

'I noticed you didn't,' said Pansy. 'That's just what I felt so bad about. Mind you, I think you're awfully right, only it takes so much livin' up to, doesn't it? with things tangled up as they are … Sure you don't mind stayin' with us, I suppose?' She asked it innocently, rolling at him a sidelong glance from her beautiful music-hall eyes.

Dixon looked at sea. 'Mind …?'

'Well, you might, mightn't you, as ours is free.' Then, at his puzzled stare, 'Why, Kitty, you surely told him!'

'I'm afraid I never thought of it,' Kitty faltered. 'She means,' she explained, turning to the two guests, 'that she and my brother aren't exactly married, you know. They can't be, because Pansy has a husband somewhere. They would if they could; they'd prefer it.'

'We'd prefer it,' Pansy echoed, a note of wistfulness in her calm voice. 'Ever so much. It's *much* nicer, isn't it? — as you were sayin'. We think so too, don't we, old man?' She turned to Anthony but he had stalked ahead, embarrassed by the turn the conversation was taking. He was angry with Kitty for not having explained the situation beforehand, angry with Pansy for explaining it now, and angry with Dixon for not understanding without explanation.

'But I do hope,' Pansy added to both her guests, slipping on her courteous and queenly manner, 'that you will allow it to make no difference.'

Dr Cross said, 'Of course not. What do you imagine?' She was a little worried by the intrusion of these irrelevant domestic details into a hitherto interesting evening. Pansy's morals were her own concern, but it was a pity that her taste should allow her to make this awkward scene.

But Dixon stopped, and, looking his hostess squarely in the face — they were exactly of a height — said, 'I am sorry, but I am afraid it does make a difference. I hate being rude, and I am most grateful to you for your hospitable invitation; but I must go to the inn instead.'

Pansy stared back, and a slow and lovely rose colour overspread her clear face. She was not used to being rebuffed by men.

'I'm frightfully sorry,' Stephen Dixon repeated, reddening too. 'But, you see, if I slept at your house it would be seeming to acquiesce in something which I believe it to be tremendously important *not* to acquiesce in … Put it that I'm a prig … anyhow, there it is … Will you apologise for me to your brother?' he added to Kitty, who was looking on helplessly, conscious that the situation was beyond her. 'And please forgive me — I know it seems unpardonable rudeness.' He held out his hand to Pansy, tentatively. She took it, without malice. Pansy was not a rancorous woman.

'That's all right, Mr Dixon. If you can't swallow our ways, you just can't, and there's an end of it. Lots of people can't, you know. Good night. I hope you'll be comfortable.'

5

Kitty looked after him with a whistle.

'I'm fearfully sorry, Pansy love. I never thought to expatiate beforehand on Tony and you … I introduced you as Miss Ponsonby — but I suppose he never noticed, or thought you were the Cheeper's governess or something. Who'd have thought he'd take on like that? But you never know, with the clergy; they're so unaccountable.'

'I'm relieved, a bit,' Pansy said. 'I was frightened of him, that's a fact.'

Dr Cross said, 'The queer thing about Stephen Dixon is that you never know when he'll take a thing in this way and when he won't. I've known him sit at tea in the houses of the lowest slum criminals — by the way, that is surely the scriptural line — and I've known him cut in the street people who were doing the same things in a different way — a sweating shop-owner, for instance. I sometimes think it depends with him on the size and comfort of the house the criminal lives in, which is too hopelessly illogical, you'd think, for an intelligent man like him. I lose my patience with him sometimes, I confess. But anyhow he knows his own mind.'

'He's gone,' Pansy said to Anthony, who was waiting for them at the gate. 'He thinks it's important not to acquiesce in us. So he's gone to the inn … By the way, I nearly told him that the innkeeper is leading a double life too — ever so much worse than ours — but I thought it would be too unkind, he'd have had to sleep on the green.'

'Well,' Anthony said crossly, 'we can get on without him. But another time, darling, I wish you'd remember that there's not the least need to explain our domestic affairs in the lane to casual acquaintances, even if they do happen to be spending the night. It's simply not done, you know. It makes a most embarrassing situation all round. I know you're not shy, but you might remember that I am.'

'Sorry, old dear,' said Pansy. 'There's been so much explainin' this evenin' that I suppose I caught it … You people,' she added to Dr Cross and Kitty, 'have got awkwarder things to explain than I have. I'd a long sight rather have to explain free love than love by Act of Parliament.'

'But on the whole,' said the doctor, relieved to have got on to that subject again after the rather embarrassing interlude of private affairs, 'I thought the meeting this evening not bad. What did you think, Miss Grammont?'

'I should certainly,' said Kitty, 'have expected it to have been worse. If I had been one of the audience, it would have been.'

6

Some of the subsequent meetings of that campaign, in fact, were. But not all. On the whole, as Dr Cross put it, they were not bad.

'It's a toss-up,' said Dixon at the end, 'how the country is going to take this business. There's a chance, a good fighting chance, that they may rise to the idea and accept it, even if they can't like it. It depends a lot on how it's going to be worked, and that depends on the people at the top. And for the people at the top, all one can say is that there's a glimmer of hope. Chester himself has got imagination; and as long as a man's got that he may pull through, even if he's head of a government department … Of course one main thing is not to make pledges; they can't be kept; everyone knows they can't be kept, as situations change, and when they break there's a row … Another thing — the rich have got to set the example; they must drop this having their fun and paying for it, which the poor can't afford. If that's allowed there'll be revolution. Perhaps anyhow there'll be revolution. And revolutions aren't always the useful things they ought to be; they sometimes lead to reaction. Oh, you Brains people have got to be jolly careful.'

A week later the Mind Training Bill became an Act. It did, in fact, seem to be a toss-up how the public, that strange, patient, unaccountable dark horse, were going to take it. That they took it at all, and that they continued to take the Mental Progress Act, was ascribed by observant people largely to the queer, growing, and quite peculiar influence of Nicholas Chester. It was an odd influence for a minister of the government to have in this country; one would have almost have supposed him instead a power of the Press, the music-hall stage, or the cinema world. It behoved him, as Dixon said to be jolly careful.

CHAPTER 6

The Simple Human Emotions

1

During the period which followed the Explanation Campaign, Kitty Grammont was no longer bored by her work, no longer even merely entertained. It had acquired a new flavour; the flavour of adventure and romance which comes from a fuller understanding and a more personal identification; from, in fact, knowing more about it at first-hand.

Also, she got to know the Minister better. At the end of August they spent a week-end at the same country house. They were a party of four, besides their host's family; a number which makes for intimacy. Their hostess was a Cambridge friend of Kitty's, their host a man high up in the Foreign Office, his natural force of personality obscured pathetically by that apprehensive, defiant, defensive manner habitual and certainly excusable in these days in the higher officials of that department and of some of the other old departments; a manner that always seemed to be saying, 'All right, we know we've made the devil of a mess for two centuries and more, and we know you all want to be rid of us. But we'd jolly well like to know if you think you could have worked things any better yourselves. Anyhow, we mean to stick here till we're chucked out.'

How soon would it be, wondered Kitty, before the officials of the Ministry of Brains wore that same look? It must come to them; it must come to all who govern, excepting only the blind, the crass, the impervious. It must have been worn by the members of the Witan during the Danish invasions; by

Strafford before 1642; by Pharaoh's councillors when Moses was threatening plagues; by M. Milivkoff before March, 1917; by Mr Lloyd George during much of the Great War.

But it was not worn yet by Nicholas Chester.

2

He sat down by Kitty after dinner. They did not talk shop, but they were linked by the strong bond of shop shared and untalked. There was between them the relationship, unlike any other (for no relationship ever is particularly like any other) of those who are doing, though on very different planes, the same work, and both doing it well; the relationship, in fact, of a government official to his intelligent subordinates. (There is also the relationship of a government official to his unintelligent subordinates; this is a matter too painful to be dwelt on in these pages.)

But this evening, as they talked, it became apparent to Kitty that, behind the screen of this relationship, so departmental, so friendly, so emptied of sex, a relationship quite other and more personal and human, which had come into embryo being some weeks ago, was developing with rapidity. They found pleasure in one another this evening as human beings in the world at large, the world outside ministry walls. That was rather fun. And next morning Chester asked her to come on a walk with him, and on the walk the new relationship burgeoned like flowers in spring. They did not avoid shop now that they were alone together; they talked of the Department, of the new Act, of the efforts of other countries on the same lines, of anything else they liked. They talked of Russian politics (a conversation I cannot record, the subject being too difficult for any but those who have the latest developments under their eyes, and, indeed, not always quite easy even for them). They talked of the National Theatre, of animals they had kept and cabinet ministers they had known; of poets, pictures, and potato puddings; of, in fact, the things one does talk about on walks. They told each other funny stories of prominent persons; she told him some of the funny stories about himself which circulated in the Ministry; he told her about his experiences when, in order to collect information as to the state of the intelligence of the country before the Ministry was formed, he had sojourned in a Devonshire fishing village disguised as a fisherman, and in Hackney Wick disguised as a Jew, and had in both places got the better of everyone round him excepting only the other Hackney Jews, who had got the better of him (It was in consequence of this that Jews — such Jews as had not yet been forcibly repatriated in the Holy City — were exempted from the provisions of the Mental Progress Act and the Mind Training Act. It would be a pity if Jews were to become any cleverer.)

It will be seen, therefore, that their conversation was of an ordinary description, that might take place between any two people of moderate intelligence on any walk. The things chiefly to be observed about it were that Chester, a silent person when he was not in the mood to talk, talked a good deal, as if he liked talking today, and that when Kitty was talking he watched her with a curious, interested, pleased look in his deep little eyes.

And that was all, before lunch; the makings, in fact, of a promising friendship.

After tea there was more. They sat in a beech wood together, and told each other stories of their childhoods. He did not, Kitty observed, mention those of his family who were less intelligent than the rest; no doubt, with his views on the importance of intellect, he found it too depressing a subject. And after dinner, when they said good-night, he held her hand but as long as all might or so very little longer, and asked if she would dine with him on Thursday. It was the look in his eyes at that moment which sent Kitty up to bed with the staggering perception of the dawning of a new and third relationship — not the official relationship, and not the friendship which had grown out of it, but something still more simple and human. He, probably, was unaware of it; the simple human emotions were of no great interest to Nicholas Chester, whose thoughts ran on other and more complex businesses. One might surmise that he might fall very deeply in love before he knew anything much about it. Kitty, on the other hand, would always know, had, in fact, always known, everything she was doing in that way, as in most others. She would track the submersion, step by step, amused, interested, concerned. This way is the best; not only do you get more out of the affair so, but you need not allow yourself, or the other party concerned, to be involved more deeply than you think advisable.

So, safe in her bedroom, standing, in fact, before the looking-glass, she faced the glimpse of a possibility that staggered her, bringing mirth to her eyes and a flutter to her throat.

'Good God!' (Kitty had at times an eighteenth-century emphasis of diction, following in the steps of the heroines of Jane Austen and Fanny Burney, who dropped oaths elegantly, like flowers.) 'Good God! He begins to think of me.' Then, quickly, followed the thought, to tickle her further, 'Is it right? Is it *convenable*? *Should* ministers look like that at their lady clerks? Or does he think that, as he's uncertificated and no hopes of an outcome can be roused in me, he may look as he likes?'

She unhooked her dress, gazing at her reflection with solemn eyes, which foresaw the potentialities of a remarkable situation.

But what was, in fact, quite obvious, was that no situation could possibly be allowed to arise.

Only, if it did ... Well, it would have its humours. And, after all, should one turn one's back on life, in whatever curious guise it might offer itself? Kitty, at any rate, never yet had done this. She had once accepted the invitation of a Greek brigand at Thermopylæ to show her, and her alone, his country home in the rocky fastnesses of Velukhi, a two days' journey from civilisation; she had spent a week-end as guest-in-chief of a Dervish at Yuzgat; she had walked unattended through the Black Forest (with, for defence, a walking-stick and a hat-pin); and she had become engaged to Neil Desmond. Perhaps it was because she was resourceful and could trust her natural wits to extricate her, that she faced with temerity the sometimes awkward predicaments in which she might find herself involved through this habit of closing no door on life. The only predicament from which she had not, so far, succeeded in emerging, was her engagement; here she had been baffled by the elusive quality which defeated her efforts not by resistance but by merely slipping out of hearing.

And if this was going to turn into another situation ... well, then, she would have had one more in her life. But, after all, very likely it wasn't.

'Ministers,' Kitty soliloquised, glancing mentally at the queer, clever, humorous face which had looked at her so oddly, 'ministers, surely, are made of harder stuff than that. And prouder. Ministers, surely, even if they permit themselves to flirt a little with the clerks of their departments, don't let it get serious. It isn't done. You flatter yourself, poor child. Your head has been turned because he laughed when you tried to be funny, and because, for lack of better company or thinking your pink frock would go with his complexion, he walked out with you twice, and because he held your hand and looked into your eyes. You are becoming one of those girls who think that whenever a man looks at them as if he liked the way they do their hair, he wants to kiss them at once and marry them at last …'

3

'What's amusing you, Kate?' her hostess enquired, coming in with her hair over her shoulders and her Cambridge accent.

'Nothing, Anne,' replied Kitty, after a meditative pause, 'that I can possibly ever tell you. Merely my own low thoughts. They always were low, as you'll remember.'

'They certainly were,' said Anne.

4

This chapter, as will by this time have been observed, deals with the simple human emotions, their development and growth. But it will not be necessary to enter into tedious detail concerning them. They did develop; they did grow; and to indicate this it will only be necessary to select a few outstanding scenes of different dates.

On September 2nd, which was the Thursday after the week-end above described, Kitty dined with Chester, and afterwards they went to a picture palace to see *The Secret of Success*, one of their own propaganda dramas. It had been composed by the bright spirits in the Propaganda Department of the Ministry, and was filmed and produced at government expense. The cinematograph, the stage, and the Press were now used extensively as organs to express governmental points of view; after all, if you have to have such things, why not make them useful? Chester smiled sourly over it, but acquiesced. The chief of such organs were of course the new

State Theatre (anticipated with such hope by earnest drama-lovers for so many years) and the various State cinemas, and the *Hidden Hand*, the government daily paper; but even over the unofficial stage and film the shadow of the State lay black.

The Secret of Success depicted lurid episodes in the careers of two young men; the contrast was not, as in other drama, between virtue and vice, but between Intelligence and the Reverse. Everywhere Intelligence triumphed, and the Reverse was shamed and defeated. Intelligence found the hidden treasure, covered itself with glory, emerged triumphant from yawning chasms, flaming buildings, and the most suspicious situations, rose from obscure beginnings to titles, honours and position, and finally won the love of a pure and wealthy girl, who jilted the brainless youth of her own social rank to whom she had previously engaged herself but who had, in every encounter of wits with his intelligent rival, proved himself of no account, and who was finally revealed in a convict's cell, landed there by his conspicuous lack of his rival's skill in disengaging himself from compromising situations. Intelligence, with his bride on his arm, visited him in his cell, and gazed on him with a pitying shake of the head, observing, 'But for the Government Mind Training Course, I might be in your shoes today.' Finally, their two faces were thrown on the screen, immense and remarkable, the one wearing over his ethereal eyes the bar of Michael Angelo, the other with a foolish, vacant eye and a rabbit mouth that was ever agape.

This drama was sandwiched between *The Habits of the Kola Bear*, and *How his Mother-in-law Came to Stay*, and after it Chester and Kitty went out and walked along the Embankment.

It was one of those brilliant, moonlit, raidless nights which still seemed so strange, so almost flat, in their eventlessness.

Instinctively they strained their ears for guns; but they heard nothing but the rushing of traffic in earth and sky.

5

'The State,' said Chester, 'is a great debaucher. It debauches literature, art, the press, the stage, and the Church; but I don't think even its worst enemies can say it has debauched the cinema stage … What a people we are; good Lord, what a people!'

'As long as we leave Revue alone, I don't much mind what else we do,' Kitty said. 'Revue is England's hope, I believe. Because it's the only art in which all the forms of expression come in — talking, music, singing, dancing, gesture — standing on your head if nothing else will express you at the moment … I believe Revue is going to be tremendous. Look how its stupidities and vulgarities have been dropping away from it lately, this last year has made a new thing of it altogether; it's beginning to try to show the whole of life as lived … Oh, we must leave Revue alone … I sometimes think it's so much the coming thing that I can't be happy till I've chucked my job and gone into it, as one of a chorus. I should feel I was truly serving my country then; it would be a real thing, instead of this fantastic lunacy I'm involved in now …'

At times Kitty forgot she was talking to the Minister who had created the fantastic lunacy.

'You can't leave the Ministry,' said the Minister curtly. 'You can't be spared.'

Kitty was annoyed with him for suddenly being serious and literal and even cross, and was just going to tell him she should jolly well leave the Ministry whenever she liked, when some quality in his abrupt gravity caught the words from her lips.

'We haven't got industrial conscription to that extent yet,' she merely said, weakly.

It was all he didn't say to her in the moment's pause that followed which was revealing; all that seemed to be forced back behind his guarded lips. What he did say, presently, was 'No, more's the pity. It'll come, no doubt.'

And, talking of industrial conscription, they walked back.

What stayed with Kitty was the odd, startled, doubtful look he had given her in that moment's pause; almost as if he were afraid of something.

6

Kitty took at this time to sleeping badly; even worse, that is to say, than usual. In common with many others, she always did so when she was particularly interested in anyone. She read late, then lay and stared into the dark, her thoughts turning and twisting in her brain, till, for the sake of peace, she turned on the light again and read something; something cold, soothing, remote from life as now lived, like Aristophanes, Racine, or Bernard Shaw. Attaining by these means to a more detached philosophy, she would drift at last from the lit stage where life chattered and gesticulated, and creep behind the wings, and so find sleep, so little before it was time to wake that she began the day with a jaded feeling of having been up all night.

On one such morning she came down to find a letter from Neil Desmond in its thin foreign envelope addressed in his flat, delicate hand. He wrote from a Pacific island where he was starting a newspaper for the benefit of the political prisoners confined there; it was to be called 'Freedom' (in the British Isles no paper of this name would be allowed, but perhaps the Pacific island censorship was less strict) and he wanted Kitty to come and be sub-editor …

Kitty, instead of lunching out that day, took sandwiches to the office and spent the luncheon-hour breaking off her engagement again. The reason why Neil never got these letters was the very reason which impelled her to write them — the lack of force about him which made his enterprises so ephemeral, and kept him ever moving round the spinning world to try some new thing.

Force. How important it was. First Brains, to perceive and know what things we ought to do, then Power, faithfully to fulfil the same. In another twenty or thirty years, perhaps the whole British nation would be full of both these qualities, so full that the things in question really would get done. And then what? Kitty's mind boggled at the answer to this. It might be strangely upsetting …

She stamped her letter and lit a cigarette. The room, empty but for her, had that curious, flat, dream-like look of arrested activity which belongs to offices in the lunch hour. If you watch an office through that empty hour of suspension you may decipher its silent, patient, cynical comment (slowly growing into distinctness like invisible ink) on the work of the morning which has been, and of the afternoon which is to be. Kitty watched it, amused, then yawned and read *Stop It*, the newest weekly paper. It was a clever paper, for it had succeeded so far (four numbers) in not getting suppressed, and also in not committing itself precisely to any direct statement as to what it wanted stopped. It was produced by the Stop It Club, and the government lived in hopes of discovering one day, by well-timed police raids on the Club premises, sufficient lawless matter to justify it in suppressing both the Club and the paper. For Dora had recently been trying to retrieve her character in the eyes of those who blackened it, and was endeavouring to act in a just and temperate manner, and only to suppress those whose guilt was proven. Last Sunday, for instance, a Stop It procession had been allowed to parade through the city with banners emblazoned with the ambiguous words. There were, of course, so many things that, it was quite obvious, should be stopped; the command might have been addressed to those of the public who were grumbling, or to the government who were giving them things to grumble at; to writers who were producing books, journalists producing papers, parliaments producing laws, providence producing the weather, or the agents of any other regrettable activity at the moment in progress. Indeed, the answer to the enquiry 'Stop what?' might so very plausibly be 'Stop it all,' that it was a profitless question.

It was just after two that the telephone on Prideaux's table rang. (Kitty was working in Prideaux's room now.) 'Hullo,' said a voice in answer to hers, 'Mr Prideaux there? Or anyone else in his room I can speak to? The Minister speaking.'

Not his PS nor his PA, but the Minister himself; an unusual, hardly seemly occurrence, due, no doubt, to lunch-time. Kitty was reminded of a story someone had told her of a pert little office flapper at one end of a telephone, chirping, 'Hullo, who is it?' and the answer, slow, dignified, and crushing, from one of our greater peers — 'Lord Blankson ...' (pause) 'HIMSELF.'

'Mr Prideaux isn't in yet,' said Kitty. 'Can I give him a message?'

There was a moment's pause before the Minister's voice, somehow grown remote, said, 'No, thanks, it's all right. I'll ring him up later.'

He rang off abruptly. (After all, how can one ring off in any other way?) He had said, 'Or anyone else in his room I can speak to', as if he would have left a message with any chance clerk; but he had not, apparently, wished to hold any parley with her, even over the telephone, which though it has an intimacy of its own (marred a little by a listening exchange) is surely a sufficiently remote form of intercourse. But it seemed that he was avoiding her, keeping her at a distance, ringing her off; his voice had sounded queer, abrupt, embarrassed, as if he was shy of her. Perhaps he had thought things over and perceived that he had been encouraging one of his clerks to step rather too far out of her position; perhaps he was afraid her head might be a little turned, that she might think he was seeking her out …

Kitty sat on the edge of Prideaux's table and swore softly. She'd jolly well show him she thought no such thing.

'These great men,' she said, 'are insufferable.'

7

When they next met it was by chance, in a street aeroplane. The aero was full, and they didn't take much notice of each other till something went wrong with the machinery and they were falling street-wards, probably on the top of that unfortunate shop, Swan and Edgar's. In that dizzy moment the Minister swayed towards Kitty and said, 'Relax the body and don't protrude the tongue,' and then the crash came.

They only grazed Swan and Edgar's, and came down in Piccadilly, amid a crowd of men who scattered like a herd of frightened sheep. No one was much hurt (street aeros were carefully padded and springed, against these catastrophes), but Kitty chanced to strike the back of her head and to be knocked silly. It was only for a moment, and when she recovered consciousness the Minister was bending over her and whispering, 'She's killed. She's killed. Oh God.'

'Not at all,' said Kitty, sitting up, very white. 'It takes quite a lot more than that.'

His strained face relaxed. 'That's all right, then,' he said.

'I'm dining in Hampstead in about ten minutes,' said Kitty. 'I must get the tube at Leicester Square.'

'A taxi,' said the Minister, 'would be better. Here is a taxi. I shall come too, in case there is another mischance, which you will hardly be fit for alone at present.' He mopped his mouth.

'You have bitten your tongue,' said Kitty, 'in spite of all you said about not protruding it.'

'It was while I was saying it,' said the Minister, 'that the contact occurred. Yes. It is painful.'

They got into the taxi. The Minister, with his scarlet-stained handkerchief to his lips, mumbled, 'That was a very disagreeable shock. You were very pale. I feared the worst.'

'The worst,' said Kitty, 'always passes me by. It always has. I am like that.'

'I am not,' he said. 'I am not. I have bitten my tongue and fallen in love. Both bad things.'

He spoke so indistinctly that Kitty was not sure she heard him rightly.

'And I,' she said, 'only feel a little sick … No, don't be anxious; it won't develop.'

The Minister looked at her as she powdered her face before the strip of mirror.

'I wouldn't put that on,' he advised her. 'You are looking too pale already.'

'Quite,' said Kitty. 'It's pink powder, you see. It will make me feel more myself.'

'You need nothing,' he told her gravely. 'You are all right as you are. It is fortunate that it is you and not I who are going out to dinner. I couldn't talk. I can't talk now. I can't even tell you what I feel about you.'

'Don't try,' she counselled him, putting away her powder-puff and not looking at him.

He was leaning forward, his elbows on his knees, looking at her with his pained-humorist's face and watchful eyes.

'I expect you know I've fallen in love with you?' he mumbled.

'I didn't mean to; in fact, I've tried not to, since I began to notice what was occurring. It's excessively awkward. But … I have not been able to avoid it.'

Kitty said 'Oh,' and swallowed a laugh. One didn't laugh when one was receiving an avowal of love, of course. She felt giddy, and seas seemed to rush past her ears.

'There are a good many things to talk about in connection with this,' said the Minister. 'But it is no use talking about them unless I first know what you feel about it — about me, that is. Will you tell me, if you don't mind?'

He asked it gently, considerately, almost humbly. Kitty, who did mind rather, said 'Oh,' again, and lay back in her corner. She still felt a little dizzy, and her head ached. It is not nice having to say what one feels; one would rather the other person did it all. But this is not fair or honourable. She remembered this and pulled herself together.

'I expect,' she said, swinging her glasses by their ribbon, cool and yet nervous, 'I expect I feel pretty much the same as you do about it.'

After a moment's pause he said, 'Thank you. Thank you very much for telling me. Then it *is* of use talking about it. Only not now, because I'm afraid we're just getting there. And tomorrow I am going to a conference at Leeds. I don't think I can wait till the day after. May I call for you tonight and we'll drive back together?'

'Yes,' said Kitty, and got out of the taxi.

8

When they were in it again they comported themselves for a little while in the manner customary on these occasions, deriving the usual amount of pleasurable excitement therefrom.

Then the Minister said, 'Now we must talk. All is not easy about our situation.'

'Nothing is easy about it,' said Kitty. 'In fact, we're in the demon of a mess.'

He looked at her, biting his lips.

'You know about me, then? That I'm uncertificated? But of course you do. It is, I believe, generally known. And it makes the position exactly what you say. It means …'

'It means,' said Kitty, 'that we must get over this unfortunate passion.'

He shook his head, with a shrug.

'One can, you know,' said Kitty. 'I've been in and out before — more than once. Not so badly, perhaps, but quite badly enough. You too, probably?'

'Yes. Oh, yes,' he admitted gloomily. 'But it wasn't like this. Neither the circumstances, nor the — the emotion.'

Kitty said, 'Probably not. Why should it be? Nothing ever is exactly like anything else, luckily … By the way, when did you begin to take notice of me? Don't worry, if you can't remember.'

He thought for a minute, then shook his head.

'I'm bad at these things. Didn't we meet at Prideaux's one night in the spring? I observed you then; I remember you amused me. But I don't think the impression went deep … Then — oh, we met about a good deal one way and another — and I suppose it grew without my noticing it. And then came that week-end, and that did the trick as far as I was concerned. I knew what I was doing after that, and I tried to stop it, but, as you see, I have failed. This evening I told you, I suppose, under the influence of shock … I am not sorry. It is worth it, whatever comes of it.'

'Nothing can come of it,' said Kitty. 'Not the least thing at all. Except being friends. And you probably won't want that. Men don't.'

'No,' he said. 'I don't want it at all. But I suppose I must put up with it.' He began to laugh, with his suppressed, sardonic laughter, and Kitty laughed too.

'We're fairly hoist with our own petard, aren't we?' he said. 'Think of the scandal we might make, if we did what we chose now … I believe it would be the *coup de grâce* for the Brains Ministry.' He stated a simple fact, without conceit.

'It's a rotten position,' he continued moodily. 'But there it is … And you're A, aren't you? You'll have to marry someone, eventually. If only you were B2 or 3 — only then you wouldn't be yourself. As it is, it would be criminally immoral of me to stand in your way. The right thing, I suppose, would be for us to clear out of each other's way and give each other a chance to forget. *The right thing* … Oh damn it all, I'm as bad as the most muddle-headed fool in the country, who doesn't care *that* for the right thing if it fights against his individual impulses and desires … I suppose moralists would say here's my chance to bear my witness, to stand by my own principles and show the world they're real … They *are* real, too; that's the mischief of it. I still am sure they matter more than anything else; but just now they bore me. I suppose this is what a moral and law-abiding citizen feels when he falls in love with someone else's wife … What are you laughing at now?'

'You,' said Kitty. 'This is the funniest conversation … Of course it's a funny position — it's straight out of a comic opera. What a pity Gilbert and Sullivan didn't think of it; they'd have done it beautifully … By the way, I don't think I shall be marrying anyone anyhow, so you needn't worry about that. I've broken off my last engagement — at least I've done my best to; it became a bore. I don't really like the idea of matrimony, you know; it would be too much of a tie and a settling down. Yes, all right, I know my duty to my country, but my duty to myself comes first … So there's no harm, from my point of view, in our going on seeing each other and taking each other out and having as good a time as we can in the circumstances. Shall we try that way, and see if it works?'

'Oh, we'll try,' he said, and took her again in his arms. 'It's all we can get, so we'll take it … my dear.'

'I think it's a good deal,' said Kitty. 'It will be fun … You know, I'm frightfully conceited at your liking me — I can't get used to it yet; you're so important and superior. It isn't every day that a Minister of a Department falls in love with one of his clerks. It isn't really done, you know, not by the best Ministers.'

'Nor by the best clerks,' he returned. 'We must face the fact that we are not the best people.'

'And here's my flat. Will you come in and have something? There's only my cousin here, and she's never surprised; her own life is too odd.'

'I think it would be inadvisable,' said the Minister discreetly. 'We don't want to coddle our reputations, but we may as well keep an eye on them.'

On that note of compromise they parted.

CHAPTER 7

The Breaking Point

1

It was six months later: in fact, April. It was a Saturday afternoon, and many people were going home from work, including Kitty Grammont and Ivy Delmer, who were again in the Bakerloo tube, on their way to Marylebone for Little Chantreys.

The same types of people were in the train who had been in it on the Monday morning in May which is described in the opening chapter of this work. The same types of people always are in tube trains (except on the air-raid nights of the Great War, when a new and less self-contained type was introduced). But they were the same with a difference: it was as if some tiny wind had stirred and ruffled the face of sleeping waters. In some cases the only difference was a puzzled, half-awakened, rather fretful look, where had been peace. This was to be observed in the faces of the impassive shopping women. Still they sat and gazed, but with a difference. Now and then a little shiver of something almost like a thought would flicker over the calm, observing, roving eyes, which would distend a little, and darken with a faint annoyance and fear. Then it would pass, and leave the waters as still as death again; but it had been there. And it was quite certain there were fewer of these ruminating ladies. Some had perhaps died of the Mind Training Course, of trying to use their brains. (They say that some poor unfortunates who have never known the touch of soap and water on their bodies die of their first bath on being brought into hospital; so these.) Some who had been in the ruminating category six months ago were now reading papers. Some others, who still gazed at their fellows, gazed in a different manner; they would look intently at someone for half a minute, then look away, and their lips would move, and it was apparent that they were, not saying their prayers, but trying to repeat to themselves every detail of what they had seen. For this was part of the Government Mind Training Course (observation and accuracy). And one large and cow-like lady with a shopping-bag containing circulating library books and other commodities said to her companion, in Kitty Grammont's hearing, two things that accorded strangely with her aspect.

'I couldn't get anything worth reading out of the library today — they hadn't got any of the ones I'd ordered. These look quite silly, I'm sure. There aren't many good books written, do you think?'

Doubtful she was, and questioning: but still, she had used the word 'good' and applied it to a book, as she might have to butter, or a housemaid, or a hat, implying a possible, though still dimly discerned, difference between one book and another. And presently she said a stranger thing.

'What,' she enquired, 'do you think about the state of things between Bavaria and Prussia? Relations today seemed more strained than ever, I thought.'

Her companion could not be said to rise to this; she replied merely (possibly having a little missed the drift of the unusual question) that in her view relations were very often a nuisance, and exhausting. So the subject was a little diverted; it went off, in fact, on to sisters-in-law; but still it had been raised.

Beyond these ladies sat another who looked as if she had obtained exemption from the Mind Training Course on the ground that her mind (if any) was not susceptible of training; and beyond her sat a little typist eating chocolates and reading the *Daily Mirror*. Last May she had been reading 'The love he could not buy'; this April she was reading 'How to make pastry out of nuts.' Possibly by Christmas she might be reading 'Which way shall I Vote and Why?'

Ivy Delmer, next her, was reading the notices along the walls. Between 'Ask Mr Punch into your home', and 'Flee from the wrath to come' there was a gap, where a Safety if Possible notice had formerly offered the counsel 'Do not sit down in the street in the middle of the traffic or you may get killed.' A month ago this had been removed. It had, apparently, been decided by the Safety if Possible Council that the public had at last outgrown their cruder admonitions. The number of street accidents was, in fact, noticeably on the decline: it seemed as if people were learning, slowly and doubtfully, to connect cause and effect. A was learning why he would be killed, B why he would not. Ivy Delmer noticed the gap on the wall, and wondered what would take its place. Perhaps it would be another text; but texts were diminishing in frequency; one seldom saw one now. More likely it would be an exhortation to Take a Holiday in the Clouds, or Get to Watford in five minutes by Air (and damn the risk).

Ivy, as she had a year ago, looked round at the faces of her fellow-travellers — mostly men and girls going home from business. Quite a lot of young men there were in these days; enough, you'd almost think, for there to be one over for Ivy to marry some day … Ivy sighed a little. She hoped rather that this would indeed prove to be so, but hoped without conviction. After all, few girls could expect to get married in these days. She supposed that if she married at all, she ought to take a cripple, or a blind one, and keep him. She knew that would be the patriotic course; but how much nicer it would be to be taken by a whole one and get kept! She looked at the pale, maimed young men round her, and decided that they didn't, mostly, look like keeping anyone at all, let alone her; they were too tired. The older men looked more robust; but older men are married. Some of them looked quite capable and pleased with themselves, as if they were saying, 'What have I got out of it, sir? Why, £100 more per annum, more self-confidence, and a clearer head.'

There was also a brilliant-looking clergyman, engaged probably in reforming the Church; but clergymen are different, one doesn't marry them. Altogether, not a hopeful collection.

The train got to Marylebone pretty quickly, because it had almost abandoned its old habit of stopping halfway between every two stations. No one had ever quite known why it had done this in the past, but, with the improvement in the brains of the employees of the electric railways, the custom had certainly gradually decreased.

Marylebone too had undergone a change: there was rather less running hither and thither, rather less noise, rather less smoke, and the clock was more nearly right. Nothing that would strike the eye of anyone who was not looking for signs, but little manifestations which made the heart, for instance, of Nicholas Chester stir within him with satisfaction when he came that way, or the way of any other station (excepting only the stations of the South Eastern line, the directors and employees of which had been exempted in large numbers from the Mind Training Act by the Railway Executive Committee, as not being likely to profit by the course).

Certainly the train to Little Chantreys ran better than of old, and with hardly any smoke. Someone had hit on a way of reducing the smoke nuisance; probably of, eventually, ending it altogether. Kitty Grammont and Ivy Delmer found themselves in the same compartment, and talked at intervals on the journey. Ivy thought, as she had thought several times during the last few months, that Kitty looked prettier than of old, and somehow more radiant, more lit up. They talked of whether you ought to wear breeches as near to town as West Ealing, and left it unsettled. They talked of where you could get the best chocolates for the least money, and of what was the best play on just now. They talked of the excess of work in the office at the present moment, caused by the new Instruction dealing with the exemption of journalists whose mental category was above B2. (This was part of the price which had to be paid by the Brains Ministry for the support of the press, which is so important.) They began to talk, at least Ivy did, of whether you can suitably go to church with a dog in your muff; and then they got to Little Chantreys.

2

Ivy found her parents in the garden, weeding the paths. Jane and John were playing football, and Jelly was trotting a lonely trail round the domains in a character apparently satisfactory to himself but which would have been uncertain to an audience.

'Well, dear,' said the vicar, looking up at Ivy from his knees. The vicarage had not yet adopted the new plan of destroying weeds by electricity; they had tried it once, but the electricity had somehow gone astray and electrified Jelly instead of the weeds, so they had given it up. The one-armed soldier whom they employed as gardener occasionally pulled up a weed, but not often, and he was off this afternoon anyhow, somewhat to the Delmers' relief. Of course one must employ disabled soldiers, but the work gets on quicker without them.

'Have you had a busy day, darling?' enquired Mrs Delmer, busy scrabbling with a fork between paving-stones.

'Rather,' said Ivy, and sat down on the wheelbarrow. 'The Department's frightfully rushed just now … Mr Prideaux says the public is in a state of unrest. It certainly seems to be, from the number of grumbling letters it writes us … You're looking tired, Daddy.'

'A little, dear.' The vicar got up to carry his basket of weeds to the bonfire. Mrs Delmer said, 'Daddy's had a worrying time in the parish. Two more poor little abandoned babies.'

'Where were they left this time?' Ivy asked with interest.

'One at the Police Station, with a note to say the government had driven the parents to this; the other just outside our garden door, with no note at all, but I suppose it's the same old story. We've no clue to either yet; they're not from Little Chantreys, of course, but I suppose we shall trace them in time. Daddy's been making enquiries among the village people; none of them will say, if they know, but Daddy says they're all in a sad state of anger and discontent about the Baby Laws; he thinks they're working up worse every day. There's so much talk of different laws for rich and poor. Of course when people say that, what they always mean is that it's the same law for both, and ought to be different. Even that isn't true, of course, in this case, as the taxes are in proportion to the income; but it certainly does come very hard on the poor. Daddy thinks it his duty to preach about it again tomorrow, and that worries him, because he may get arrested and fined. But he feels it's right. He thinks the country is in real danger of risings and revolts if this goes on. He says the Stop It League is doing its best to stir up rebellion, poor little babies abandoned or disowned all over the country; it goes to one's heart … Don't talk about it, darling, it worries Daddy so … And poor Brown is little use with the vegetable garden. His Mind Training Course seems really to have quite upset him; he talks and looks so strangely now. And Daddy's worried about Mr Hawtrey,' (the curate) 'who's joined the Church Improvement Society and has become dreadfully restless, and keeps saying Daddy ought to join it too.'

Mrs Delmer sighed, and changed the subject, as the vicar came back, to the amount of blossom there was on the white-heart cherry.

Ivy went indoors. She went up to the room she shared with

Betty. Betty was there, staining a straw hat with Jackson's nut-brown hat-polish.

Ivy said, 'A nice mess you're making. I should think you might remember it's my room as well as yours,' and Betty said, 'Socks.' From which it may be inferred that these sisters, good-humoured in the main to others, were frequently short-tempered to one another.

Ivy said next, opening a drawer, 'I won't stand it. You've been pinching my handkerchiefs.'

Betty replied absently, and as if from habit rather than from reflection, 'Haven't been near your old drawer.'

'Liar. There were twelve here this morning and now there are only ten. I've told you before I won't stand having my things pinched. If you're too slack to earn enough to keep yourself in handkerchiefs, you must do without, that's all.'

'I suppose you'd rather I'd used my sleeve at the Whites' tennis this morning, wouldn't you?'

'I shouldn't care if you had … Tennis in the morning's a pretty rotten idea anyhow, if you ask me. You're the biggest slacker I ever came across. If I was Daddy I wouldn't keep you eating your head off, even if you aren't clever. You're going on like a girl before the war. Your Training Course doesn't seem to have done you the slightest good, either. It's people like you who'll rot up the whole plan.'

'It's rot anyhow,' Betty returned, without interest, turning her hat about critically. 'You should just hear the way they're all going on about it in the village. Stuff and nonsense, I call it. And as long as people like me and the village — normal, ordinary people — think it's stuff and nonsense … well, it *will* be stuff and nonsense, that's all.'

'People like you,' Ivy retorted witheringly, as she changed her skirt for her country breeches.

But, after all, that retort didn't dispose of Betty, or the people like Betty … or the whole vicarage family … or most of Little Chantreys … Those people, after all, were going to take more disposing of than that … They were, quite possibly, going to take more disposing of than anyone yet knew.

'Silly ass,' said Ivy, but with a touch of doubt.

She thought her new green breeches were rather nice, anyhow, and that seemed to matter more.

3

Kitty found her brother Cyril at the End House. Cyril was in a poor way. His publishing business was on the edge of bankruptcy.

'So much for your abominable Brains Ministry,' he complained. 'The mass of safe, mediocre stuff on which publishers count for a living while they adventure with the risks is being gradually withdrawn. It simply doesn't come in. Its producers are becoming — many of them — just too intelligent. I'm not imagining this; I know of several cases in which it has happened; of people who have developed just enough distaste for their own work to dry them up altogether. What's worse, there isn't the same sale for such stuff as there was. When the process has gone much further (if ever it does) — so far that a lot of really good stuff is turned out, and read by large numbers of people, business will be all right again. Till then, publishers are in a poor way … Verse is dropping off, too, like autumn leaves. That's all to the good … I daresay in another year or two (unless you're wrecked first, which seems probable, by the way) there'll only be about a hundred people left in the country writing anything at all … Newspapers, of course, go on much the same; that's because you're afraid of them and exempt their staff. Insignificant verse and meaningless novels may die a natural death (though I think it improbable), but *Myosotis* and the *Patriot* and the *Daily Idiot* will go on for ever. You're all such cowards at Whitehall.

You dare to ruin unoffending publishers, to browbeat the poor and simple, and to extract gold from the innocent babe unborn, but you daren't risk the favour of the press.'

'No,' Kitty agreed. 'We certainly daren't … Not that we've got it, you know, quite the contrary; but we strive for it. I was reading the *Herald* and *Stop It* in the train, till I was cold with fear. *Stop It* veils its meaning delicately, as usual; but it means business … However, I thought we should have been downed six months ago, yet here we are still. It's like skating on rotten ice so fast that it never breaks. It's fun; it's exciting. And I believe if we go on skating fast, it won't break at all. You see, the government are getting cleverer and cleverer themselves, which will help them to do it skilfully. Chester says his head really does feel clearer after taking the Course; he says so in private life, I mean, not only when he's soft-soaping the public.'

'He'll need,' said Anthony, 'a jolly clear head before he's through with this job. With every door-step in our towns and villages piled with exposed babies … it's worse than China. Much worse, because I believe in China they don't get put on door-steps, but left harmlessly out of the way in open fields and no one meddles with them. It's becoming a public nuisance.'

'There is a new branch at the Ministry,' said Kitty, 'which is concerned exclusively with Uncertificated Babies, how to deal with them.'

'An' how *do* they deal with them, the poor little ducks?" enquired Pansy, who had just come in from the garden looking more than usually gay and lovely and fantastic in a pink sunbonnet and the kind of dress affected by milkmaids in a chorus.

Kitty looked at her thoughtfully.

'I should hardly like to tell you. You mightn't like it. Besides, it's a private department, like the secret room in jam factories where they make the pips. No, Pansy love, I can't possibly tell you … But they *do* deal with them, quite effectively.'

Pansy tossed her Cheeper up and down to a gentle music-hall ditty.

> 'Who'll buy babies —
> Babies better dead?
> Here's every mental category,
> From C3 down to Z … '

It was a taking song as she crooned it on the stage, nursing an infant on each arm, and with a baby chorus crying behind her.

4

After breakfast on Sunday morning Kitty remarked that she was going by train to Beaconsfield, where she had arranged to meet Chester for a walk through Burnham Beeches. She as a rule made no secret of her walks with Chester, only occasionally, when self-consciousness took her. After all, why should she? One went walks with all sorts of people, with any man or woman who liked walking and talking and whom one liked as a companion; it implied nothing. Kitty at times, with all it meant in this instance burning and alive in her consciousness, had to pause to tell herself how little it did imply to others, how she might mention it freely and casually, without fear. Yet might she? The intimacy of the Minister of a Department with one of his clerks was, no doubt, out of the ordinary, not quite like other intimacies; perhaps it did seem odd, and imply things. Perhaps Kitty might have thought so herself, in another case.

She announced her plan this morning with an extra note of casualness in her voice.

Pansy said, 'Oh, you two. You'll be goin' baby-huntin' in

the ditches, I should think, instead of pickin' primroses. I should say you jolly well ought, and you'd better take the Cheeper's pram with you.'

Anthony said, 'Exactly what I always try *not* to do, going out on Sundays with the people from my shop. It spoils the Sabbath rest, the Pisgah's mountain touch. You'd much better come out with Cyril and Pansy and me.'

'I,' said Cyril, in his detached manner, 'shall be going to Mass.'

5

They walked up through the depraved mushroom growth round Beaconsfield station to the old town, that city set on a hill, lying wide and spacious, with its four Ends stretched out like a cross. Old Beaconsfield is an enchanted city; as it was in the seventeenth and eighteenth centuries, so it is today, an ancient country town, full of brick walls and old houses, and courtyards and coaching inns, and dignity and romance and great elms. But they left it behind them, and took the lane that runs to Hedgerley, with the cold April wind in their faces.

They came, four miles on, to the forest of great beeches, where broad glades and grassy rides run in and out through thickets of wild undergrowth and bracken, and ancient twisted boles and slim smooth grey-green stems are set close together under a rustling singing roof of brilliant green, the young, new-born, radiant green of beeches in April. In every hollow and dip of the forest's mossy floor, primroses glimmered in pale pools.

They sat down by one of these pools to have their lunch.

After lunch they lay on there and smoked. Chester lay on his back, his hands clasped behind his head, staring up at the green roof. Kitty, her round chin cupped in her two hands, lay and watched his lean, sallow, clever face, foreshortened, with the shadows of the leaves moving on it and his eyes screwed against the sun.

'Kitty,' said Chester presently; 'I want to talk to you."

'M — m.' Kitty, having finished her cigarette, was chewing grass.

He sat up and looked at her, and as he looked his face grew more sallow and his smile died. He stabbed into the soft, damp earth with his stick, and frowned.

'It's this, my dear. I can't go on any longer with this — this farce. We must end it. I've been meaning to tell you so for some time, but I thought I'd give it a fair trial, just to satisfy us both. Well, we've given it a trial, and it won't work. It isn't good enough. We've got to be more to each other — or less. This — this beastly half-way house was all right for a bit; but we've got on too far now for it ... I should like to know what *you* think about it.'

Kitty pulled a primrose to pieces, petal by petal, before she answered.

'One thing I think,' she said slowly, 'is that I'm different from you. Or is it that women are different from men? Never mind; it doesn't really matter which. But I fancy it's women and men. Anyhow there it is. And the difference is that for me a half-way house would always be better than nothing, while for you it would be worse. Men seem to value being married so much more than women do — and friendship, going about together, having each other to talk to and play with, and all that, seems to matter to them so little. Love seems to take different forms with men and women, and to want different ways of expression ... So it's not much use trying to understand one another about it ... That's the chief thing I think, Nicky.'

He moved impatiently.

'In fact, you're contented with the present state of things.'

'Oh, no. Not a bit. I want much more. But — if it's all we can have ...'

'It isn't,' he said. 'We can get married.'

She shook her head, with decision. 'No. No. No.'

'Quite quietly,' he pleaded. 'No one would know but ourselves and the registrar and a witness whom we'd murder after the ceremony. Why shouldn't we? What are the reasons why not? There are only two; you ought to marry a certificated person and have an intelligent family; and I oughtn't to have a family at all. Well, you say you don't mean to marry anyone else; so you may as well marry me. So much for the first reason. And of course we wouldn't have a family; so much for the second. Well, then?'

'There's a third,' said Kitty. 'And the only important one. There's the look of the thing. I don't care how many people we murder, the secret will leak out. Things always do leak out. Never, in the course of twenty-nine years of endeavour, have I been able to keep anything shady from coming to light sooner or later. It isn't done. You ought to know that, as a government servant. Has any government ever succeeded in keeping its own dark doings secret for long? No; they come out like — like flowers pushing up towards daylight; and then there's the devil to pay. All our shadiest departmental transactions emerge one by one; nothing is hid that shall not be revealed. And our marriage would be the same. Be sure our sin would find us out. And that would be the end of your career, and probably of the Ministry as well; I believe the Ministry will stand or fall with you; and it's already pretty tottery ... It's a pity you can't get exemption; but of course your case is one in which it's absolutely never given ... No, we can't do this thing. You're the Minister of Brains first, and poor Nicky Chester, who would like to marry his girl, a long, long way behind. And the poor girl who would like to marry Nicky Chester — she's not got to count at all ... I don't want to be high-falutin and to talk about principles, only to have a little sense.'

He was watching her moodily from under bent brows, leaning back against a beech-trunk and pulling up little handfuls of damp moss with his thin, unusual fingers.

'Sense,' he repeated. 'It is sense, to have what one wants, if it doesn't harm anything or anyone. And I'll tell you another thing — not having it is rotting me up altogether — me and my work. I didn't want to fall in love again; I hoped I'd done with all that; I tried not to take any notice of you. But it was no go, and I can't fall out again, and I'm dead sick of going on like this. And my experience of life, both private and public, has been longer than yours, and, as it happens, I've known of several transactions which haven't come to light and never will; I've perpetrated some myself in the Ministry, which even that clear light which beats upon a hotel hasn't yet exposed, and, heaven helping us, won't. You don't suppose all the dark secrets of the war ever came out? Of course they didn't. There are some that will wait till ... well, till the next war, let's say ... Kitty, let's try it. It's worth the risk, surely. Let's be sporting. We're missing — we're missing the best thing in the world, just out of funk. I thought you always did things, just for the sake of doing them. I thought you never turned your back on life. It isn't like you.'

'Oh,' murmured Kitty. 'Life ... There's so much of that. This is just one thing out of it.'

'While you want it,' he returned, indubitably correct as to this, 'it seems a long way the most important thing.'

'It does,' she agreed. 'There's no comparison at all ... It's queer, isn't it, how strong it is, this odd, desperate wanting of one person out of all the world. It's an extraordinary, enormously strong thing ... But there *are* other things. There are jokes, and shops, and music, and plays, and pictures, and nice clothes, and Russian politics, and absurd people, and

Greek poetry, and the world's failures caged together on one island, and things to eat and to drink, and our careers, and primroses in woods, and the censor … Good gracious, it's all like an idiotic, glorified revue. We mustn't let the one thing, just because it matters most, matter alone. It's so commonplace. Our hearts aren't broken, and won't break. We're out to have a good time, and we'll let love and marriage go to the — anywhere they like, if we can't have them … By the way, if it's any comfort to you (it is to me) I shouldn't make at all a good wife; I'm much nicer as a friend. I want too much out of life. I'm grasping and selfish. You'd find me tiring.'

'I do,' he returned. 'You're tiring me to death now. I've plenty of friends already, thank you. And what does it matter to me what sort of a wife you'd make? You talk as if you were refusing a secretarial appointment. I want you, not a wife.'

'You've got me,' said Kitty, 'only not as a wife … If that's no use to you, we'll give it up. Nicky, I suppose we'd *better* give it up. It isn't working. I'll go right away. I'll get another job.'

'No,' he said gloomily. 'There's no need for that. Why should you mess up your career? We needn't meet. We shouldn't naturally meet, unless we made opportunities. I think you're right, that we'd better not meet. What's the good of meeting, just to repeat this sort of scene again and again, and hurt each other? We've reached the breaking point; I can't bear any more … I think we'd better leave it that you let me know when you change your mind and will marry me. You will, won't you, when you do?'

'Yes,' said Kitty, and could say no more than that because she was on the edge of tears.

For a moment they clung together, holding each other close. He said, 'My dearest dear, I love you. Can't you? … can't you?' and she whispered, very pale, 'I love you. I think I worship you,' and laid her cheek on his hand, so that he felt her tears.

They walked on together through the April afternoon, and it cried to them like a child whom they were betraying and forsaking. There would not be another day like this day, through all the lovely awakening spring and summer.

6

Ivy and Betty Delmer, who had been spending the afternoon at Beaconsfield, saw them at Beaconsfield station.

Betty said, 'Surely that's your Minister with Miss Grammont.'

Ivy looked at them, down the length of the platform. It seemed to her that Miss Grammont's walk with the Minister hadn't been altogether a success; they both looked so pale and tired, and Miss Grammont, surely, had been crying.

Something suddenly passed into Ivy's consciousness about these two people whom she admired, and her soft mouth dropped open a little with the amazement of her thoughts. The Minister — and Miss Grammont! It was surely incredible. Ministers didn't; they were too high, too superior. Besides, what had love to do with this Minister, who was uncertificated for matrimony? Ivy told herself she was mistaken, she had misread the look with which they had looked at each other as they parted.

'Are they thick?' Betty was asking, with careless, inquisitive interest. Betty wouldn't think it odd; Betty didn't know anything about ministers in general or this minister in particular.

'Oh, I think they know each other quite well,' replied Ivy. 'Miss Grammont's jolly clever, you know. I shouldn't wonder if he talks about quite important things to her.'

'How dull,' returned Betty, swinging her primroses. 'Don't

let's get into the same carriage as her. I never know if I know those End House people or not; Daddy and mother think I don't, and it's awkward … I'd rather enjoy knowing Miss Ponsonby and that ducky baby, even if they aren't respectable, she looks so sweet, and I'd like to hear all about the stage. But I've no use for your Miss Grammont. Her clothes are all right, but I'm sure she's stuck up … Fancy going out for Sunday with the Minister of a government department! Rather her than me.'

Ivy said, 'Don't you worry, my child. No Minister'll ever trouble *you* to go out with him. As for Chester, I should think he'd have you executed after one talk; he's great on ridding the world of the mentally deficient.' But what she was thinking was, 'How fearfully interesting if there is anything between them.' She wondered what the other people at the office thought about it, or if they had ever thought about it at all.

CHAPTER 8

On Fixed Hearts and Changing Scenes

1

To Kitty it was manifest that the time had come for a change of employment. Such times came frequently in her life; often merely because she got bored, yawned, wanted a change, heard life summoning her to fresh woods and pastures new, and obeyed the call. Many occupations she had thus thrown up lightly; this is one reason why those who regard life as a variety entertainment do not really get on; they forget that life is real, life is earnest, and departing leave behind them no footprints on the sands of time. They do not make a career; they do not make good; they do not, in the long run, even make much money, though that rolls in by fits and starts, and at times plentifully. They do not so much hide their talents in napkins as play ball with them.

This is as much as to say that it was not to Kitty Grammont the effort and the wrench that it would have been to many people to contemplate a change of avocation. And it certainly seemed desirable. Chester had said, 'We needn't meet'; but the fact remained that when two people who love each other work in the same building, however remote their spheres, they disturb each other, are conscious of each other's nearness. And Chester's presence pervaded the whole Ministry; he had stamped himself everywhere; there was no getting away from him. His name was constantly on the lips and on the pens of his subordinates, and clicked forth from every typewriter; you could not so much as write an official letter without beginning 'I am directed by the Minister of Brains to state,' and signing it 'for the Minister of Brains'. Besides which, he was to be seen going out and coming in, to be met in passages and lifts, to be observed taking his food in the canteen, and his Personal Assistant demanded continual attention to him on the telephone. No, there was no getting away from the Minister. And that meant no peace of mind, none of the old careless light-hearted living and working; nothing but a continual, disturbing, restless, aching want. Kitty had no intention of facing this, so she told Vernon Prideaux that when she found another job she was going to leave. He looked at her in annoyance and dismay, and said, 'Good lord, why?'

Kitty said, 'I'm bored. I want a change. I'm tired of working for this autocratic government. I want something with more variety in it, and more soul — a travelling circus, or a companionship to a rich American seeing the world; or any old thing, so long as it amuses me.'

'There's going to be quite enough amusement in *this* circus,' said Prideaux, 'before we're through with it, to satisfy anyone, I should say … Really, Kitty, I think you're foolish. You're throwing up your chances; you're climbing up, and will climb higher if you stay. Even if the thing founders, as is quite likely, you'll climb out of it into another job, you're good enough. You ought to think of your career. And besides, you can't be spared. Who on earth do you think is going to do your job? I think you ought to see this thing through.'

But Kitty did not think so. 'It will go to its own place quite quickly enough without my help. And as for my career — funny word — I'm not sure I've got one. If I have it's such a chequered one that a few more ups and downs won't make much difference to it. And as for being spared, oh anyone can be spared, out of any ministry; there are too many of us. Anyhow — well anyhow I must go.'

Prideaux thought this so frivolous, so foolish, so unworthy, so tiresome, and so like a woman, that he was exasperated. He rang for a shorthand typist, remarking, 'If you must you must. Miss Egerton,' (Miss Egerton had succeeded Miss Pomfrey, and was better) 'send to the Establishment Branch for Miss Grammont's papers sometime,' which closed the subject for the present.

Kitty went back to her table and wrote a letter to the ASE about some unfortunate agreement which had been made with them concerning the exemption of some of their members from the Mind Training Course. Personally Kitty was of the opinion that it was a pity the agreement had not been made as extensive as the ASE desired; she thought that this Union were already too clever by half. She almost went to the length of thinking it was a pity the promises made to them had not been kept; a revolutionary opinion which in itself indicated that it was time she left. Having dealt with the ASE she turned her attention to a file sent down from MBI and minuted 'Passed to you to deal with this man's imaginary grievance.' The imaginary grievance was that the wife of the man in question had been killed by a motor bus, and he wanted a week's postponement of his Mind Training Course in order that he might arrange about the funeral. MBI were like that; they did not mean to be unkind, but were a little lacking in flexibility and imagination.

Ivy Delmer, who had answered Prideaux's bell, sat with her pencil ready and her round face bent over her notebook. She had heard Prideaux's order to his secretary, and concluded, correctly, that Miss Grammont was either going to have her pay raised or to leave, and from Prideaux's manner and voice she thought it was the second. She wondered whether this could have anything to do with the Minister, and what he had been saying to Miss Grammont on Sunday. She was curious and interested, even more so than she had been on Sunday, because the people to whom she had mentioned the subject had all noticed the intimacy; everyone seemed to have seen the Minister out with Miss Grammont at one time or another. No one but Ivy thought it was anything more than friendship, but no one else had seen them look at one another on Beaconsfield platform. Ivy had, and said so …

Kitty was right; nothing remained hidden in government departments, or, indeed, anywhere else. Healthily, persistently, inevitably, everything pushed up towards the clear light of day; and quite right, too.

2

In the evenings Kitty, seeking jobs, studied the advertisement columns of the daily papers. She had always read them; they, with Mr Selfridge and the Pelman system, form the lighter and more entertaining part of any daily paper; but now she took to perusing them with care. The personal column of the *Times* she found peculiarly edifying.

'Quiet, refined gentleman (served in war, musical) would like to get into touch with bright and sympathetic lady.' Kitty rejected that; she was not sure that she was sympathetic, and the terms were too vague. Better was 'Lady, high standard of taste and culture and large means, wants capable travelling companion. Knowledge of art essential, good breeding preferred. Must talk continental languages fluently and understand railway guides.' Kitty, making a mental note of that (for, with the possible exception of the breeding, she had all these qualifications), ran her eyes down the column, past 'Write to me, darling, all is forgiven', 'Will the lady in a fur toque riding in a Hammersmith aero on Saturday last at 3.30 communicate with AC', 'No man hath seen God at any time', until she came to 'Young, accomplished, well-educated War Widow would like position as secretary or confidential clerk to nobleman, member of parliament, or gentleman.' She rested her finger on that. 'I'll put one in like this,' she remarked to her cousin. 'War Widow. That's what I've always wanted to be. It sounds so well. Elspeth, I shall buy some weeds and commence widow. A war widow …'

'If you want a new job, and a job with travel and life in it,' said her cousin, sounding her, 'I don't know why you don't go out to the Pacific Islands and join Neil. You may be sure that wherever Neil is there'll be travel enough and life enough.' She watched Kitty idly through a little whirl of cigarette smoke. But Kitty looked no more than bored, bending over the *Times* and manicuring her nails.

'Neil would tire me. I've grown too old for Neil. Besides, it wouldn't be proper; I've broken off my engagement. I've not had the last letter back yet, you know, so he may have got it. Besides …' Kitty paused only for a moment, and added in the same casual tone, 'besides, I'm too much in love with Nicky Chester, though I can't have him, to have any use for anyone else just now.'

Her cousin nodded. 'I knew that, darling, of course. And so you've renounced each other. How silly. But it won't last. It never does. Go and be a Young Accomplished War Widow, then, to pass the time.'

3

But there were hours of the night when it seemed to Kitty that she could not go and be a Young Accomplished War Widow, that she could not be companion, however capable, to any travelling lady of taste, culture and means, or clerk, however confidential, to any peer, MP, or even gentleman;

that none of these careers (were they careers? She still sought to define that word) would pass the time at all; that nothing, in fact, would pass it except working for Nicholas Chester, seeing him some times, hearing his voice … Always addicted to metaphysical speculation in the night, even in nights of anguish, she would speculate on this queer disease, so common to the race, which had overtaken (and not, as they had both candidly remarked, for the first time, possibly not even for the last) herself and Nicholas Chester. What was it, this extraordinary driving pressure of emotion, this quite disproportionate desire for companionship with, for contact with, one person out of all the world; of people and things, which made, while it lasted, all other desires, all other emotions, pale and faint beside it? Which so perverted and wrenched from its bearings the mind of a man like Nicholas Chester that he was for throwing overboard the cherished principles which were the cargo he had for long been so desperately bent on carrying, through storm and stress, to the country of his dreams? Which made him say, 'No one will find out, and if they do, let them and be damned to them'? … Desire for a person; it had, it had always had, an extraordinarily dynamic effect on the lives of men and women. When it came into play, principle, chivalry, common sense, intellect, humour, culture, sweetness and light, all we call civilisation, might crumple up like match-board so this one overwhelming desire, shared by all the animal creation, might be satisfied. On this rock the world, the pathetic, eager, clever, foolish, so heavily handicapped world, might be wrecked. It was, perhaps, this one thing that would always prevent humanity from being, in fact, a clever and successful race, would always keep them down somewhere near the level of the other animals.

Faces passed before Kitty's wakeful eyes; the fatuous, contented faces of mothers bending over the rewards of love clinging to their breasts; slow, placid, married faces everywhere … This thing was irresistible, and certainly inevitable; if it ceased, humanity itself would cease, since it is the one motive which impels the continued population one had to accept it; there was, perhaps, no one who grew to years of maturity who escaped it, no one whose life would not, at some period, be in some degree disorganised by this strange force. It was blind instinct; its indulgence did not, in the end, even make for good, so far as good meant adventure, romance, and the gay chances of life, the freedom of the cities of the world — anything beyond mere domesticity. For what, after all, was marriage? A tying down, a shutting of gates, the end of youth, the curbing of the spirit of adventure which seeks to claim all the four corners of the world for its heritage. It meant a circumscribed and sober life, in one place, in one house, with, perhaps, children to support and to mind; it meant becoming respectable, insured, mature, settled members of society, with a stake in the country. No longer may life be greeted with a jest and death with a grin; both these (of course important but not necessarily solemn) things have come to matter too much to be played with.

To this sedate end do the world's gay and careless free-lances come; they shut the door upon the challenging spirit of life, and Settle Down. It is to this end that instinct, not to be denied, summons men and women, as the bit of cheese summons the mouse into the trap.

Musing thus, Kitty turned her pillow over and over, seeking a softer side. How she detested stupidity! How, even more, Nicholas Chester loathed stupidity! To him it was anathema, the root of all evil, the Goliath he was out to destroy, the blind beast squatting on men's bones, the idiot drivelling on the village green. And here he was, caught in the beast's destroying grip, just because he had, as they call it, fallen in love … What a work is man! … And here was Kitty herself, all her gay love of living in danger, tottering unsteadily on its foundations, undermined by this secret gnawing thing.

At last, as a sop to the craving which would not be denied, she sat up, with aching, fevered head, and turned the light on, and wrote on a piece of paper, 'Nicky, I'll marry you any time you like, if you want me to,' and folded it up and laid it on the table at her side, and then lay quite quiet, the restless longing stilled in her, slow tears forcing themselves from under her closed lashes, because she knew she would not send it. She would not send it because Chester too, in his heart, knew that they had better part; he too was fighting for the cause he believed in; he wanted her, but wanted to succeed in doing without her. She must give him his chance to stick by his principles, not drag him down below them.

There were moments when Kitty wished that she could believe in a God, and could pray. It must, she thought, be a comfort. She even at times wished she were a Christian, to find fulfilment in loss. That was, at least, what she supposed Christians to do.

But she could not be a Christian, and she could not pray; all she could do was to nerve herself to meet life in the spirit of the gay pierrette, with cap and bells on her aching head, and a little powder to hide the tears, and to try not to snap at Elspeth or the people at the office. This last endeavour usually failed. The little gaping messengers who answered (when they thought they would) Miss Grammont's bell, told each other Miss Grammont was cross. The typists grew tired of having letters sent back to be retyped because of some trifling misapprehension of Miss Grammont's calligraphy or some trifling misspelling on their own account. Surely these things could be set right with a pen and a little skill.

These moods of impatience, when frustration vented itself in anger, alternated with the gaiety, the irreverent and often profane levity, which was Kitty's habitual way of braving life in its more formidable aspects. Some people have this instinct, to nail a flag of motley to the mast of the foundering ship and keep it flying to the last.

4

While Kitty was debating as to her future, toying with the relative advantages and entertainment to be derived from the careers of War Widow, Confidential Clerk, Travelling Companion, archaeological explorer in Macedonia or Crete, beginner on the music-hall stage, under Pansy's auspices, all of which seemed to have their bright sides, two suggestions were made to her. One was from a cousin of hers who was sub-editor of *Stop It*, and offered to get her a place on the staff.

'Would it bind me to a point of view?' Kitty enquired. 'I can't be bound to a point of view.'

'Oh dear no,' her cousin assured her. 'Certainly not. Rather the contrary,' and Kitty said, 'All right, I'll think it over.' She was rather attracted by the idea.

You cannot, of course, exactly call it being bound to a point of view to be required to hint every week that certain things want stopping, in a world whose staunchest champions must admit that this is indeed so.

Stop It was certainly eclectic, in its picking out, from all the recognised groups associated for thought and action, activities whose cessation seemed good to it. The question that rather suggested itself to its readers was, if *Stop It* had its way, what, if anything, would be left?

'Very little,' the editor would have answered. 'A clean sheet. Then we can begin again.'

Stop It had dropped some of the caution with which it had begun: it was now quite often possible to deduce from its still cryptic phraseology what were some of the things it wanted stopped. Having for some time successfully dodged Dora, it was now daring her. As in all probability it would not have a long life, and appeared to be having a merry one, Kitty thought she might as well join it while she could.

To desert abruptly from the ranks of the bureaucracy to those of the mutineers seemed natural to Kitty, who had always found herself at home in a number of widely differing situations. Really this is perhaps the only way to live, if all the various and so greatly different needs of complicated human nature are to be satisfied. It is very certain that they cannot be satisfied simultaneously; the best way seems, therefore, to alternate. It is indeed strange that this is not more done, that Radicals, Tories, and Labour members, for instance, do not more frequently interchange, play general post, to satisfy on Tuesday that side of their souls and intellects which has not been given free play on Monday; that Mr Ramsay Macdonald and Lord Curzon do not, from time to time, deliver each other's speeches, not from any freakish desire to astonish, but from the sheer necessities of their natures; that Mr Massingham and Mr Leo Maxse, or Mr A G Gardiner and Mr Gwynne, or Mr J C Squire and Mr J St Loe Strachey, or Mr Garvin and Mr J A Spender, do not from time to time arrange together to change offices and run each other's papers; or that Mr Arthur Ransome and Mr Stephen Graham do not, during their tours of Russia, sometimes change pens with each other when they write home. There must be in many people some undemocratic instinct of centralisation, of autocratic subversion of the horde of their lesser opinions and impulses to the most dominant and commanding one, a lack of the true democrat's desire to give a chance to them all. They say with the Psalmist, 'My heart is fixed,' and 'I have chosen the way and I will run it to the end,' and this is called, by some, finding one's true self. Perhaps it may be so; it certainly entails the loss of many other selves; and possibly the dropping of these, or rather their continual denial and gradual atrophy, simplifies life.

But Kitty, whose heart was not fixed, entered upon all the changing scenes of life with a readiness to embrace any point of view, though not indeed to be bound to it, and an even greater willingness to tell anything in earth or heaven that it ought to be stopped.

She told Prideaux that she was considering this offer. Prideaux said, 'That thing! Its very name condemns it. It's on the wrong tack. You shouldn't be out to stop things; they've got to go on ... If it's journalism you want, why don't you apply for a job on *Intelligence*?' *Intelligence*, or the Weekly Bulletin of the Brains Ministry (to give it its subtitle, humorously chosen by one who visualised either the public or the Ministry as a sick man) was a weekly journal issued by the Ministry, and its aim was, besides reporting the Ministry's work, decisions and pronouncements for each week, to correlate all its local activities and keep them in touch with headquarters, and to collect reports from over the country as to the state of the public mind. It was for official circulation only. 'Why not?' repeated Prideaux, struck by this idea. 'It would be quite enough of a change: you would probably be one of the travelling reporters and send bright little anecdotes from the countryside; I know they want some more reporters. Why don't you apply? I'll speak to MBB about you if you like.' (MBB was the department which edited the Bulletin.)

'Would it be interesting?' Kitty wondered.

Prideaux thought it would. 'Besides,' he added, 'you'd remain attached to the Ministry that way, and could return to headquarters later on if you wanted to ... And meanwhile you'd see all the fun ... We're in for a fairly lively time, and it would be a pity to miss it. We're bound to slip up over the ASE before the month's over. And probably over the exemption of Imbeciles and the Abandoned Babies, too. And the journalists; that's going to be a bad snag. Oh, it'll be interesting all right. If it wasn't for Chester's remarkable gift of getting on people's right side, it would be a poor look-out. But Chester'd pull most things through. If they'd put him at the head of the Recruiting job during the war, I believe he'd have pulled even the Review of Exceptions through without a row … Well now, what about trying for this job?'

'All right,' Kitty agreed. 'If you think there's any chance of my getting it. I don't mind much what I do, so long as I have a change from this hotel.'

On Prideaux's recommendation she did get the job, and was transferred from her branch to MBB as a travelling reporter for *Intelligence*. She renounced *Stop It* with some regret; there was a whimsical element about *Stop It* which appealed to her, and which must almost necessarily be lacking in an official journal; but the career of travelling reporter seemed to have possibilities. Besides the more weighty reports from the countryside, a page of *Intelligence* was devoted each week to anecdotes related in the engagingly sudden and irrelevant manner of our cheaper daily Press; as, 'A woman appealed before the Cuckfield Tribunal for exemption from the Mind Training Course on the grounds that she had made an uncertificated marriage and had since had twins, and must, therefore, be of a mental level which unfitted her to derive benefit from the Course.' 'Three babies have been found abandoned in a ditch between Amersham and Chesham Bois.' 'The Essex Farmers' Association have produced a strain of hens which lay an egg each day all the year round. The farmers ascribe this to the improvement in their methods caused by the Mind Training Course.' 'In reply to a tinplate worker who applied for Occupational Exemption from the Mental Progress Act, the Chairman of the Margam Tribunal said …' (one of the witty things which chairmen do say, and which need not here be reported). It was, apparently, the business of the reporters to collect (or invent) and communicate these trivial anecdotes, as well as more momentous news, as of unrest at Nottingham, the state of intelligence or otherwise among Suffolk agriculturists, and so forth.

Kitty rather hoped to be sent to Ireland, which was, as often, in an interesting and dubious state. Ireland was excluded from the Brains Acts, as from other Acts. But she was being carefully watched, with a view to including her when it seemed that it might be safe to do so. Meanwhile those of her population who were considered by the English government to be in no need of it were profiting by the Mind Training Course, while the mass of the peasantry were instructed by their priests to shun such unholy heretic learning as they would the devil. But on the whole it seemed possible that the strange paths pointed out by the Brains Ministry might eventually lead to the solution of the Irish Question. (What the Irish Question at that moment was, I will not here attempt to explain: it must be sufficient to remark that there will always be one.)

5

But Kitty was not sent to Ireland. She was sent about England; first to Cambridge. Cambridge was not averse to having its mind improved; there is a sweet reasonableness about Cambridge. It knows how important brains are. Also it had an affection for Chester, who had been at Trinity. So reports from Cambridge as regards the Brains Acts were on the whole favourable, in spite of some unrest (for different reasons) at Kings, Downing, and Trinity Hall, and slight ferment of revolt down at Barnwell. There was, indeed, a flourishing branch of the SIL (Stop It League) in the University, but its attention was not directed at the moment particularly to stopping the work of the Ministry of Brains.

It was, of course, a queer and quite new Cambridge which Kitty investigated. She had known the pre-war Cambridge; there had intervened the war Cambridge, that desolated and desolating thing, and now there had sprung up, on the other side of that dividing gulf, a Cambridge new and without precedent; a Cambridge half full of young war veterans, with the knowledge of red horizons, battle, murder, and sudden death, in their careless, watchful, experienced eyes; when they lounged about the streets or hurried to lectures, they dropped, against their will, into step; they were brown, and hard, and tired, and found it hard to concentrate on books; they had forgotten their school knowledge, and could not get through Littlegoes, and preferred their beds to sleeping in the open, that joy of pampered youth which has known neither battlefields or Embankment seats.

The other half were the boys straight from school; and between these two divisions rolled the Great European War, across which they could with difficulty make themselves understood each by the other.

It was a Cambridge which had broken with history, for neither of these sections had any links with the past, any traditions to hand down. They only people who had these were the dons and Fellows and the very few undergraduates who, having broken off their University career to fight, had, after long years, returned to it again. These moved like ghosts among their old haunts; but their number was so inconsiderable as hardly to count. It was, to all intents and purposes, a new Cambridge, a clean sheet; and it was interesting to watch what was being inscribed upon it.

But such observations, apart from those of them which were connected with the attitude of Cambridge towards the Brains Ministry, neither Kitty nor this story are concerned. The story of the new Cambridge will have to be written some day by a member of it, and should be well worth reading.

From Cambridge Kitty went to travel in Cambridgeshire, which was in a state of quiet, albeit grudging, East Anglian acceptance and slow assimilation.

Far different were the northern midlands, which were her next destination. Here, indeed, was revolt in process of ferment; revolt which had to be continually uncorked and aired that it might not ferment too much. The uncorking and airing was done by means of conferences, at which the tyrannised and the tyrants each said their say. These heart-to-heart talks have a soothing effect (sometimes) on the situation; at other times not. As conducted by the Minister of Brains, they certainly had. Chester was something more than soothing; he was inspiring. While he was addressing a meeting, he made it believe that intelligence was the important thing; more important than liberty, more important than the satisfaction of immediate desires. He made intelligence a flaming idea, like patriotism, freedom, peace, democracy, the eight hour day, or God; and incidentally he pointed out that it would lead to most of these things; and they believed him. When he showed how, in the past, the lack of intelligence had led to national ruin, economic bondage, war, autocracy, poverty, sweating, and vice, they believed that too. When he said, 'Look at the European War,' they looked. When he went on, 'Without centuries of stupidity everywhere the war would never have been; without stupidity the war, if it had been, would have been very differently conducted; without stupidity we need never have another war, but with stupidity we inevitably shall, League of Nations or not,' they all roared and cheered.

So he went about saying these things, convincing and propitiating labour everywhere; labour, that formidable monster dreaded and cajoled by all good statesmen; labour, twice as formidable since in the Great War it had learned the ways of battle and the possibility and the power of the union of arms and the man.

CHAPTER 9

The Common Herd

1

It was after such a meeting, at Chesterfield, at the end of July, that Kitty and the Minister next met. Kitty was at that time writing up the Derbyshire towns for the Bulletin. She attended the Chesterfield meeting officially. It was a good one; Chester spoke well, and the audience (mainly colliers) listened well.

It was a very hot evening. The Town Hall was breathless, and full of damp, coal-grimed, imperfectly-cleaned faces. Kitty too was damp, though she was wearing even less than usual. Chester was damp and white, and looked, for all his flame and ardour, which carried the meeting along with him, fatigued and on edge. Kitty, herself fatigued and on edge, watched him, seeing the way his hands moved nervously on the table as he spoke.

It was while he was talking about the demand for increased wages among colliers to facilitate the payment of the taxes on uncertificated babies, that he saw Kitty. His eyes stayed on hers for a moment, and he paused in the middle of a sentence ... 'defeat the whole purpose of the Act,' he finished it, and looked elsewhere. Kitty was startled by his pause; it was not like him. Normally he, so used to public speaking, so steeled against emergencies, so accustomed to strange irruptions into the flow of his speech, would surely have carried on without a break or a sign. That he had not done so showed him to be in a highly nervous state, thought Kitty, something like her own in this hot weather, through her continual travellings by train and staying in lodgings and writing absurd reports.

Across the length of the hall she saw nothing now but that thin, slouching figure, the gestures of those nervous, flexible hands, that white, damp face, with its crooked eyebrows and smile.

It was so long since she had seen him and spoken to him; something in her surged up at the sight of him and turned her giddy and faint. It was perilously hot; the heat soaked all one's will away and left one limp … Did he too feel like that?

2

He looked at her once more, just before the end, and his eyes said, 'Wait for me.'

She waited, in the front of a little group by the door through which he was to come out. He came out with his secretary, and the mayor, and others; he was talking to them. When he saw her he stopped openly, and said, so that all could hear, 'How do you do, Miss Grammont. I haven't seen you for some time. You're doing this reporting work for the Bulletin now, aren't you? I want to talk to you about that. If you'll give me the address I'll come round in about half an hour and see you about it.'

She gave him the address of her rooms in Little Darkgate Street, and he nodded and walked on. He had done it well; no one thought it strange, or anything but all in the way of business. Ministers have to be good at camouflage, at throwing veils over situations; it is part of their job.

Kitty went back to her lodgings, and washed again, for the seventeenth time that day, and tried if she would feel less hot and less pale and more the captain of her soul in another and even filmier blouse. But she grew hotter, and paler, and less the captain of anything at all.

At 9.30 Chester came. He too was hot and pale and captain of nothing. He had not even the comfort of a filmy blouse.

He said, 'My dear — my dear,' and no more for a little time. Then he said, 'My dearest, this has got to stop. I can't stand it. We've got to marry.'

Kitty said, 'Oh well. I suppose we have.' She was too hot, too limp, too tired, to suppose anything else.

'At once,' said Chester. 'I'll get a licence … We must get it done at some small place in the country where they don't know who we are. I must take another name for it … There's a place I sometimes stay at, in the Chilterns. They are rather stupid there — even now,' he added, with the twist of a rueful smile. 'I think it should be pretty safe. Anyhow I don't think I much care; we're going to do it.'

They spoke low in the dim, breathless room, with its windows opened wide on to the breathless street.

'I have wanted you,' said Chester. 'I have wanted you extremely badly these last three months. I have never wanted anything so much. It has been a — a hideous time, taking it all round.'

'You certainly,' said Kitty, 'look as if it had. So do I — don't I? It's partly heat and dirt, with both of us — the black of this town *soaks* in — and partly tiredness, and partly, for you, the strain of your ministerial responsibilities, no doubt; but I think a little of it is our broken hearts … Nicky, I'm too limp to argue or fight. I know it's all wrong, what we're going to do; but I'm like you — I don't think I much care. We'll get married in your stupid village, under a false name. That counts, does it? Oh, all right. I shouldn't particularly mind if it didn't, you know. I'll do without the registry business altogether if you think it's safer. After all, what's the odds? It comes to the same thing in the end, only with less fuss. And it's no one's business but ours.'

'No,' Chester said. 'I think that would be a mistake. Wrong. I don't approve of this omitting of the legal bond; it argues a lack of the sense of social ethics; it opens the door to a state of things which is essentially uncivilised, lacking in self-control and intelligence. I don't like it. It always strikes me as disagreeable and behind the times; a step backwards. No, we won't do that. I'd rather take the greater risk of publicity. I'm dropping one principle, but I don't want to drop more than I need.'

Kitty laughed silently, and slipped her hand into his. 'All right, you shan't. We'll get tied up properly at your country registry, and keep some of our principles and hang the risk … I oughtn't to let you, you know. If it comes out it will wreck your career and perhaps wreck the Ministry and endanger the intellect of the country. We may be sowing the seeds of another World War; but — oh, I'm bored with being high-principled about it.'

'It's too late to be that,' said Chester. 'We've got to go ahead now.'

He consulted his pocket-book and said that he was free on August 10th, and that they would then get married and go to Italy for a fortnight's holiday together. They made the other arrangements that have to be made in these peculiar circumstances, and then Chester went back to his hotel.

The awful, airless, panting night through which the Chesterfield furnaces flamed, lay upon the queer, crooked black city like a menace. Kitty, leaning out of her window and listening to Chester's retreating steps echoing up the street, ran her fingers through her damp dark hair, because her head ached, and murmured, 'I don't care. I don't care. What's the good of living if you can't have what you want?'

Which expressed an instinct common to the race, and one which would in the end bring to nothing the most strenuous efforts of social and ethical reformers.

3

They got married. Chester took, for the occasion, the name of Gilbert Lewis; it was surprising how easy this was. The witness looked attentively at him, but probably always looked like that at the people getting married. Neither he nor the registrar looked intelligent, or as if they were connecting Chester's face with anything they had seen before.

After the performance they went to Italy for a fortnight. Italy in August is fairly safe from English visitors. They stayed at Cogoleto, a tiny fishing town fifteen miles up the coast from Genoa, shut in a little bay between the olive hills and the sea. To this sheltered coast through the summer months people come from the hot towns inland and fill every lodging and inn and pitch tents on the shore, and pass serene, lazy, amphibious days in and out of a sea which has the inestimable advantage over English seas that it is always at hand.

The Chesters too passed amphibious days. They would rise early, while the sea lay cool and smooth and pale and pearly in the morning light, and before the sand burnt their feet as they walked on it, and slip in off the gently shelving shore, and swim and swim and swim. They were both good swimmers. Chester was the stronger and faster, but Kitty could do more tricks. She could turn somersaults like an eel, and sit at the bottom of the sea playing with pebbles, with open eyes gazing up through clear green depths. When they bathed from a boat, she turned head over heels backwards from the bows, and shot under the boat and came up neatly behind the stern. Chester too could perform fairly well; their energy and skill excited the amazed admiration of the bagnanti, who seldom did more than splash on the sea's edge or bob up and down with swimming belts a few yards out. Chester and Kitty would swim out for a mile, then lie on their backs and float, gazing up into the sea-blue sky, before the sun had climbed high enough to burn and blind. Then they would swim back and return to the inn and put on a very few clothes and have their morning coffee, and then walk up the coast, taking lunch, to some little lonely cove in the shadow of rocks, where they would spend the heat of the day in and out of the sea. When they came out of the water they lay on the burning sands and dried themselves, and talked or read. When the heat of the day had passed a little, and the sea lay very smooth and still in the late afternoon, with no waves at all, only a gentle, whispering swaying to and fro, they would go further afield; climbing up the steep stone-paved mule-tracks that wound up the hills behind, passing between grey olive groves and lemon and orange gardens and vineyards of ripening vines and little rough white farmhouses, till they reached the barer, wilder hill slopes of pines and rocks, where the hot sweetness of myrtle and juniper stirred with each tiny moving of sea air.

They would climb often to the top of one or other of this row of hills that guarded the bay, and from its top, resting by some old pulley well or little shrine, they would look down over hills and sea bathed in evening light, and see to the east the white gleam of Genoa shimmering like a pearl, like a ghost, between transparent sea and sky, to the west the point of Savona jutting dark against a flood of fire.

There was one hill they often climbed, a steep little pine-grown mountain crested by a little old chapel, with a well by its side. The chapel was dedicated to the Madonna della Mare, and was hung about inside with votive offerings of little ships, presented to the Madonna by grateful sailors whom she had delivered from the perils of the sea. Outside the chapel a shrine stood, painted pink, and from it the mother and child smiled kindly down on the withered flowers that nearly always lay on the ledge before them.

By the shrine and the well Chester and Kitty would sit, while the low light died slowly from the hills, till its lower slopes lay in evening shadow, and only they on the summit remained, as if enchanted, in a circle of fairy gold.

One evening while they sat there a half-witted contadino slouched out of the chapel and begged from them. Chester refused sharply, and turned his face away. The imbecile hung about, mouthed a confused prayer, bowing and crossing, before the shrine, got no help from that quarter either, and at last shambled disconsolately down the hillside, crooning an unintelligible song to himself.

Kitty, looking at Chester, saw with surprise that his face was rigid with disgust; he looked as if he were trying not to shudder.

'How you hate them, Nicky,' she said curiously.

He said 'I do,' grimly, and spoke of something else.

But a little later he said abruptly, 'I've never told you much about my people, Kitty, have I, or what are called my early years?'

'You wouldn't, of course,' she replied, 'any more than I should. We're neither of us much interested in the past; you live in the future, and I live in the present moment … But I should be interested to hear, all the same.'

'That imbecile reminded me,' Chester said grimly. 'I had a twin sister like that, and a brother not very far removed from it. You know that, of course; but you'll never know, no one *can* ever know who's not experienced it, what it was like … At first, when I began to do more than just accept it as part of things as they were, it only made me angry that such things should be possible, and frightfully sorry for Joan and Gerald, who had to go about like that, so little use to themselves or anyone else, and so tiresome to me and Maggie (she's my eldest sister; I'd like you to meet her one day). I remember even consulting Maggie as to whether it wouldn't be a good thing to take them out into a wood and lose them, like the babes in the wood. I honestly thought it would be for their own good; I knew I should have preferred it if I had been them. But Maggie didn't agree; she took a more patient line about it than I did; she always does. Then, as I grew older, I became angry with my parents, who had no right, of course, to have had any children at all; they were first cousins, and deficiency was in the family ... It was that that first set me thinking about the whole subject. I remember asking my father once, when I was about seventeen, how he had reconciled it with his conscience (he was a dean at that time) to do such a thing. I must have been an irritating young prig, of course; in fact, I remember that I was. He very properly indicated to me that I was stepping out of my sphere in questioning him on such a point, and also that whatever is must be sent by Providence, and therefore right. I didn't drop it at once; I remember I argued that it hadn't 'been' and therefore had not necessarily been right, until he and my mother made it so; but he closed the conversation; quite time too, I suppose. It was difficult to argue with my father in those days; it's easier now, though not really easy. I think the reduction of the worldly condition of bishops has been good for him; it has put him in what I suppose is called a state of grace I don't believe he'd do it now, if he lived his life again. However, he did do it, and the result was two deficient children and one who grew up loathing stupidity in the way some few people (conceivably) loathe vice, when they've been brought into close contact with its effects. It became an obsession with me; I seemed to see it everywhere, spoiling everything, blocking every path, tying everyone's hands. The Boer War happened while I was at school ... Good Lord ... Then I went to Cambridge, and it was there that I really began to think the thing seriously out.

What has always bothered me about it is that human beings are so astoundingly *clever*; miraculously clever, if you come to think of it, and compare us with the other animals, so like us in lots of ways. The things we've done; the animal state we've grown out of; the things we've discovered and created — it makes one's head reel. And if we can be clever like that, why not be a little cleverer still? Why be so abysmally stupid about many things? The *waste* of it … The world might get anywhere if we really developed our powers to their full extent. But we always slip up somewhere: nothing quite comes off as it should. Think of all these thousands of years of house-managing, and the really clever arrangements which have been made in connection with it — and then visit a set of cottages and see the mess; a woman trying to cook food and clean the house and look after children and wash clothes, all by hand, and with the most inadequate contrivances for any of it. Why haven't we thought of some way out of that beastly, clumsy squalor and muddle yet? And why do houses built and fitted like some of those still exist? If we're clever enough to have invented and built houses at all, why not go one better and do it properly? It's the same with everything. Medical science, for instance. The advances it's made fill one with amaze and admiration; but why is there still disease? And why isn't there a cure for every disease? And why do doctors fail so hopelessly to diagnose anything a little outside their ordinary beat? There it is; we've been clever about it in a way, but nothing like clever enough, or as clever as we've got to be before we've done. The same with statesmanship and government; only there we've very seldom been clever at all; that's still to come. And our educational system … oh Lord … The mischief is that people in general don't *want* other people to become too clever; it wouldn't suit their turn. So the popular instinct for mucking along, for taking things as you find them (and leaving them there), the popular taste for superficial twaddle in literature and politics and science and art and religion is pandered to on its own level …

'But I didn't mean to go off on to all this; I merely meant to tell you what first started me thinking of these things.'

'Go on,' said Kitty. 'I like it. It makes me feel at home, as if I was sitting under you at a meeting … What I infer is that if your parents *hadn't* been first cousins and had deficiency in their family, there would have been no Ministry of Brains. I expect your father was right, and whatever is is best … Of course the interesting question is, what would happen if ever we *were* much cleverer than we are now? What would happen, that is, besides houses being better managed and disease better treated and locomotion improved and books better written or not written at all, and all that? What would happen to nations and societies and governments, if people in general became much more intelligent? I can't imagine. But I think there'd be a jolly old row … Perhaps we shall know before long.'

'No,' said Chester. 'We shan't know that. There may be a jolly old row; I daresay there will; but it won't be because people have got too clever; it will be because they haven't got clever enough. It'll be the short-sighted stupidity of people revolting against their ultimate good.'

'As it might be you and me.'

'Precisely. As it might be you and me … What we're doing is horribly typical, Kitty. Don't let's ever blind ourselves to its nature. We'll do it, because we think it's worth it; but we'll do it with our eyes open. Thank heaven we're both clear-headed and hard-headed enough to know what we're doing and not to muddle ourselves with cant about it … That's one of the things that I suppose I love you for, my dear — your clear-headedness. You never muddle or cant or sentimentalise. You're hard-headed and clear-eyed.'

'In fact, cynical,' said Kitty.

'Yes. Rather cynical. Unnecessarily cynical, I think. You could do with some more faith.'

'Perhaps I shall catch some from you. You've got lots, haven't you? As the husband is the wife is; I am mated to, etc ... And you're a lot cleverer than I am, so you're most likely right ... We're awfully different, Nicky, my love, aren't we?'

'No doubt we are. Who isn't?'

For a while they lay silent in the warm sweetness of the hill-top, while the golden light slipped from them, leaving behind it the pure green stillness of the evening; and they looked at one another and speculated on the strange differences of human beings from each, and the mystery of personality, that tiny point on to which all the age-long accumulated forces of heredity press, so that you would suppose that the world itself could not contain them, and yet they are contained in one small, ordinary soul, which does not break under the weight.

So they looked at one another, speculating, until speculation faded into seeing, and instead of personalities they became to one another persons, and Chester saw Kitty red-lipped and golden-eyed and black-lashed and tanned a smooth nut-brown by sun and sea, and Kitty saw Chester long and lean and sallow, with black brows bent over deep, keen, dreaming eyes, and lips carrying their queer suggestion of tragedy and comedy.

'Isn't it fun,' said Kitty, 'that you are you and I am I? I think it must be (don't you?) the greatest fun that ever was since the world began. That's what I think ... and everywhere millions of people are thinking exactly the same. We're part of the common herd, Nicky — the very, very commonest herd of all herds. I think I like it rather — being so common, I mean. It's amusing. Don't you?'

'Yes,' he said, and smiled at her. 'I think I do.'

Still they lay there, side by side, in the extraordinary

hushed sweetness of the evening. Kitty's cheek was pressed against short warm grass. Close to her ear a cicale chirped, monotonously bright; far off, from every hill, the frogs began their evening singing.

Kitty, as she sometimes did, seemed to slip suddenly outside the circle of the present, of her own life and the life around her; far off she saw it, a queer little excited corner of the universe, where people played together and were happy, where the funny world spun round and round and laughed and cried and ran and slept and loved and hated, and everything mattered intensely, and yet, as seen from outside the circle, did not matter at all … She felt like a soul unborn, or a soul long dead, watching the world's antics with a dispassionate, compassionate interest …

The touch of Chester's hand on her cheek brought her back abruptly into the circle again.

'Belovedest,' he said, 'let's come down the hill. The light is going.'

4

One day they had a shock; they met someone they knew. They met him in the sea; at least he was in a boat and they were in the sea. They were swimming a mile from shore, in a pearl-smooth, golden sea, in the eye of the rising sun. Half a mile out from them a yacht lay, as idle as a painted ship upon a painted ocean. From the yacht a boat shot out, rowed by a man. It shot between the swimmers and the rising sun. Chester and Kitty were lying on their backs, churning up the sun's path of gold with their feet, and Kitty was singing a little song that Greek goat-herds sing on the hills above Corinth in the mornings.

Leaning over the side and resting on his oars, the man in the boat shouted, '*Hullo*, Chester!'

An electric shock stabbed Kitty through at the voice, which was Vernon Prideaux's. Losing her nerve, her head, and her sense of the suitable, she splashed round on to her chest, kicked herself forward, and dived like a porpoise, travelling as swiftly as she could from Chester, Prideaux, and the situation. When she came back up it was with a splutter, because she had laughed. Glancing backwards over her shoulder, she saw Chester swimming towards the boat. What would he say? Would he speak of her, or wrap her in discreet silence? And had Prideaux recognised her or not?

'Lunatic,' said Kitty. 'Of course he did. I have taken the worst way, in my excitement.'

Promptly she retraced her path, this time on the water's surface, and hailed Prideaux as she came.

'Hullo, Vernon. The top of the morning to you. I thought I'd show you I could dive ... What brings you here? Oh, the yacht, of course ...' She paused, wondering what was to be their line, then struck one out on her own account. 'Isn't it odd; Mr Chester and I are both staying near here.'

Prideaux's keen, well-bred, perfectly courteous face looked for one moment as if it certainly was a little odd; then he swallowed his surprise.

'Are you? It's a splendid coast, isn't it? Cogoleto in there, I suppose? We're not stopping at all, unfortunately; we're going straight on to Genoa ... I'm coming in.'

He dived neatly from the bows, with precision and power, as he wrote minutes, managed deputations, ignored odd situations, and did everything else. One was never afraid with Prideaux; one could rely on him not to bungle.

They bathed together and conversed, till Kitty said she must go in, and swam shoreward in the detached manner of one whose people are expecting her to breakfast. Soon afterwards she saw that Prideaux was pulling back to the yacht, and Chester swimming westward, as if he were staying at Varazze.

'Tact,' thought Kitty. 'This, I suppose, is how people behave while conducting a vulgar intrigue. Ours is a vulgar marriage; there doesn't seem much difference … I rather wish we could have told Vernon all about it; he safe enough, and I should like to have heard his comments and seen his face. How awful he would think us … I don't know anyone who would disapprove more … Well, I suppose it's more interesting than a marriage which doesn't have to be kept dark, but it's much less peaceful.'

They met at the inn, at breakfast.

'Did you have to swim right across the bay, darling?' Kitty enquired. 'I'm so sorry. By the way, I noticed that Vernon never asked either of us where we were staying, nor invited us to come and visit the yacht. Do you suppose he believed a word we said?'

Chester lifted his eyebrows. 'His mental category is A, I believe,' he replied.

'Well,' said Kitty, 'anyhow he can't know we're married, even if he does think we've arranged to meet here. And Vernon's very discreet; he won't babble.'

Chester ate a roll and a half in silence. Then he remarked, without emotion, 'Kitty, this thing is going to come out. We may as well make up our minds to it. We shall go on meeting people, and they won't all be discreet. It will come out, as certainly as flowers in spring, or the Clyde engineers next week.'

They faced one another in silence for a moment across the coffee and rolls. Then, because there seemed nothing else which could meet the situation, they both began to laugh helplessly.

Three days later they returned to England, by different routes.

CHAPTER 10

A Ministry at Bay

1

That autumn was a feverish period in the Ministry's career. Many persons have been called upon, for one cause or another, to wait in nervous anticipation hour by hour for the signal which shall herald their own destruction. Thus our ancestors at the latter end of the tenth century waited expectantly for the crack of doom; but the varying emotions with which they awaited it can only be guessed at. More vivid to the mind and memory are the expectant and waiting first days of August 1914. On the other hand, the emotions of cabinets foreseeing their own resignation, of the House of Lords anticipating abolition, of criminals awaiting sentence, of newspapers desperately staving off extinction, of the crews of foundered ships struggling to keep afloat, of government departments anticipating their own untimely end, are mysteries veiled from the outside world, sacred ground which may not be trodden by the multitude.

The Ministry of Brains that autumn was fighting hard and gallantly for its life. It was an uphill struggle; Sisyphus pushing up the mountain the stone of human perverseness, human stupidity, human self-will, which threatened all the time to roll back and grind him to powder. Concessions were made here, pledges given there (even, here or there, occasionally fulfilled). New Instructions were issued daily, old ones amended or withdrawn, far-reaching and complicated arrangements made with various groups and classes of people, 'little ministries' set up all over the country to administrate the acts regionally, soothing replies and promises dropped like leaves in autumn by the Parliamentary Secretary, to be gathered up, hoarded, and brooded over in many a humble, many a stately home. It is superfluous to recapitulate these well-worn, oft-enacted, pathetic incidents of a tottering ministry. Ministries, though each with a special stamp in hours of ease, are all much alike when pain and anguish wring their brows. With arts very similar each to other they woo a public uncertain, coy and hard to please; a public too ready to believe the worst of them, too pitiless and unimaginative towards their good intentions, too extreme to mark what is done amiss, too loth to admit success, too ready to condemn failure without measuring the strength of temptation.

Ministries have a bitter time; their hand is against every man and every man's hand against them. For their good men return them evil and for their evil no good. And — let it not be forgotten — they are really, with all their faults, more intelligent, and fuller of good intentions, than the vast majority of their critics. The critics cry aloud 'Get rid of them,' without always asking themselves who would do the job any better, always providing it has to be done. In the case of the Ministry of Brains, the majority of the public saw no reason why the job should be done at all, which complicated matters. It was like the Directorate of Recruiting during the war, or the Censor's office, or the Ministry of Food; not merely its method but its function was unwelcome. As most men did not want to be recruited by law, or to have their reading or their diet regulated by law, so they did not want to be made intelligent by law. All these things might be, and doubtless were, for the ultimate good of the nation, but all were inconvenient at the moment, and when ultimate good (especially not necessarily one's own good) and immediate convenience come to blows, it is not usually ultimate good which wins.

So the Ministry of Brains, even more than other ministries, was fighting against odds. Feverish activity prevailed, in all departments. From morning till night telephones telephoned, clerks wrote, typists typed against time, deputations deputed, committees committeed, officials conferred with each other, messengers ran to and fro with urgent minutes and notes by hand. Instructions and circular letters poured forth, telegrams were despatched in hot haste to the local Ministries and to the Brains Representatives on the local tribunals, the staff arrived early and stayed late, and often came on Sundays as well, and grew thin and dyspeptic and nervy and irritable.

2

Even Ivy Delmer grew pale and depressed, not so much from official strain as from private worries. These she confided one day to Kitty, who had got transferred back to headquarters through a little quiet wire-pulling (it is no use being married to a Minister if little things like that cannot easily be arranged), and was now working in her old branch. They were travelling together one Monday morning up from Little Chantreys.

'Now I ask you, Miss Grammont, what would you do? I'm B3 and he's C1 (I'm certain they've classified him wrong, because he's not a bit stupid really, not the way some men are, you know, he's jolly clever at some things — ideas, and that) , but of course it's against the regulations for us to marry each other. And yet we care for each other, and we both of us feel we always shall. And we neither of us want a bit to marry an A person, besides, I don't suppose an A would ever think of us in *that* way, you know what I mean, Miss Grammont, don't laugh, and to give each other up would mean spoiling both our lives … Yet I suppose everyone would think it awfully wrong if we got regularly engaged, and me working at the Ministry too. I suppose I ought to leave it really, feeling the way I do … The fact is, I've come to feel very differently about the Ministry, now I've thought it more over, and — you'll be horrified, I know — but I'm not at all sure I approve of it.'

'Good gracious no,' Kitty said. 'I never approve of any Ministries. That isn't what one feels for them. Sympathy; pity; some affection, even; but approval — no.'

'Well, you see what I mean, it's all very well in theory, but I do honestly know so many people whose lives have been upset and spoilt by it — and it does seem hard. Heaps of people in Little Chantreys alone; of course we come across them rather a lot, because they tell father and mother about it … And all the poor little deserted babies … Oh I suppose it's all right … But I'm feeling a bit off it just now … Now I ask you, feeling as I do about it, and meaning to do what I'm going to do (at least we hope we're going to do it sometime), ought I to go on at the Ministry? Is it honest? Would *you*, Miss Grammont?'

Kitty blushed faintly, to her own credit and a little to Ivy's surprise. She did not associate blushing with Miss Grammont, and anyhow there seemed no occasion for it just now.

'Well, yes, I think I would. I don't see that you're called on to give it up — unless, of course, you hate it, and want to … After all, one would very seldom stick to any work at all if one felt obliged to approve entirely of it. No, I don't think there's much in that.'

'You truly don't? Well, I expect I'll carry on for a bit, then. I'd rather, in one way, of course, especially as we shall need all the money we can get if we ever do marry. Not that I'm saving; I spend every penny I get, I'm afraid. But of course it takes me off father's hands … Don't *you* feel, Miss Grammont, that all this interference with people's private lives is a mistake? It's come home to me awfully strongly lately. Only when I read the Minister's speeches I change my mind again; he puts it so rippingly, and makes me feel perhaps I'm being simply a selfish little beast. I don't care what anybody says about him, I think he's wonderful.'

'I suppose he is,' said Kitty.

'My word, he jolly well *would* despise me if he knew, wouldn't he?'

'Well …' said Kitty. And perhaps it was well that at that moment they reached Marylebone.

That conversation was typical, even as Ivy Delmer's standpoint was itself typical, of a large body of what, for lack of a better name, we must call thought, all over the country. Laws were all very well in theory, or when they only disarranged the lives of others, but when they touched and disorganised one's own life — hands off. Was the only difference between such as Ivy Delmer and such as Nicholas Chester that Ivy deceived herself ('It's not that I care a bit for myself, but it's the principle of the thing') and that Chester fell with open eyes? Which was perhaps as much to say that Ivy was classified B3 and Chester A.

All over the country people were saying, according to their different temperaments, one or another of these things. 'Of course I don't care for myself, but I think the system is wrong', or (the other way round) 'It may be all right in theory, but I'm jolly well not going to stand being inconvenienced by it', or 'I'm not going to stand it *and* it's all wrong'. Of course there were also those more public-spirited persons who said, 'It's a splendid system and I'm going to fall in with it', or 'Though it's a rotten system I suppose we must put up with it'. But these were the minority.

3

Up till November the campaign against the Brains Ministry was quite impersonal, merely resentment against a system. It was led, in the press, by the Labour papers, which objected to compulsion, by the *Nation*, which objected to what it, rightly or wrongly, called by that much-abused name, Prussianism, by the *New Witness*, which objected to interference with the happy stupidity of merry Gentiles (making them disagreeably clever like Jews), and by *Stop It*, which objected to everything. It was supported by the more normal organs of opinion of the kind which used before and during the war to be called conservative and liberal. And, of course, through thick and thin, by the *Hidden Hand*.

But in the course of November a new element came into the attack — the personal element. Certain sections of the Press which supported the Ministry began to show discontent with the Minister. The *Times* began to hint guardedly that new blood might perhaps be desirable in certain quarters. The *Daily Mail*, in its rounder and directed manner, remarked in large head-lines that 'Nicky is played out'. Ministers have to bear these intimations about themselves as they walk about London; fleeing from old gentlemen selling the *Daily Mail* outside Cox's, Chester was confronted in the Strand by the *Herald* remarking very loudly 'CHESTER MUST GO'. And then (but this was later), by the *Patriot*, which was much, much worse.

The *Patriot* affair was different from the others. The *Patriot* was, in fact, a different paper. The *Patriot* had the personal, homely touch; it dealt faithfully not only with the public misdemeanours of prominent persons, but with the scandals of their private lives. It found things out. It abounded in implications and references, arch and jocose in manner and not usually discreet in matter. The *Patriot* had been in the law courts many times, but as it remarked, 'We are not afraid of prosecution'. It had each week a column of open letters addressed to persons of varying degrees of prominence, in which it told them what it thought of them. The weak point of these letters was that the *Patriot* was not a paper which was read by persons of prominence; its readers were the obscure and simple, who no doubt extracted much edification from them. Its editor was a Mr Percy Jenkins, a gentleman of considerable talents, and, it was said, sufficient personal charm to be useful to him. What he lacked in aesthetic taste he made up in energy and patriotism, and the People hailed him affectionately as the People's friend. Throughout October Mr Jenkins suffered apparently from a desire to have a personal interview with the Minister of Brains. He addressed private letters to him, intimating this desire, which were answered by his secretary in a chilly negative strain. He telephoned, enquiring when, if at all, he could have the pleasure of seeing the Minister, and was informed that the Minister had, unfortunately, no time for pleasures just now. He called at the Ministry and sent up his card, but was told that, as he had no appointment it was regretted that he could not penetrate further into the Ministry than the waiting-room. He called in the evening at the Minister's private address, but found him engaged.

After that, however, the Minister apparently relented, for Mr Jenkins received a letter from his secretary informing him that, if he wished to see the Minister, he might call at his house at 9.30 pm on the following Monday. Mr Jenkins did so. He was shown into the Minister's study. Chester was sitting by the fire, reading *Tales of my Grandfather*. He was never found writing letters, as one might expect a public man to be found; his secretary wrote all his official letters, and his unofficial letters were not written at all, Chester being of the opinion that if you leave the letters you receive long enough they answer themselves.

Mr Jenkins, having been invited to sit down, did so, and said, 'Very kind of you to give me this interview, sir.'

Chester did not commit himself, however, to any further kindness, but said stiffly, 'I have very little time. I am, as you see, occupied' — he indicated *Tales of my Grandfather* — 'and I shall be glad if you will state your business at once, sir, and as plainly as you can.'

Mr Jenkins murmured pleasantly, 'Well, we needn't be blunt, exactly … But you are quite right, sir; I have business. As you are no doubt aware, I edit a paper — the *Patriot* — it is possible that you are acquainted with it.'

'On the contrary,' said Chester, 'such an acquaintance would be quite impossible. But I have heard of it. I know to what paper you refer. Please go on.'

'Everybody,' retorted Mr Jenkins, a little nettled, 'does not find close acquaintance with the *Patriot* at all impossible. Its circulation …'

'We need not, I think, have that, Mr Jenkins. Will you kindly go on with your business?'

Mr Jenkins shrugged his shoulders.

'Your time appears to be extremely limited, sir.'

'All time,' returned the Minister, relapsing, as was often his habit, into metaphysics, 'is limited. Limits are, in fact, what constitute time. What "*extremely* limited" may mean, I cannot say. But if you mean that I desire this interview to be short, you are correct.'

Mr Jenkins hurried on.

'The *Patriot*, as you may have heard, sir, deals with truth. Its aim is to disseminate correct information with regard to all matters, public and private. This, I may say, it is remarkably successful in doing. Well, Mr Chester, as of course you are aware, the public are very much interested in yourself. There is no one at the present moment who is more to the fore, or if I may say so, more discussed. Naturally, therefore, I should be glad if I could provide some items of public interest on this subject, and I should be very grateful for any assistance you could give me … Now, Mr Chester, I have heard lately a very interesting piece of news about you. People are saying that you are being seen a great deal in the company of a certain lady.' He paused.

'Go on,' said Chester.

'It has even been said,' continued Mr Jenkins, 'that you have been seen staying in the country together … alone together, that is … for week-ends …'

'Go on,' said Chester.

Mr Jenkins went on. 'Other things are said; but I daresay they are mere rumour. Queer things get said about public men. I met someone the other day who lives in Buckinghamshire, somewhere in the Chilterns, and who has a curious and no doubt entirely erroneous idea about you … Well, in the interests of the country, Mr Chester (I have the welfare of the Ministry of Brains very much at heart, I may say; I am entirely with you in regarding intelligence as the Coming Force), I should like to be in a position to discredit these rumours. If you won't mind my saying so, they tell against you very seriously. You see, it is generally know that you are uncertificated for matrimony and parentage, if I may mention it. And once people get into their heads the idea that, while forcing these laws on others, you are evading them yourself … well, you may imagine it might damage your work considerably. You and I, Mr Chester, know what the public are … I should be glad to have your authority to contradict these rumours, therefore.'

Chester said, 'Certainly. You may contradict anything you please. I shall raise no objection. Is that all?'

Mr Jenkins hesitated. 'I cannot, of course, contradict the rumours without some assurance that they are false …'

[1] 'No? And what form would you suggest that that assurance should take?'

Mr Jenkins shrugged his shoulders, and replied with his

1 With this sentence the original material from the 1918 edition is reinstated.

pleasant smile, 'The form usual in such cases, Mr Chester … Beyond that I leave it to you.'

The Minister leant forward confidentially.

'Now, Mr Jenkins, speak straight out. What are your terms? You intend to spread scandal about me in your paper unless I give you — how much? Don't be afraid to say: you shall have it if it's at all reasonable … It's no use your putting it too high, you know, or you won't get it.'

'Five hundred?' murmured Mr Jenkins tentatively, after a moment's hesitation.

The Minister rose to his feet.

'Thank you very much, Mr Jenkins. I don't think we need trouble you any further, need we, Oxford?'

Two persons stepped into view from behind a screen — a shrewd-faced lawyer, and a youth with a shorthand notebook.

'Thank you Mr Jenkins. We have all we require for a very nice blackmail case,' the lawyer said. 'I can't say I ever thought Mr Chester would succeed in making you commit yourself — I thought you were too old a hand. A very clever draw.'

'Such an action in the courts,' Mr Jenkins remarked suavely (he had learnt long since to bear such incidents without too great discomposure) 'would be, I fancy, the end of your public career, Mr Chester. The truth would then all come out, as of course you are aware.'

'I am aware,' Mr Chester said tranquilly. 'But there will be an action, all the same. Not yet. I shall wait until I am less busy. You may go now, and disseminate all the truth you like. Good evening.'

So that was that, and that was how the *Patriot* campaign started.

Having started, it flourished. If the *Patriot* was going in the end to have to pay, it intended anyhow to have a run for its money.

It began with an Open Letter.

[2] *'To the Minister of Brains.*

'Dear Mr Nicholas Chester,

'There is a saying "Physician, heal thyself". There is also, in the same book (a book which, coming of clerical, even episcopal, parentage, you should be acquainted with), "Cast out the beam which is in thine own eye, and then thou shalt see more plainly to pull out the mote which is in thy brother's eye". We will on this occasion say no more than that we advise you to take heed to these sayings before you issue many more orders relating to matrimony and such domestic affairs. And yet a third saying, "Can the blind lead the blind? Shall they not both fall into the ditch?" you would do well to ponder in your heart.'

That was all, that week. But it was enough to start speculation and talk among the *Patriot's* readers. Next week and other weeks there were further innuendoes, and more talk. One week there was a picture of Chester with several unmistakable, but also unmistakably deficient, little Chesters clinging to his coat. This picture was called 'Following the dear old dad. What we may expect to see in the near future.'

Mr Percy Jenkins knew his business. And, during his interview with the Minister of Brains, he had conceived an extreme dislike towards him.

2 The 1919 edition reverts to the 1918 text from this point.

4

'He'll feel worse before I've done with him,' Chester said to Kitty. They were sitting together on Kitty's sofa, with a copy of the *Patriot* between them. Kitty was now alone in her flat, her cousin having suddenly taken it into her head to get married.

'I always said it would come out,' was Kitty's reply. 'And now you see.'

'Of course I knew it would come out,' Chester said calmly. 'It was bound to. However, it hasn't yet. All this is mere talk. It's more offensive, but not really so serious, as the Labour attacks on the Ministry, and the *Stop It* campaign, and the cry for a Business Government. Business Government, indeed! The last word in inept futility …'

'All the same,' Kitty said, rather gravely, 'you and I have got to be rather more careful, Nicky. We've been careful, I think, but not enough, it seems.'

'There's no such thing,' said Chester, who was tired, 'as being careful enough, in this observant world, when one is doing wrong. You can be too careful (don't let's, by the way) but you can't be careful enough.'

5

But Chester did not really see Kitty very often in these days, because he had to see and confer with so many others — the Employers' Federation, and the Doctors, and the Timber Cutters, and the Worsted Industries, and the Farmers, and the Cotton Spinners, and the Newspaper Staffs, and the Church, and the Parents, and the Ministerial Council, and the Admiralty, and the Board of Education, and the War Office, and the Ministry of Reconstruction, and the Directorate of Propaganda. And the ASE.

It is much to be hoped that conferences are useful; if they are not, it cannot, surely, be from lack of practice.

Prideaux also, and the other heads of sections, on their humbler scale received deputations and conferred. Whether or not it was true to say of the Ministry (and to do Ministries justice, these statements are usually not true) that it did not try to enter sympathetically into the difficulties and grievances of the public, it is anyhow certain that the difficulties and grievances entered into the Ministry, from 9.30 am until 7 pm. After 7 no more difficulties were permitted to enter; but the higher staff remained often till late into the night to grapple with those already there.

Meanwhile the government laid pledges in as many of the hands held out to them as they could. Pledges, in spite of a certain boomerang quality possessed by them, are occasionally useful things. They have various aspects; when you give them, they mean a little anger averted, a little content generated, a little time gained. When you receive them, they mean, normally, that others will (you hope) be compelled to do something disagreeable before you are. When others receive them, they mean that there is unfair favouritism. When (or if) you fulfil them, they mean that you are badly hampered thereby in the competent handling of your job. When you break them, they mean trouble. And when you merely hear about them from the outside they mean a moral lesson — that promises should be kept if made, but certainly never, never made.

It is very certain, anyhow, that the Ministry of Brains made at this time too many. No Ministry could have kept so many. There was, for instance, the Pledge to the Married Women, that the unmarried women should be called up for their Mind Training Course before they were. There was the Pledge to the Mining Engineers, that unskilled labour should take the Course before skilled. There was the Pledge to the Parents of Five, that, however high the baby taxes were raised, the parents of six would always have to pay more on each baby. There was the Pledge to the Deficient, that they would not have to take the Mind Training Course at all. This last pledge was responsible for much agitation in Parliament. Distressing cases of imbeciles harried and bullied by the local Brains Boards were produced and enquired into. (Question, 'Is it not the case that the Ministry of Brains has become absolutely soulless in this matter of harrying the Imbecile?' Answer, 'I have received no information to that effect'. Question, 'Are enquiries being made into the case of the deficient girl at Perivale Halt who was rejected three times as unfit for the Course and finally examined again and passed, and developed acute imbecility and mumps half-way through the Course?' Answer, 'Enquiries are being made'. And so on, and so on, and so on.)

But, in the eyes of the general public, the chief testimony to the soullessness of the Ministry was its crushing and ignoring of the claims of the human heart. What could one say of a Ministry who deliberately and coldly stood between lover and lover, and dug gulfs between parent and unborn child, so that the child was either never born at all, or abandoned, derelict, when born, to the tender mercies of the state, or retained and paid for so heavily by fine or imprisonment that the parents might well be tempted to wonder whether after all the unfortunate infant was worth it?

'Him to be taxed!' an indignant parent would sometimes exclaim, admiring her year-old infant's obvious talents. 'Why he's as bright as anything. Just look at him … And little Albert next door, what his parents got a big bonus for, so as you could hear them for a week all down the street drinking it away, he can't walk yet, nor hardly look up when spoke to. Deficient, *I* calls him. It isn't fair dealing, no matter what anyone says.'

'All the same,' said Nicholas Chester to his colleagues, 'there appears to me to be a considerably higher percentage of intelligent looking infants of under three years of age than there were formerly. Intelligent looking, that is to say, *for* infants. Infants, of course, are not intelligent creatures. Their mental level is low. But I observe a distinct improvement.'

A distinct improvement was, in fact, discernible. But, among the Great Unimproved, and among those who did not want improvement, discontent grew and spread; the slow, aggrieved discontent of the stupid, to whom personal freedom is as the breath of life, to whom the welfare of the race is as an idle, intangible dream, not worth the consideration of practical men and women.

CHAPTER II

The Storming of the Hotel

1

In December Dora did a foolish thing. It is needless to say that she did other foolish things in other months; it is to be feared that she had been born before the Brains Acts; her mental category must be well below C3. But this particular folly is selected for mention because it had a disastrous effect on the already precarious destiny of the Ministry of Brains. Putting out a firm and practised hand, she laid it heavily and simultaneously upon four journals who were taking a rebellious attitude towards the Brains Act — the *Nation*, *Stop It*, the *Herald*, and the *Patriot*. Thus she angered at one blow considerable sections of the Thoughtful, the Advanced, the Workers (commonly but erroneously known as the proletariat) and the Vulgar.

'Confound the fools,' as Chester bitterly remarked; but the deed was then done.

'How long,' Vernon Prideaux asked, 'will it take governments to learn that revolutionary propaganda disseminated all over the country don't do as much harm as this sort of action?'

Chester was of opinion that, give the Ministry of Brains its chance, let it work for, say, fifty years, and even governments might at the end of that time have become intelligent enough to acquire such elementary pieces of knowledge. If only the Ministry were given its chance, if it could weather the present unrest, let the country get used to it … Custom: that was the great thing. People settled down under things at last. All sorts of dreadful things. Education, vaccination, taxation, sanitation, representation … It was only a question of getting used to them.

2

Though the authorities were prepared for trouble, they did not foresee the events of Boxing Day, that strange day in the history of the Ministry.

The Ministry were so busy that many of the staff took no holiday beyond Christmas Day itself. Bank Holidays are, as everyone who has tried knows, an excellent time for working in one's office, because there are no interruptions from the outside world, no telephoning, no visitors, no registry continually sending up incoming correspondence. The clamorous, persistent public fade away from sound and sight, and ministries are left undistracted, to deal with them for their good in the academic seclusion of the office. If there was in this world an eternal Bank Holiday (some, but with how little reason, say that this awaits us in heaven) ministries would thrive better; governing would then become like pure mathematics, an abstract science unmarred by the continual fret and jar of contact with human demands, which drag them so roughly, so continually, down to earth.

On Boxing Day the Minister himself worked all day, and about a quarter of the higher staff were in their places. But by seven o'clock only the Minister remained, talking to Prideaux in his room.

The procession, at first in the form of four clouds each no bigger than a man's hand, trailed from out the north, south, east and west, and coalesced in Trafalgar Square. From there it marched down Whitehall to Westminster, and along the Embankment. It seemed harmless enough; a holiday crowd of men and women with banners, like the people who used to want Votes, or Church Disestablishment, or Peace, or Cheap Food. The chief difference to be observed between this and those old processions was that a large number in this procession seemed to fall naturally and easily into step, and marched in time, like soldiers. This was a characteristic now of most processions; that soldier's trick, once learnt, is not forgotten. It might have set an onlooker speculating on the advantages and the dangers of a nation of soldiers, that necessary sequence to an army of citizens.

The procession drew up outside the Ministry of Brains, and resolved itself into a meeting. It was addressed in a short and stirring speech from the Ministry steps by the president of the Stop It League, a fiery young man with a megaphone, who concluded his remarks with 'Isn't it up to all who love freedom, all who hate tyranny, to lose no time, but to wreck the place where these things are done? That's what we're here to do to-night — to smash up this hotel and show the government what the men and women of England mean! Come on, boys!'

Too late the watching policemen knew that this procession and this meeting meant business, and should be broken up.

The Minister and Prideaux listened, from an open window, to the speaking outside. 'Rendle,' said Prideaux. 'Scandalous mismanagement. What have the police been about? It's too late now to do much … Do they know we are here, by the way? Probably not.'

'They shall,' replied Chester, and stepped out on to the balcony.

There was a hush, then a tremendous shout.

'It's the Minister! By God, it's Nicky Chester, the man who's made all the trouble!'

A voice rose above the rest.

'Quiet! Silence! Let him speak. Let's hear what he's got to say for himself.'

Silence came, abruptly; the queer, awful, terrifying silence of a waiting crowd.

Into it Chester's voice cut, sharp and incisive.

'You fools. Get out of this and go home. Don't you know that you're heading for serious trouble — that you'll find yourselves in prison for this? Get out before it's too late. That's all I have to say.'

'That's all he's got to say,' the crowd took it up like a refrain. '"That's all he's got to say, after all the trouble he's made!'

A suave, agreeable voice rose above the rest.

'That is *not* quite all he's got to say. There's something else. He's got to answer two plain questions. Number one: *Are you certificated for marriage, Mr Chester, or have you got mental deficiency in your family?*'

There was an instant's pause. Then the Minister, looking down from the balcony at the upturned faces, white in the cold moonlight, said, clearly, 'I am not certificated for marriage, owing to the cause you mention.'

'Thank you,' said the voice. 'Have you all noted that, boys? The Minister of Brains is not certificated for marriage. He has deficiency in his family. Now, Mr Chester, question number two, please. *Am I correct in stating that you — got — married — last — August?*'

'You are quite correct, Mr Jenkins.'

Chester heard beside him Prideaux's mutter — 'Good God!' and then, below him, broke the roar of the crowd.

'Come on, boys!' someone shouted. 'Come on and wreck the blooming show, and nab the blooming showman before he slips off!'

Men flung themselves up the steps and through the big doors, and surged up the stairs.

'This,' remarked Prideaux, 'is going to be some mess. I'll go and get Rendle to see sense, if I can. He's leading them up the stairs, probably.'

'I fancy that won't be necessary,' said Chester. 'Rendle and his friends are coming in here, apparently.'

The door was burst open, and men rushed in. Chester and Prideaux faced them, standing before the door.

'You fools,' Chester said again. 'What good do you think you're going to do yourselves by this?'

'Here he is, boys! Here's Nicky Chester, the married man!"

Chester and Prideaux were surrounded and pinioned.

'Don't hurt him,' someone exhorted. 'We'll hang him out over the balcony and ask the boys down there what to do with him.'

They dragged him on to the balcony and swung him over the rail, dangling him by a leg and an arm. One of them shouted, 'Here's the Minister, boys! Here's Nicky, the Minister of Brains!'

The crowd looked up and saw him, swinging in mid air, and a great shout went up.

'Yes,' went on the speaker from the balcony, 'Here's Nicky Chester, the man who dares to dictate to the people of Britain who they may marry and what kids they may have, and then goes and gets married himself, breaking his own laws, and hushes it up so that he thought it would never come out.' ('I always knew it would come out,' the Minister muttered, inarticulately protesting against the estimation of his intelligence.) 'But it *has* come out,' the speaker continued. 'And now what are we to do with him, with this man who won't submit to the laws he forces on other people? This man who dares to tell other people to bear what he won't bear himself? What shall we do with him? Drop him down into the street?'

For a moment it seemed that the Minister's fate, like himself, hung suspended.

They swung him gently to and fro, as if to get an impetus …

Then someone shouted, 'We'll let him off this time, as he's just married. Let him go home to his wife, and not meddle with government any more!'

The crowd rocked with laughter; and in that laughter, rough, good-humoured, scornful, the Ministry of Brains seemed to dissolve.

They drew Chester in through the window again. Someone said, 'Now we'll set the blooming hotel on fire. No time to waste, boys.'

Chester and Prideaux were dragged firmly but not unkindly down the stairs and out through the door. Their appearance outside the building, each pinioned by two stalwart ex-guardsmen, was hailed by a shout, partly of anger, but three parts laughter. To Chester it was the laughter, good-humoured, stupid, scornful, of the British public at ideas, and particularly at ideas which had failed. But in it, sharp and stinging, was another, more contemptuous laughter, levelled at a man who had failed to live up to his own ridiculous ideas, the laughter of the none too honest world, which yet respected honesty, at the hypocrisy and double-dealing of others.

'They're quite right to laugh,' thought Chester. 'It is funny: damned funny.'

And at that, standing pinioned on the steps of his discredited Ministry, looking down on the crowd of the injured, contemptuous British public, who were out to wreck the things he cared for, he began to laugh himself.

His laughter was naturally unheard, but they saw his face, which should have been downcast and ashamed, twist into his familiar, sad, cynical smile, which all who had heard him on platforms knew.

'Laughing, are you,' someone shouted thickly. 'Laughing at the people you've tricked! You've ruined me and my missus — taken every penny we had, just because we had twins — and you — you stand there and laugh! You — you bloody married imbecile!'

Lurching up the steps, he flung himself upon Chester and wrenched him from the relaxed hold of his captors. Struggling together, the Minister and his assailant stumbled down the steps, and then fell headlong among the public.

3

When the mounted police finally succeeded in dispersing the crowd, the Ministry of Brains was in flames, like Sodom and Gomorrah, those wicked cities. Unlike Sodom and Gomorrah, the conflagration was at last quenched by a fire engine. But far into the night the red wreckage blazed, testimony to the wrath of a great people, to the failure of a great idea, to the downfall of him who, whatever the weakness he shared in common with the public who downed him, was yet a great man.

CHAPTER 12

Debris

1

Chester lay with a broken head and three smashed ribs in his flat in Mount Street. He was nursed by his elder sister Maggie, a kind, silent, plain person with her brother's queer smile and more than his cynical patience. With her patience took the form of an infinite tolerance; the tolerance of one who looks upon all human things and sees that they are not much good, nor likely to be. (Chester had not his fair share of this patience: hence his hopes and his faiths, and hence his downfall.) She was kind to Kitty, whose acquaintance she now made. (The majority of the Ministry of Brains staff were having a short holiday, during the transference to other premises.)

Maggie said to Kitty, 'I'm not surprised. It was a lot to live up to. And it's not in our family, living up to that. Perhaps not in any family. I'm sorry for Nicky, because he'll mind.'

She did not reproach Kitty; she took her for granted. Such incidents as Kitty were liable to happen, even in the best regulated lives. When Kitty reproached herself, saying, 'I've spoilt his life,' she merely replied tranquilly, 'Nicky lets no one but himself spoil his life. When he's determined to do a thing, he'll do it.' Nor did she commit herself to any indication as to whether she thought that what Nicky had gained would be likely to compensate for what he had lost.

For about what he had lost there seemed no doubt in anyone's mind. He had lost his reputation, his office, and, for the time being, his public life. The Ministry of Brains might continue, would in fact, weakly continue, without power and without much hope, till it trailed into ignominious death; even the wrecked Hotel would continue, when repaired; but it was not possible that Chester should continue.

The first thing he did, in fact, when he could do anything at all intelligent, was to dictate a letter to the Ministerial Council tendering his resignation from office. There are, of course, diverse styles adopted by the writers of such letters. In the old days people used to write (according to the peculiar circumstances of their case) —

> 'Dear Prime Minister,
>
> 'Though you have long and often tried to dissuade me from this course … etc., etc. … I think you will hardly be surprised … deep regret in severing the always harmonious connection between us …,' and so forth.

Or else quite otherwise —

> 'Dear Prime Minister,
>
> 'You will hardly be surprised, I imagine, after the strange occurrence of yesterday, when I had the interest of reading in a daily paper the first intimation that you desired a change at the Ministry I have the honour to adorn …'

Neither of these styles was used by Chester, who wrote briefly, without committing himself to any opinion as to the probable surprise or otherwise of the Ministerial Council —

> 'Dear Sirs,
>
> 'I am resigning my office as Minister of Brains, owing to facts of which you will have doubtless heard, and which make it obviously undesirable for me to continue in the post.'

Having done this, he lay inert through quiet, snow-bound days and nights, and no one knew whether or not he was going to recover.

2

After a time he asked after Prideaux, and they told him Prideaux had not been hurt, only rumpled.

'He calls to ask after you pretty often,' said Kitty. 'Would you like to see him sometime? When the doctor says you can?'

'I don't care,' Chester said. 'Yes, I may as well.'

So Prideaux came one afternoon (warned not to be political or exciting) and it was a queer meeting between him and Chester. Chester remembered the last shocked words he had had from Prideaux — 'Good God!' and wondered, without interest, what Prideaux felt about it all now.

But it was not Prideaux's way to show much of what he felt.

They talked mainly of that night's happenings. Chester had already had full reports of these; of the fire, of the fight between the police and the crowd, in which several lives had been lost, of the arrest of the ringleaders and their trials. To Chester's own part in the proceedings they did not refer, till, after a pause, Chester suddenly said, 'I have been wondering, but I can't make up my mind about it. How much difference to the business did the discovery about me make? Would they have gone to those lengths without it?'

Prideaux was silent. He believed that Chester that night on the balcony, had his hands been clean, could have held the mob.

Chester interpreted the silence.

'I suppose they wouldn't,' he said impassively. 'However, I fancy it only precipitated the catastrophe. The Ministry was down and under, in any case. People were determined not to stand laws that inconvenienced them — as I was. I was merely an example, not a cause, of that disease …'

That was the nearest he ever got with Prideaux to discussion of his own action.

'Anyhow,' said Prideaux sadly, ;the Ministry is down and under now. Imagine Frankie Lyle, poor little beggar, trying to carry on, after all this!' (This gentleman had been nominated as Chester's successor.)

Chester smiled faintly. 'Poor little Frankie … I hear Monk wouldn't touch it, by the way. I don't blame him … Lyle won't hold them for a week; he'll back out on every point.'

There was regret in his tired, toneless voice, and bitterness, because the points on which Lyle would back out were all points which he had made. He could have held them for a week, and more; he might even — there would have been a fighting chance of it — have pulled the Ministry through altogether, had things been otherwise. But things were not otherwise, and this was not his show any more. He looked at Prideaux half resentfully as Prideaux rose to leave him. Prideaux had not wrecked his own career …

To Kitty, the first time he had met her after the events of Boxing Night, Prideaux had shown more of his mind. He had come to ask after Chester, and had found Kitty there. He had looked at her sharply and coolly, as if she had made a stupid mistake over her work in the office.

'So you didn't guess, all this time,' she had said to him, coolly too, because she resented his look.

'Not,' he had returned, 'that things had gone as far as this. I knew you were intimate, of course. There was that time in Italy … But — well, honestly, I thought better of both your brains.'

She gave up her momentary resentment, and slipped again into remorse.

'We thought better of them too — till we did it … Have I spoilt his life, Vernon? I suppose so.'

He shrugged his shoulders. 'You've spoilt yours, and he's spoilt his own, career as Minister of Brains. There are other things, of course. Chester can't go under; he's too good a man to lose. They'll stick on to him somehow … But … well, what in heaven or earth or the other place possessed you both to do it, Kitty?'

To which she had no answer but 'We just thought we would,' and he left her in disgust.

Even in her hour of mortification and remorse, Kitty could still enjoy getting a rise out of Prideaux.

3

Pansy, who called often with showers of hot-house flowers, which Chester detested, was much more sympathetic. She was frankly delighted. She could not be allowed to see Chester; Kitty was afraid that her exuberance might send his temperature up.

'You won't mind my tellin' you now, darlin', but I've been thinkin' it was free love all this time. I didn't mind, you know. But this is more respectable. This family couldn't really properly afford another scandal; it might lose its good name, then what would Cyril say? It would come hard on the Cheeper too. Now this is some marriage. So *sensible* of you both, to throw over those silly laws and do the jolly thing and have a good time. As I said to Tony, what *is* the good of making laws if you can't break them yourself? Now that your Nicky's set a good example, it really does seem as if all this foolishness was goin' to dwine away and be forgotten … I guess it's doin' what we like and havin' a good time that matters in the long run, isn't it. Not keepin' laws or improvin' the silly old world.'

'Ask me another,' said Kitty. 'I haven't the slightest idea, Pansy, my love. You're usually right, so I daresay you're right about this. But you mustn't talk like that to Nicky, or he'll have a relapse.'

'And fancy,' Pansy mused, 'me havin' got the great Minister of Brains for a brother-in-law! Or anyhow somethin' of the sort; as near as makes no difference. I shall never hear the last of it from the girls and boys … Good-bye, old thing; I'm ever so pleased you're a happy wife now as well as me.'

4

Chester handed Kitty a letter from his mother, the wife of a struggling bishop somewhere in the west country. It said, 'Directly you are well enough, dear, you must bring Kitty to stay with us; she won't, I am sure, mind our simple ways … My dear, we are so thankful you have found happiness. We are distressed about your accident, and about your loss of office, which I fear you will feel … But, after all, love and happiness are so much more important than office, are they not? …'

'Important,' Kitty repeated. 'Queer word. Just what love and happiness aren't, you'd think. Comfortable — jolly — but not important … Never you mind, Nicky, you'll be important always: Vernon is right about that. They'll put you somewhere where 'domestick selvisheness' doesn't matter: perhaps they'll make you a peer …'

Chester said he would not be at all surprised.

Kitty said, 'Shall we go and see your people?' and he replied gloomily, 'I suppose we must. It will be … rather trying.'

'Will they condole with you?' she suggested and he returned, 'No. They'll congratulate me.'

A fortnight later they went down to the west. Bishop Chester lived in a little old house in a slum behind his cathedral. Bishops' palaces were no longer bishops' homes; they had all been turned into community houses, clergy houses, retreat houses, alms houses, and so forth. Celibate bishops could live in them, together with other clergy of their diocese, but bishops with families had to find quarters elsewhere. And, married or unmarried, their incomes were not enough to allow of any style of living but that apostolic simplicity which the Church, directly it was freed from the State and could arrange its own affairs, had decided was right and suitable.

Not all bishops took kindly to the new regime; some resigned, and had to be replaced by bishops of the new and sterner school. But, to give bishops their due, which is too seldom done, they are for the most part good Christian men, ready to do what they believe is for the good of the Church. Many of their detractors were surprised at the amount of good-will and self-sacrifice revealed in the episcopal ranks when they were put to the test. If some failed under it — well, bishops, if no worse than other men, are human.

Bishop Chester had not failed. He had taken to plain living and plainer thinking (how often, alas, these two are to be found linked together!) with resignation, as a Christian duty. If it should bring any into the Church who had been kept outside it by his purple and fine linen, he would feel himself more than rewarded. If it should not, that was not his look-out. Which is to say that Bishop Chester was a good man, if not clever.

He and his wife were very kind to Chester and Kitty. Chester said he could not spare more than a day and night; he had to get back to town, where he had much business on hand, including the instituting of an action for malicious libel against Mr Percy Jenkins and the publishers and proprietors of the *Patriot*. Kitty was not surprised at the shortness of the visit, for it was a humiliating visit. The bishop and Mrs

Chester, as their son had known they would, approved of his contravention of his own principles. They thought them, had always thought them, monstrous and inhuman principles.

The bishop said, 'My dear boy, I can't tell you how thankful I am that you have decided at last to let humanity have its way with you. Humanity; the simple human things; love, birth, family life. They're the simple things, but, after all, the deep and grand things. No laws will ever supersede them.'

And Mrs Chester looked at Kitty with the indescribable look of mothers-in-law who hope they may be grandmothers, and whispered to her when she said good-night, 'And some day, dear …'

And they saw Chester's twin sister. She was harmless; she was even doing crochet work; and her face was the face of Chester uninformed by thought. Mrs Chester said, 'Nicky will have told you of our poor ailing girl …'

5

They came away next morning. They faced each other in the train, but they read the *Times* (half each) and did not meet each other's eyes. They could not. They felt as thieves who still have consciences must feel when congratulated on their crimes by other thieves, who have not. Between them stood and jeered a Being with a vacant face and a phrase which it repeated with cynical reiteration. 'You have let humanity have its way with you. Humanity; the simple human things … No laws will ever supersede them …' And the Being's face was as the face of Chester's twin sister, the poor ailing girl.

To this they had come, then; to the first of the three simple human things mentioned by the bishop. What now, since they had started down the long slope of this green and easy hill, should arrest their progress, until they arrived, brakeless and unheld, into the valley where the other two waited, cynical, for all their simplicity, and grim?

Kitty, staring helplessly, into the problematical future, saw, as if someone had turned a page and shown it to her, a domestic picture — herself and Chester (a peer, perhaps, why not?) facing one another not in a train but in a simple human home, surrounded by Family Life; two feckless, fallen persons, who had made a holocaust of theories and principles, who had reverted to the hand-to-mouth shiftlessness and mental sloppiness of the primitive Briton. Kitty could hear Chester, in that future, vaguer, family, peer's voice that might then be his, saying, 'We must just trust to luck and muddle through somehow.'

Even to that they might come …

In the next Great War — and who should stay its advent if such as these failed? — their sons would fight, without talent, their daughters would perhaps nurse, without skill. And so on, and so on, and so on …

So turned the world around. Individual desire given way to, as usual, ruining principle and ideals by its soft pressure. What would ever get done in such a world? Nothing, ever.

Suddenly, as if both had seen the same picture, they met one another's eyes across the carriage, and laughed ruefully.

That, anyhow, they could always do, though sitting among the debris of ruined careers, ruined principles, ruined Ministries, ruined ideals. It was something; perhaps, in a sad and precarious world, it was much …

THE END

Notes

BY KATE MACDONALD

Jesus, son of Sirach: the author of Ecclesiasticus, in the Apocrypha, verses 6:22 and 16:1.

Chapter 1

the captains and the kings: from Rudyard Kipling's poem 'Recessional' (1897); 'The tumult and the shouting dies — / The captains and the kings depart — / Still stands thine ancient Sacrifice / An humble and a contrite heart / Lord God of Hosts, be with us yet / Lest we forget – lest we forget'.

Bakerloo tube: the Bakerloo line of the London Underground was opened between 1905 and 1915. It serves stations between the mainline train stations of Baker Street and Waterloo, and includes Marylebone, from which the Buckinghamshire commuters alighted.

League of Nations: The League of Nations, the intergovernmental organisation which eventually evolved into the United Nations, was founded in January 1920 as a result of the Paris Peace Conference that ended the First World War, after at least two years of campaigning.

Doris Keane: an American stage and film actress (1881–1945).

Teddie Gerrard: an Argentinian film actress (1890–1942).

spud: a hooked tool used for howking out very deeply-rooted weeds.

Struma: a river running through Greece and Bulgaria, whose valley was part of the Macedonian Front in the First World War.

Saturday: in the early twentieth century it was normal for office staff to work on Saturday mornings.

Nature made him and then broke the die: from Ariosto's epic poem *Orlando Furioso* (1532).

purple paper cover: this is clearly a Christian devotional book

Regicide Peace: Edmund Burke's *Letters ... on the Proposals for Peace with the Regicide Directory of France* was published in 1796, opposing the British government's intentions of seeking an accord with the Revolutionary rulers of France.

Robert Hall: Hall was a Baptist minister, whose sermon 'Sentiments proper to the present crisis' was published in 1803 as a response to the Revolutionary leadership in France.

having sold her own copy at Blackwell's: Blackwells was the principal bookseller at Oxford, and bought back textbooks from departing graduates.

the Poetry Bookshop: this shop and focus for new poetry was founded in 1913 by Harold Monro, an influential critic of new poetry in Britain, and run by Alida Klementaski.

***The Dangers of Dora*:** This is a joke title, using Dora (the acronym for the Defence Of the Realm Act) and popular film titles such as *The Perils of Pauline* and *The Exploits of Elaine* (both 1914).

Kerensky: Kerensky was a leading political figure in the October 1917 Russian Revolution.

the Geddes family: while candidates for this reference are many, it is likely that Macaulay meant the brothers Auckland Campbell Geddes, who had been part of Lloyd George's coalition government during the war, and Eric Campbell-Geddes, who served as First Lord of the Admiralty in the war, and was later notorious for his retrenchment on public expenditure, leading to the phrase 'the Geddes axe'.

Chapter 2

Nelson Keys: a British stage and screen actor (1886–1939).

Lee White: American revue actress and singer (1886–1927).

Icilma: Icilma was a well-known and heavily advertised cosmetics brand.

pierrot: pierrots (and their female variant, the pierrettes) are the white-faced clowns wearing voluminous black and white outfits and conical black or white hats, whose look had a vogue in the early twentieth century as fancy-dress costumes.

agnogger: agnostic, a person who does not believe that God can be proved to exist.

Discobolus: a classical statue of a naked young male athlete stooping as he prepares to turn and throw the discus.

Salonika Force: the Allied forces sent to fight the Turks in northern Greece, also called the Macedonian Front (see 'Struma' above).

Amphipolis: a classical Greek city, later also a Roman colony, with many historical associations.

Carlo Dolci: a seventeenth-century Italian painter, notable for his Baroque style.

Chapter 3

a dress of motley: a dress of many colours.

hockey for Bucks: she played hockey at county level for Buckinghamshire.

Little Go: the slang name for Responsions, the first exam taken by a newly matriculated undergraduate at Cambridge, to verify their suitability for the work. It was abolished in 1960.

Arnold Bennett: prolific and popular novelist, editor and critic.

cornering: stockpiling supplies to release them for sale when there is a shortage, at high prices.

Lord Roberts: The Boer War general Lord Roberts died of pneumonia in November 1914 and was mourned as a national hero, so the date of June 1915 is likely to be Macaulay's indication that she is not writing about the actual past, but an alternate past and speculative future. The quotation that Prideaux objects to is from the 1878 song by McDermott and Hunt with the well-known chorus 'We don't want to fight but by Jingo if we do / We've got the ships, we've got the men, we've got the money too'.

small island: this group exile did not happen, another subtle indication of the alternative history that Macaulay was creating.

Chapter 4

Petrograd: the name for St Petersburg that lasted from 1914 to 1924.

obiter dicta: a remark given by a presiding judge but not considered to be essential for the final decision of the court.

minuted down: Macaulay describes the standard civil service means of communication between departments, which leaves a paper trail, and can be followed minutely, but is also long-winded and liable to circularity.

Exemptions: Macaulay worked for the War Office from 1917, in the section dealing with exemptions from military service.

My Lords Commissioners: serving admirals of the Royal Navy who direct the operational affairs of the Navy through the Admiralty.

QMG touch: the Quartermaster-General is in charge of all logistics and supplies for the British Army, and thus has a finger in every pie, and knowledge of everything that goes on.

the Oaks: an annual horse race held at Epsom in early June.

little PS: his personal secretary.

Sinn Feiner or a Bolshevist: at the end of the First World War, these stereotypes of Irish Republicanism and Russian Revolution were the two most likely to disrupt society.

muff things: to make a mess of, to fail.

Carson's rebels: the Ulster Volunteer Force who were formed by the unionist MP Sir Edward Carson to resist Home Rule for Ireland, and the establishment of an Irish Free State.

Sir Roger Casement: human rights campaigner and activist in the fight for Irish independence from Britain. He attempted to smuggle weapons into Ireland to support the Easter Rising of 1916. His last adventure was execution in London in 1916.

Protopopoff: Protopopov was a Russian Tsarist politician, briefly Minister for the Interior after the Revolution and even more briefly the self-proclaimed dictator deposing the Russian government, before his execution in 1917.

Kaledin: general of the Cossack cavalry, who killed himself in 1918 when his counter-revolutionary movement had lost all hope of success against the Communist forces.

Arthur Ransome: most famous now for his Swallows and Amazons books, Ransome was one of the few western correspondents in Russia at the time of the Revolution, a Bolshevik sympathiser, and a friend of Lenin and Trotsky.

Korniloff: engineer of the Kornilov Affair which backfired on his patron, Kerensky, and led to his imprisonment. He fought against the Bolsheviks and died under shell attack in 1918. It will be noted that Macaulay has chosen failed revolutionaries for Neil's lost causes.

Chapter 5

sweating shop: small-scale manufacturing workshop with overcrowding, poor pay, dreadful conditions and no health or safety provision. The owners made the money, not the workers.

Chapter 6

Witan, Strafford, Pharaoh's councillors, Milivkoff, Lloyd George: all leaders facing times of grave danger for their country (though Milivkoff is more obscure than the others).

National Theatre: there had been a campaign to establish a national theatre in Britain since the 1850s, but this was not achieved until 1949.

raidless nights: one of Macaulay's most anthologised poems is 'The Shadow', about the horror of air raids on London in the First World War.

listening exchange: the early telephone system connected callers to each other manually by exchange operators, who could and did listen in to calls: many light novels of the early twentieth century create comic and dramatic moments out of this.

Gilbert and Sullivan: the Victorian dramatist W S Gilbert and composer Arthur Sullivan created immortal operettas by combining the exaggerated conventions of melodrama with fantastical plots and memorable music.

Chapter 7

that city set on a hill: a quotation from Matthew 5:14, from Christ's Sermon of the Mount, a metaphor for 'the light of the world'.

'are they thick?': are they thick as thieves, close, intimate?

Chapter 8

Pelman: a system of self-help and mental discipline, widely advertised in newspapers, much like the adverts for Selfridge's department shop.

Ramsay Macdonald and Lord Curzon: in 1918 MacDonald and Curzon were both strong contenders for the leaderships of, respectively, the Labour Party and the Conservative Party, but Curzon did not achieve this expectation.

Massingham and Maxse: Henry Massingham was the editor of *The Nation*, the leading Radical weekly newspaper, and Maxse was the editor of the highly conservative *National Review*.

Gardiner and Gwynne: A G Gardiner was a journalist and essayist ('Alpha of the Plough'), notable for his liberal views. Macaulay probably means Howell Arthur Gwynne, editor of the conservative *Morning Post*.

J C Squire and St Loe Strachey: Squire was a celebrated essayist and journalist, and (when *What Not* was being written) was acting editor of the *New Statesman*, a weekly left-wing newspaper. Strachey was the editor of the *Spectator*, the leading Conservative weekly paper.

Garvin and Spender: James Garvin was the long-standing editor of the *Observer*, a left-leaning Sunday newspaper. Spender was the editor of the highly influential *Westminster Gazette*, a London evening paper that had published Macaulay's first poems.

Ransome and Graham: Arthur Ransome sent reports on the Russian Revolution to the radical *Daily News*, whereas Stephen Graham wrote his reports for the *Times*.

She had known the pre-war Cambridge: so had Macaulay, whose father taught English literature at Trinity College from 1906.

Chapter 9

amphibious days: Macaulay wrote often in her later journalism of the delights of swimming off the Genoese coast.

bagnanti: other, Italian, bathers.

contadino: farmer.

cicale: cicada, large Mediterranean insect that 'sings' loudly by resonating vibrations through its body.

Chapter 10

***Tales of my Grandfather*:** the correct and often forgotten title is *Tales of A Grandfather*, by Sir Walter Scott, which are episodes of Scottish history. In the circumstances this is an unlikely book for Chester to be reading, so it is probably another Macaulay joke.

'... that they are false.': The replacement text inserted to avoid a libel charge reads as follows:

'They had an interesting conversation on this topic for ten minutes more, which I do not intend to record in these pages.

So many conversations are, for various reasons, not recorded. Conversations, for instance, at Versailles, when the allied powers of the world sit together there behind impenetrable curtains, through the rifts of which only murmurs of the unbroken harmony which always prevails between allies steal through to a waiting world. Conversations between M Trotzky and the representatives of the German Government before the Treaty of Brest-Litovsk. Conversations between the President of the Board of Trade and the railway Companies when the price of travel is being increased; between governments and the capitalists when elections are to be fought or newspapers to be bought; between Jane Austen's heroes and heroines in the hour when their passion is declared.

For quite different reasons, all these conversations are left to the imagination, and I propose to leave to the same department of the reader's mind the interview between Mr Percy Jenkins and the Minister of Brains. I will merely mention that the talking was, for the most part, done by Mr Jenkins. The reasons for this were two. One was that Mr Jenkins was a fluent talker, and the Minister capable of a taciturnity not invariably to be found in our statesmen. Both have their uses in the vicissitudes of public life. Both can be,
if used effectively, singularly baffling to those who would probe the statesman's mind and purposes. But fluency is, to most (it would seem) the easier course.

***

Anyhow this was how the *Patriot* campaign started. It began with an Open Letter.'

Chapter 11

ex-guardsmen: soldiers in the Grenadier Guards were required to be taller than most other regiments, with 6'2" being the traditional entry height.

Try some other Handheld Classics

Save Me The Waltz

by Zelda Fitzgerald

Zelda Fitzgerald's only novel, *Save Me The Waltz* (1932) was written in six weeks and covers the period of her life that her husband F Scott Fitzgerald had been drawing on for years while writing *Tender is the Night* (1934). She died in 1948. *Save Me The Waltz* is now recognised as a classic novel of the woman's experience in fast-moving American Jazz Age society.

The novel opens during the First World War. Alabama Beggs is a Southern belle who makes her début into adulthood with wild parties, dancing and drinking, and flirting with the young officers posted to her home town. When the artist Lieutenant David Knight arrives to join her line of suitors, Alabama marries him. Their life in New York, Paris and the South of France closely mirrors the Fitzgeralds' own life and their prominent socialising in the 1920s and 1930s as part of what was later called the Lost Generation.

Like Zelda, Alabama became passionate about dance. She attends ballet class in Paris every day. She refuses to accept that

she might not become the great dancer that she ardently longs to be, and this threatens her mental health and her marriage.

The introduction to the novel by Erin E Templeton, Professor of English at Converse College, shows how these struggles to become a dancer were the result of Zelda's need to have a life of her own rather than living in her husband's shadow.

£12.99, ISBN 978-1-9998280-4-2

What Might Have Been: The Story of a Social War

by Ernest Bramah

This new edition of Ernest Bramah's speculative fantasy *What Might Have Been* (1907) was reviewed enthusiastically in the *Times Literary Supplement*: 'abounds in humour and wit ... Bramah's condemnation of the power of the press to corrupt and mislead is as pertinent today as it was in 1907'.

This satirical novel of Conservative resistance to Labour rule is better known in its abridged form as *The Secret of the League* (1909). It mixes social realism with office espionage, and accurately predicted the invention of the fax

machine and the ascendancy of Labour politics. *What Might Have Been* is a political thriller, with a nail-biting Buchanesque car chase, a sea battle that C S Forester could have written, and dramatic rescue missions on the wing.

Now, for the first time since 1907, *What Might Have Been* is available at its original length, with 7000 words restored to recreate this lost landmark in British speculative fiction. Ernest Bramah's other literary works include the Kai Lung short stories of fantasy *chinoiserie*, and the *Max Carrados* tales of a blind Edwardian detective.

£13 paperback, ISBN 978-1-9998280-0-4

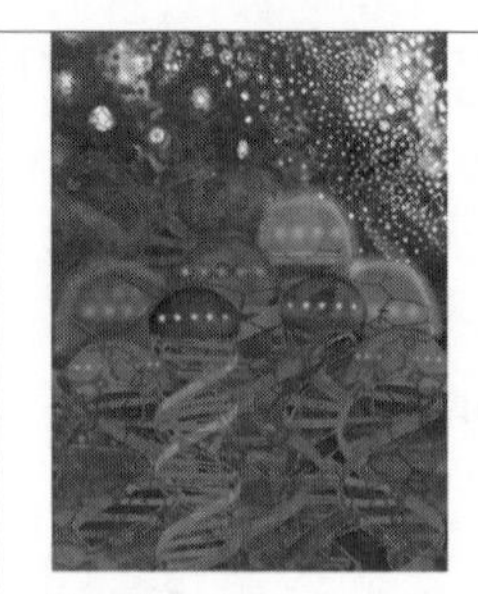

The Exile Waiting

by Vonda N McIntyre

The Exile Waiting was the first novel by the Hugo and Nebula award-winning novelist Vonda N McIntyre, published in 1975. It introduces the world that McIntyre later made famous with her multi-award-winning *Dreamsnake*: a post-apocalyptic world in which Center, an enclosed domed city, is run by slave-owning families who control the planet's resources, and are strangling the city's economy by their decadence.

Mischa is a thirteen-year old thief, struggling to support her drug-addict elder brother Chris, and their predatory uncle who uses their telepathic link with their captive younger sister Gemmi to control them. The alien pseudosibs Subone and Subtwo have come to Earth to take over Center's resources. When Mischa defends Chris from Subone's malice, Subtwo hunts her beneath Center's foundations, and discovers how cruel Center has been to its inhabitants with genetically distorted bodies and minds. They have to rescue them and leave, but how?

Also included in this edition, the first republication of McIntyre's short story 'Cages', originally published in *Quark 4* in 1972, in which she first created the pseudosibs and their terrible origins.

New York Times best-selling sf author Una McCormack wrote the Afterword.

£12.99, ISBN 978-1-912766-09-3